Wolf Dreams

by the Author

Yasmina Khadra

WOLF DREAMS

TRANSLATED BY
Linda Black

The Toby Press

The Toby Press LLC, 2007

POB 8531, New Milford, CT 06776-8531, USA
& POB 2455, London WIA 5WY, England

www.tobypress.com

ISBN 1 59264 187 3, *paperback*

A CIP catalogue record for this title
is available from the British Library

Typeset in Garamond by Jerusalem Typesetting

Printed and bound in the United States by
Thomson-Shore Inc., Michigan

For my children,
and for all children the world over

Contents

The police are no longer shooting. I can see one of their snipers behind a washhouse, above a shack. He is observing us through the sights of his gun, his finger on the trigger. Below, in the besieged city, apart from the armored vehicle and two cars with shattered windows, there is no sign of life. It is 6 A.M., and the daylight is not strong enough to venture into the streets. Since Algiers renounced its saints, the sun prefers to remain out at sea, waiting for the menace of night to withdraw.

The apartment block was evacuated at the beginning of the clash, in an apocalyptic panic. Despite appeals for calm, with each burst of fire, the staircase echoed with the screams of women and children. Alik was hit as he peered through the spy hole trying to see what was happening on the landing. The glass exploded in his face. He fell backwards, his eye blown out, the back of his head ripped open. Then a graveyard silence fell over the deserted corridors. The gas and electricity were cut off, and then the water. To isolate us. We tried several diversion tactics, in vain. An officer appealed to us to put down our weapons and surrender. I called him a traitor bastard and emptied a magazine in his direction.

"You've got it coming to you!" cried the officer. There was such contempt in his voice!

It's over.

The prophets have abandoned us. Everything around us is collapsing. It is as though the world is taking a vicious pleasure in disintegrating, slipping between our fingers like curls of smoke.

There is little left of the apartment where my group has taken cover. The windows have been blown out and the walls are crumbling from the frenzied shooting. Rafik is no longer moving. He is lying in a pool of blood, his eyes wild and his neck ludicrously contorted. Doujana stares at the ceiling, shot to pieces by a grenade. Handala lies dead in the hall, his face turned towards his shoe, his clenched fingers on the floor. His younger brother died at 3 A.M. Only Abou Tourab is still breathing, crumpled under the kitchen sink, his pump-action shotgun across his knees. He gives me a pathetic wink.

"I told you it wasn't a good idea."

He is wild-eyed with pain. His chest contracts as he musters all his innermost strength to take a gulp of air to help him swallow. With infinite precaution, he stretches his leg out towards a chair and shifts onto his side to face me.

"You should see your face," he gasps. "You look like a sweep stuck up a chimney."

"Save your breath," I advise.

"True. We've got a long journey ahead."

A thread of saliva hangs quivering from his lip and dribbles down onto his beard. With his right hand he opens his bloodstained shirt revealing the hideous wound eating up his side.

"My guts are spilling out and I can't feel a thing."

The rumble of a caterpillar tank outside made the walls shudder.

"They're bringing in the heavy artillery."

"I thought they would. Do you think people will remember us?"

A glimmer lights up his almost glassy eyes for a second. He clenches his jaws and mutters:

"Oh yes! They'll never forget us. Our names will be in the history books and on the monuments. Boy scouts will sing our praises in the woods. On public holidays, people will lay wreaths on our tombs. And

meanwhile, what will the glorious martyrs be doing? We'll be grazing peacefully in the eternal gardens."

My look of disapproval makes him laugh. He knows how I abhor blasphemy. People are usually careful what they say in front of me. For the first time, Abou Tourab, the most loyal of my men, dares to offend my sensibility. He wipes his nose on his shoulder, and torments me again with that look from beyond the grave. His hollow voice comes in vexed gasps:

"Up there, we'll only need to clap our hands for our every wish to be fulfilled. We'll choose our harem from the thousands of houris who live in Eden and, every night, when the angels lay down their flutes, we'll go and gather suns by the basketful in the Lord's orchards."

The Special Intervention Group sharpshooters pour onto the terraces all around, bounding swiftly and nimbly into position, as elusive as shadows.

"Keep away from the window, emir. You might catch cold."

Sirens wail in the distance, weaving through the streets to converge on our refuge. Abou Tourab frowns and begins to beat time weakly with his finger.

"The last symphony... Listen to that. Suddenly I can think of names for everything. The Last Symphony... I couldn't have found a name like that at a more relaxed moment even if I'd been paid a fortune. I didn't know that being at death's door sharpened your wits."

"Don't distract me."

"I missed my vocation."

"Will you shut up?"

He laughs, shuts up for a couple of minutes, clutching his gun, then recites:

"'My wrongs, I regret not. My joys are of no worth. History will be no older than my memories, and Eternity will have the falseness of my sleep.' He had something up there all right, dammit. Sid Ali was a true poet. It's incredible how people are full of surprises. I thought of him as mentally backward, rather spineless, but when the moment of truth came, somehow or other he found the most extraordinary courage.

3

Do you remember? He refused to go down on his knees. He didn't even flinch when I shoved my gun in his temple. 'Go on', he said, 'I'm ready.' His head exploded like a great big boil. But even that didn't wipe that goddamn smile off his face."

No, I don't remember. I wasn't there. But I haven't forgotten.

How can you forget when you spend your time betraying your memory, and your nights trying to piece it together again like a cursed jigsaw, only for it to go hazy again when dawn comes, over and over again. Every day. Every night. Endlessly.

We call that obsession, and we think that naming it is sufficient to triumph over despair.

What do we really know about obsession?

Why did the Archangel Gabriel not stay my hand as it was poised to slit the throat of that baby? The rain threatened to wash away the entire earth that night. The heavens fulminated. For a long time, I waited for the thunder to deflect my hand, for a flash of the lightning to release me from the shadows that held me captive in their hell. And yet this was me, Nafa, who had once been convinced that I had been born to delight and charm, who dreamed of vanquishing hearts through my talents alone.

I killed my first man on Wednesday 12 January 1994 at 7.35 A.M. He was a magistrate. He had come out of his house and was walking towards his car. His six-year-old daughter was ahead of him, her braids tied with blue ribbons, her satchel on her back. She passed me without seeing me. The magistrate was smiling, but there was something tragic in his eyes. He looked like a hunted animal. He started when he discovered me lurking in the doorway. I don't know why he continued on his way as though nothing were amiss. Perhaps he thought that in shrugging off the danger, he might allay it. I took out my revolver and ran after him. He stopped and turned to face me. In a fraction of a second, the blood had drained from his face and his features were blotted out. For a moment, I was afraid I had got the wrong person.

"Khodja?" I asked him.

"Yes," he answered flatly. His naiveté—or assurance—unnerved me. I had the greatest difficulty raising my arm. My finger froze on the trigger.

Abou Tourab begins to cough. A spasm racks his body, flinging him backwards. He grips the butt of his gun, and stretches out his legs, moaning. His urine spurts through his trousers and spreads in a puddle on the floor.
   "That's all I need! Now I've pissed myself. The taghut will think I'm scared. What the hell are my guardian angels doing? Isn't it enough for them that I'm dying?"
   "Shut the hell up!"
   He was silent.
   The caterpillar tank enters the square, the gun pointing at our hideout. A megaphone blast outs: This is the your last warning! Give yourselves up!
   "Shit!" gasps Abou Tourab. "It was different in Afghanistan. Whenever the Mujahideen were caught, sand storms covered their retreat, mysterious breakdowns immobilized the enemy tanks and clouds of birds attacked the Soviet helicopters. Why don't miracles happen here?"
   He raises the butt of his gun to his temple. His smile widens, simultaneously grotesque and pathetic. I watch him as if in a dream, without even trying to dissuade him.
   "I'll go first chief. You never know…"
   The report blew off his skull in a gruesome explosion of flesh and blood, splattering his brains on the ceiling and causing heavy shooting to start outside the door.

"What are you waiting for?" yelled Sofiane, "shoot the bastard!"
   The little girl did not seem to realize what was going on. Or refused to admit it.
   "I don't believe it," fumed Sofiane. "You're not going to bottle out now. He's nothing but a swine."
   The ground threatened to give way under me. I was overcome with nausea, my guts were in a knot, and I was paralyzed. Sensing my

indecision, the magistrate thought he had a chance to get away. If he had kept still, I don't think I would have had the courage to go through with it. With each shot, I trembled from head to foot. I couldn't stop firing. I was oblivious both to the detonations and to the little girl's screams. I crashed through the sound barrier like a meteorite, beyond the point of no return: I had just stepped, body and soul, into a parallel world from which I would never come back.

Part one:
Grand-Algiers

'Whoever fights monsters
Should see to it
That in the process,
He does not become a monster…'

Frederick Wilhelm Nietzche,
Jenseits von Gut und Böse (1886)

Chapter one

Your application is convincing, Mr. Walid," the agency manager said at last. "I hope you won't let us down. Our firm's credibility relies entirely on our reputation."

His immaculately clean fingers turned over the sheets with a delicate flutter. He lingered over my photo, and picked up on a remark at the bottom of the index card.

"You worked as a driver at the National Tourist Office for nine months. Why did you give it up?"

"I was offered a part in a movie. I thought I'd be able to make a career in the cinema."

"How many movies?"

"Just one."

His auburn mustache curled around his pursed lips. He leaned back in his chair and said:

"It's not enough, but it could help. Our agency is offering what could be the chance of a lifetime. You will be well paid and it will be an opportunity for you to get yourself noticed by people who may have connections in showbiz."

Once again his shifty eyes bored into me.

"Cute looks," he admitted. "And a pretty face gets you a long way... do you speak French fluently?"

"I get by."

"Don't be vague, Mr. Walid. Be clear, specific and concise. The people you're going to work for hate woolliness."

"Got it."

"That kind of language is also inappropriate. From now on, you will only need one phrase: 'Very good, Sir.' Being the chauffeur to one of the most prestigious families in Grand Algiers is no picnic. You'll be expected to be polite, attentive, obsequious and always available. Have I made myself clear?"

"Very good, Sir."

"I'm glad to see you learn fast."

He slammed the file shut.

"My chauffeur will drive you to your new employers. You may leave."

As the car pulled away, I sensed that my life was changing direction. I felt light, relaxed, almost joyful. Already the nerve-racking streets of the city were behind us, while ahead, rather like the Red Sea in front of Moses, the wide boulevards opened their arms to greet me. I had never experienced anything like it before. And yet I often had felt within inches of reaching for the moon. But this time, I felt an extraordinary inner energy, more than euphoria, and the firm conviction that this March morning was making itself beautiful for me.

When Dahmane had offered me the job of chauffeur for one of the most affluent families in the land, I had immediately turned it down. I found it hard to picture myself waiting patiently behind the wheel for Madame to finish her aerobics class, or stoically sitting outside the school gates for Monsieur's brats, who were in no hurry to leave. I believed I deserved better. Since being offered a bit part in a movie by a desperate director, I dreamed non-stop of fame. I spent most of my waking hours fantasizing about bringing the house down, signing autographs on every street corner, driving a convertible, my smile broader than the horizon, my eyes as huge as my appetite for success.

Born on a day of storms, as the earth spilled its guts, I'd grown up without ever doubting my wildest hopes. I was convinced that, sooner or later, the limelight would pick me out of the wings and propel me towards the firmament. At school, I dreamed only of what I thought was the ultimate success. Sent before the school disciplinary board in disgrace, I kept my head in the clouds, heedless both of my teachers' anger and my parents' increasing anxiety. I was the obdurate dunce, always at the back of the classroom picking my nose and rolling my eyes. I was only comfortable behind the barricade of my obsession. My satchel was stuffed with movie magazines; my exercise books were filled with addresses of movie stars and press cuttings about their love lives and future projects. In a country where eminent university professors willingly became street vendors to make ends meet, the idea of studying didn't particularly appeal to me. I wanted to be an actor. The walls of my room were plastered with life-size posters. James Dean, Omar Sharif, Alain Delon and Claudia Cardinale surrounded me, warding off the poverty of my family: three waiting sisters, a mother who had become repulsive as a result of resigning herself to being a beast of burden, and an elderly, retired father who was irascible and demanding. All he did was complain and curse each time his gaze had the misfortune to light on one of us. So I swore to myself that I would not be like him, or inherit his poverty, or merely accept life's ups and downs as if there were no choice. I didn't have a bean, but I had more than my share of class and talent. Wherever I went—into the Casbah, to Bab El Oued, Soustara or even the gates of Bachjarah—I embodied a nascent legend in all its splendor. I just had to stand in the middle of the street for it to be lit up by my azure gaze. The virgins on their balconies were filled with longing at the sight of me, the local losers took their cue from my cavalier attitude and adopted an air of composure, and nothing seemed impervious to the quiet force of my irresistible charm.

"Bring a piece back for me," the driver shook me.

"Sorry?"

"I asked you to bring a piece back for me."

"A piece of what?"

"The moon. I've been trying to get through to you for a while, but you're on another planet."

"I'm sorry."

He turned down the volume of his radio. His big hairy hand landed on my knee.

"Don't worry, son. It'll be all right. Is it the first time you've worked for such high-up people?"

"Yes."

"I can tell." He overtook a lorry and accelerated to catch up with a line of buses. The breeze twirled the single strands of hair that were desperately attempting to cover his baldness. Sunk in his seat, his paunch resting on his knees, he looked uncomfortable in his shiny suit, like a worker all dressed up in his Sunday best, his crumpled tie adding a pathetic note.

"At first, you're a tiny bit out of your depth," he confided. "But you'll soon get into your stride. You'll stick it out, don't worry. The rich aren't as bad as they say. Fortune sometimes gives them wings, but they keep their heads screwed on."

He pointed to an ivory box on the dashboard.

"Those are American cigarettes in there. They belong to the boss, but he doesn't count them."

"No thanks. I'm trying to give up."

He nodded as he slowed down and turned onto a slip road leading off the bypass. Ahead of us, far behind the splashes of daylight, the first sculpted slopes of the Algerian Olympus began to reveal their splendors in the manner of an odalisque shedding her clothes at her sultan's feet.

"I'm Bouramane. At the agency they call me Adel. They say it sounds less like a peasant."

"Nafa Walid."

"Well, Nafa, if you play by the rules, you'll go far with that stuck-up bunch. In less than three years you'll be able to set up your own company. Our manager started out as a work-hand for the upper crust. Nowadays, he has no cause to be jealous of his former bosses. He drives a Merc, has a healthy bank balance, and his villa is just over that hill. He comes to the office once a week. The rest of the time, he travels all over the place bashing away on his calculator."

"So why don't you play the game too, if you want no cause to be jealous of him one day?"

He blew out his cheeks and gave a resigned nod.

"It's not the same. I'm forty, I've got seven kids and I'm hopelessly unlucky. Physically, nature hasn't exactly been kind to me. Looks count in business. If you don't make a good first impression, you'll never be able to make up for it. There are people born that way," he added, philosophically. "No point pushing their luck. If you have ideas above your station, you're likely to come a cropper."

The car somehow managed to extricate itself from the clamor of the slum districts and reach the motorway. We skirted the hill and arrived at a little corner of paradise with immaculate roads and pavements as wide as esplanades bordered with tall palm trees. The streets were empty, free from the swarms of impish brats that scour the streets of overcrowded cities. There wasn't even a grocer's shop or a kiosk. Taciturn villas turned their backs to us, their tall railings silhouetted against the sky, as if they were keen to set themselves apart from the rest of the world, to keep out the rot of a place that was in perpetual decline.

"Welcome to Beverly Hills," whispered the driver.

The Rajas' residence unfurled its fairytale splendor on the other side of the city, facing the sun, with its blue-tinted marble swimming pool and flagged courtyards visible from the street. Standing at the center of the gardens, like a god watching over his paradise, was a palace straight out of an oriental tale.

The driver dropped me off in front of the wrought-iron gate. His good-naturedness suddenly vanished and his lips curled in a wry smile. He gazed at the fortune of others all around him—martial, unassailable, so heavy that his shoulders bowed under the weight. He was suddenly cold and hostile, and a pale glimmer flickered in his eyes. For a second, I thought he resented me for not being able to go back with him to the chaos and foul stench of the slums.

"If you need a stand-in, you know where to find me," he said unconvincingly.

I nodded.

The car sped off and disappeared. Behind me, two terrifying Dobermans began to bark their heads off.

The butler refrained from shaking my hand or offering me a chair. He gave me a frosty reception in his office, which was illuminated by a wan light filtering through the heavy curtains over the French windows. Past sixty, with a starchy demeanor, he stood as straight as a ramrod in the center of the room. There was a vacant look in his eyes. He sought from the start to dominate me physically and mentally, to reduce me to the role of a subordinate.

"Is this a congenital disorder?" he inquired, alluding to my nonchalance.

"I..."

"Please stand up straight," he interrupted curtly. "You're not in front of a bank clerk."

His expert, impartial eyes looked me quickly up and down, penetrated my mind as if to read my thoughts—critical of my shoes, even though I'd polished them; my brand-new tie and my jacket, bought the day before from a luxury dry cleaner's.

"Do you have a telephone at home?"

"We've been bribing the underlings at the Post Office for ten years to get a line put in..."

"Keep it brief, please."

"No."

"Give my secretary your address."

"How do you keep an address brief?"

He didn't even register my impertinence. He was already ignoring me.

"You start on Tuesday, at 6 A.M. on the dot. You will have a room in Pavilion Two. My secretary will instruct you in your various domestic duties."

He pressed a buzzer. The lady on the ground floor appeared immediately to see me out.

"Is this place a boarding school?" I asked, at the other end of the corridor.

She smiled.

"Don't take any notice of him. Mr. Fayçal is a delightful man, even if he does tend to take himself too seriously. Have faith. You're going to like it here. The Rajas are charming, generous people."

She showed me into her little office, invited me to sit on a sofa and began by writing down my address in her notepad. She was well-groomed and kind, and it was partly thanks to her thoughtfulness that I decided not to allow a snooty, jumped-up servant to ruin my day.

"What's this business about a room in Pavilion Two?"

"You don't have to move in. It's just so that we know where to find you when we need you. I'd advise you to keep a few things there. Sometimes you'll be required to work very late. It will save you having to make your way home in the middle of the night."

I nodded.

"So what's your first name?"

"We don't use first names here, Mr. Walid," she replied in a clear, sharp voice, but with a sufficiently embarrassed smile not to offend me.

"Very good, Madame."

"I'm sorry. We have to comply strictly with our employers' instructions."

"Don't worry. What happened to the previous chauffeur?" I asked to dispel the awkwardness.

"He had an accident, I believe."

"What kind of accident?"

"That's all I know. Come, Mr. Walid, I'll show you your room."

We left through the tradesman's entrance. In silence, we walked around the edge of the paved courtyards, the patio and the swimming pool, as if this part of the property did not concern us. Pavilion Two was set back behind a border of bougainvillea, in a squat old building reserved for the servants. My room lay at the end of the corridor. It was pretty, with an ivy-garlanded window and a view over the magnificent gardens. The walls were papered; there was a fitted carpet on the floor and blue sheets on the bed. There was also a chest of drawers, a rocking chair in a corner facing a TV, and a wardrobe. This comfort added to the feeling that had been growing inside me in the morning since the agency car had driven me away from the stench and ugliness of the little back-street eateries.

"It's quiet here," the lady reassured me.

Telling me.

Dahmane asked me to meet him at the Lebanon, a snack bar that had once been a meeting place for intellectuals and artists, and whose clientele was now made up of losers enduring grisly hangovers or people with suspicious needle marks on their arms. Before, actors and writers met there to protest at the decline of culture, mindless censorship, and the mediocrity that was threatening to turn bookshops into havens for spiders. In those days you could sit at the table of a screenwriter or a gagged poet and listen for hours while he vented his spleen against a predatory society paying no more attention to the destruction of its elites than to the cracks surreptitiously undermining its foundations. The beer tasted like horse piss, but the place had the virtue of allowing us to forget our troubles, which paled in comparison with those of our neighbors.

There were other reasons why I went to the Lebanon. First of all because the cafés of Bab El Oued were sinister, and then because the movie-makers were no better catered for elsewhere, and I hoped to be able to collar one of them and persuade him to give me the part that would allow my dreams to come true. Unfortunately, since the junkies and transvestites had ruined the place, few movie directors still dared venture there. From time to time, between two bouts of excessive drinking, a fight would break out, and sometimes you might even stumble over a battered corpse in the toilets. No matter how often the police tried to close the place down, the Lebanon always managed to reopen its doors, like a magistrate his files. One case hadn't yet been processed when there was already another on its heels, certain to monopolize everyone's attention. I often wondered why I kept coming back to this illicit den haunted by junkies, lesbians and convalescent crooks. Perhaps it was that smoke-filled atmosphere that makes anything seem possible, for every regular would give rein to his fantasies. Hidden away in my corner, I would observe this bunch of losers with a great deal of interest, their facades and affectations providing an amazing cast of characters that was very useful for my training as an actor.

Dahmane was waiting for me by the bay window; his nose buried in a handkerchief and his face flushed. Laid low by his perpetual cold, he feebly shuffled along the battered bench to make room for me and blurted out:

"I hope you didn't do anything stupid."

"Not this time."

He breathed out a sigh of relief and relaxed.

"I couldn't have stood it."

"Me neither."

Dahmane was my lifelong friend. Born in the same cul-de-sac in the heart of the Casbah, we'd spent our early years hanging around the same streets and infuriating our schoolteachers, for we were considered hopeless pests. Then his father died in an accident, and Dahmane started to behave. Head of the family at the age of thirteen, he promised his mother never to let her down again. While I was dreaming on my cloud, he worked night and day to fulfill his family obligations, and managed to pass his baccalaureate with honors. After a training course at the catering institute in Tizi Ouzou, he had worked for several tourist complexes, networking among the Algiers bourgeoisie. Now, he ruled at the Varan Roi, a trendy cabaret on the coastal road, and had bought himself a magnificent apartment in rue Didouche Mourad. I owed him all the casual jobs that I had never managed to hold down, including the part that Rachid Derrag had given me in his third-rate movie *Children of the Dawn*. He clasped my hand. "Nafa, my friend, luck is a fickle companion. Don't let her leave your side. She rarely returns." His fingers were digging into me. "Are you listening to me?"

"I think I'll get used to it."

"You only think?"

I managed to extricate my numb hand.

"You don't sound too thrilled," he prodded.

"You can't have it all," I said with a hint of bitterness.

"Meaning?"

"Don't tell me you were expecting me to jump for joy at being the servant of a rich family. Do you realize? Me, Nafa Walid—a chauffeur?!"

"And who is Nafa Walid?" He fumed. "Someone who dips into his mother's miserable savings to buy a pair of imitation trainers, that's all. There's no point walking around in a silk tie and hunger in your belly. Not every bumpkin can strut around showing off."

"I'm not a bumpkin."

"Prove it. How much have you got in your pocket? Go on, show me. I bet you haven't even got enough for a taxi fare. I don't know whether it's my flu or your nonchalance that's getting on my nerves, but you're beginning to exasperate me. Time is flying past, and you do nothing. You have no right to complain when you're nothing, Nafa. If you want to make something of yourself, leap at the first opportunity that comes your way."

"I tell you I'm going to give it a try."

He buried his nose in his handkerchief again, and fastidiously wiped his nostrils. His feverish eyes glared at me, trapping my gaze. He went back on the offensive.

"I know a lot of people who started at the bottom of the ladder. Now you can't catch up with them. Not even with a rocket. All the fat cats who make you green with envy today were nobodies—not even ten years ago. Do you want to make it too? Do you want to succeed?"

"Yes," I almost shouted.

"Well, it's already a first step."

There was no point arguing. Dahmane was unaware that there are people who are born upright, who are allergic to subservience, people who snap; that I was one of those people who snap in two if they have to bow down to anyone. He did not understand that what he called laziness in others was actually pride, a distancing from the mundane. I wasn't one of those people who wanted to get rich. My ambition had never been to make a fortune or to be high up in an influential position. I wanted to be an actor until the day I died, to carve out a legend for myself larger than life, and claim divine privileges—otherwise how else should I interpret the fact that nature had made me as beautiful and healthy as a god?

To placate me, Dahmane took me out for dinner to a restaurant in Riad El Fath. During the evening, he bombarded me with advice and examples that were supposed to reassure me. Each time I threatened to blow a gasket, he bought me a beer. Around midnight, I was plastered. No way could I go home in that state. My father was very strict on some matters, and I didn't want to upset the family. Dahmane offered to put me up for the night. Early the next morning he drove me home. The minute my father saw me on the landing, he started shouting at me:

"I won't pay a cent, I'm warning you. I didn't ask for anything and I don't give a shit about your stupid bell."

He stepped aside to disclose the telephone sitting on a chest in the hall. I stood there pensively for a moment. For the last three years, I had been filling in application after application, bribing every clerk and underling, sending reminder after reminder to have a line put in, without any success. Yet, all I had to do was leave my address with the Rajas' secretary for a telephone to be installed the same day.

"You see?" exclaimed Dahmane. You'll soon start to appreciate the privileges that money brings."

I nodded. If money doesn't buy happiness, it's through no fault of its own.

Chapter two

I arrived at the Rajas' on Tuesday at 6 A.M. sharp. Mr. Fayçal made a show of checking his watch and gave a satisfied nod. He led me to a huge garage where five brand-new, powerful cars sat, and explained the use of each one. Then he began to instill into me the ground rules of the chauffeur's profession.

"Never look the boss in the eyes, and never hold out your hand to him," he stressed.

He showed me where I should stand, how to open the door, and how to close it. "Gently," he added. "Don't slam it. Walk round the front of the car, never the back. When you're at the wheel, look straight ahead. When someone speaks to you, don't turn around. A glance in the rear view mirror is enough. Not more than twice on any one journey."

He gave me a tour of the property, showed me where I was allowed to walk, and pointed out the one-way routes.

"To get out to the street, there's no point going past the swimming pool. There's a little door over there under the mimosa." At around 9 A.M., he sent me out to a menswear shop. I was entitled to half a dozen identical but immaculate suits, three pairs of Italian shoes, a pile of underwear, shirts, black ties and shades. The next day, driving a gleaming Peugeot, I was sent to deliver letters to a dozen important figures, to familiarize myself with the most important itineraries. Five days later, I could find the right house with my eyes shut and without wasting time getting lost. In these high spheres, punctuality is a virtue; there is no worse crime than keeping a *nabob* waiting.

The Rajas were away on a business trip. Mr. Fayçal was keen to train me before their return. He gave me briefings each morning, made me recite the names and addresses, timed my journeys and corrected my log sheets, fuming at every mistake. When he blew his top, his back swelled and his face reddened so quickly that he looked as if he were about to have a heart attack. Meanwhile, I took refuge behind a stalwart obsequiousness. In the evening, exhausted by my marathon day, I returned to Pavilion Two with my head about to explode. Shut up in my room, I felt as if I were going mad. Even sleep was elusive. I lay on the bed, my hands clasped behind my head, staring at the ceiling. I tried to cheer myself up by laughing at myself as a child, the scrapes I had got into and my big secrets. It was no use. Something wasn't right. I was already missing the noises of my streets, the warmth of my own people, the bond of poverty. At this hour, in the Casbah, I usually went out for a breath of air on the terrace, or I'd have gone to Sid Ali the poet's place to watch him dragging on a joint and reciting his lines between two puffs. Here, the silence, the absence, and the coldness almost poisoned my breath. I shrank inwardly with the feeling that I could gather the drops of solitude in the palm of my hand. My "cubicle" was like a sterile chrysalis from which no butterfly would emerge.

Every evening, the servants would gather at 7 P.M., to eat in a gloomy recess opposite the kitchens.

Three men and two women ate around a big oak table, paying as little attention to each other as a group of gargoyles. The gardener was a wizened old man, a bunch of bones thrown higgledy-piggledy into threadbare overalls. With his hoary head and exhausted eyes, it took him longer to raise the spoon to his mouth than for someone with a squint to thread a needle. He kept to himself, wraith-like, hunched over his plate, refusing, with a kind of obdurate hostility, to talk to anyone. The two cleaning women huddled in their corner, their faces wrinkled and their chins sunken, visibly irritated by the proximity of the men. Annoyed by my curiosity, the two other servants wolfed down their food, clearly in a hurry to get away.

People are always wary of a new recruit at first. I thought that eventually I would manage to get a smile out of someone, or at least get the quiver of an eyebrow. Yet after a week, I was still being treated to the same frosty welcome, the same animosity. It was all very well me saying "Good morning", "Good evening", "Hello everyone", but I received not the faintest look, not the slightest mumble, except perhaps the creaking of a chair or the momentary pause of a fork betraying the tension that my untimely arrival had created. I sat down at the other end of the table; I was served furtively, in a meaningful silence, and sometimes the table was cleared before I had finished eating. In no time at all, my neighbors tiptoed out of the room; I found myself alone in the middle of the kitchens with a sinking feeling that would develop into a sense of deep despair as the evening wore on.

Sid Ali, the bard of the Casbah, told me that Algeria was the biggest archipelago in the world—made up of twenty-eight million or so islands. He neglected to add that the oceans of misunderstanding that divide us are the darkest and vastest of the entire planet.

On the eighth day, when I was seriously thinking of dropping the whole thing and returning to the maze of the Casbah, a man burst into my room.

"Are you the new fellow?"

Without giving me time to rise, he grabbed a bottle of mineral water from my bedside table and raised it to his lips. He was a strapping black guy, built like a brick outhouse, with Herculean arms and a massive, battered face. He crushed the bottle in his hands, threw it into the wastepaper basket and wiped his lips on his wrist. His intense eyes swept me up and down.

"I've been looking for you for the last fifteen minutes."

"I was eating with the others."

"With those creeps? Are you kidding? That's no place for you, man. There's a snack bar at 61 rue Fakhar. Fouquet's. It belongs to Junior. From now on, you'll eat there."

"I didn't know," I said, relieved.

"Well, now you do." He suddenly put out his hand. "I'm Hamid. I work for the boss's son. Let's not hang around. I can feel my hair turning gray just standing here."

We left via the little door under the mimosa. Night had conquered the streets and was about to defeat the last pockets of heat. In the sky, a potbellied moon was reviewing its platoons of stars. Hamid invited me to clamber aboard a monumental Mercedes, ensconced himself behind the wheel and drove off at speed along the deserted highways.

"I've seen you somewhere before," I said after a long, awkward silence.

He bared his big teeth in a grin:

"Gold medal at the Mediterranean Games, vice-champion of the military world, vice-champion of Africa, twice champion of the Arab world, took part in the Olympic Games twice…"

I struck my forehead with the palm of my hand.

"Hamid Sallal, the boxer."

"I didn't think you'd recognized me."

"Didn't you decide to go professional?"

"Yes, but the fat cats at the Federation were too greedy. I said: I'm not sharing. So they gave me the boot. I spent two years in Marseille. I won my first fights within the distance. And then, suddenly, I found myself doing the washing-up in a café."

"How come?"

"They tried to exploit me. Rich pickings. I get punched, they get rich. That's how it is in the Federation. 'Canonball' Bilal, Rachid Yanes and 'Left Hook' were potential world champions. But they were destroyed because they refused to take part in the scams run by the gangsters of the sports world. Bilal went off on a training course in Canada and cleared out. Rachid is a mechanic in Boufarik. Only

'Left Hook' has found himself a home, near Relizane. He coaches kids in the morning, and in the evening he hits the bottle. The back of beyond, it's no place for thoroughbreds, my friend. To survive there, you have to be a donkey or an old nag. Hey! Stop me if I'm boring you! When it comes to chatting, I'm unbeatable—the heavyweight champion!"

"You're not boring me. I've been champing at the bit for the last week."

"Maybe, but that's no reason for me to take advantage. Do you know what Junior does when I go on too much, he slams his fist in my mouth to shut me up."

Before I could respond, he continued:

"I've dragged around all over the place, done every shitty job there is. I even spent months being tossed around on a trawler. One evening, when I was drowning my sorrows in drink, a cabaret boss offered me a job as a bouncer. It was a notorious district. The real low lives. They'd slit your throat over nothing. I soon sorted them out. Not that I hit hard. I didn't need to. The punters respect a champion. In this backwater, the ordinary people are the ones who still worship you. They're the only ones who recognize your worth. The officials, they congratulate you one day and forget you the next. They've got other things to think about. Bunch of bastards... At the club, I met Junior. He was looking for a bodyguard. He said: show me your fists. I showed him my fists. He said: They're made of bronze; now open them. I opened them. Junior said: Inside, there's nothing but air. Then he showed me his fists. I said: they're pretty, but made of porcelain. Junior laughed, then opened them. Inside, there was dough. I'm a boxer. With all the knocks I've taken, I've become cautious. But that night, it didn't need to be spelled out. I twigged at once. That was how Junior hired me."

We had arrived at a chalet concealed by a young tropical forest. The car crunched the gravel and pulled up beside a bay window. A superior-looking man wearing a kimono was lounging in a rocking chair by a swimming pool, puffing on a cigar as scary as a ghost.

"That's Junior," Hamid informed me.

27

I straightened my suit and stood to attention at the foot of the marble steps. Junior looked me up and down. When he moved his pudgy, hairy legs, his bathrobe parted, revealing dark red boxer shorts. With his ruddy complexion and regal paunch, everything about him reeked of wealth. He was aged between twenty-five and thirty, but he clearly considered himself old enough to affect a patriarchal air.

"Come nearer so I can have a good look at you," he commanded.

I walked up the four steps that separated us and stood a good distance from him, as Mr. Fayçal had instructed me. Junior placed his cigar in an ashtray in the shape of a water lily, stared at me, his lips drooping. He casually flipped a business card with a sketch on it to me.

"You're to bring me a lady. She's waiting for you in Fouka Marine. Do you know where that is, at least?"

"Sixty to eighty kilometers from here."

"Here we talk timing. Your dashboard is your watch face. Have I made myself clear?"

"Yes, Sir."

"The route is on this map. I want you back here by 10 P.M. You're already three minutes late."

Hamid picked up the map, stuffed it into my pocket and shoved me into the Mercedes.

"Top speed!"

I revved the engine.

"Where are the documents for the car?"

"The Rajas don't need them. Go, go…"

It took me an hour to get to Fouka, with the accelerator hard down all the way. I didn't want to screw up my first job. The map took me to a villa on the edge of town. I had barely pulled up when a woman appeared out of the dark and slid surreptitiously onto the back seat.

"You should turn off your headlights, you cretin," she grumbled.

"I'm new, Madame."

"That's no excuse."

Her pale, scowling face filled the rear-view mirror.

"For goodness sake, get moving!" she screeched in French.

Her curtness threw me into a panic. I was all fingers and thumbs, and hit the pavement as I moved off, throwing the lady against the door.

"Idiot," she fumed. "Go back to your village and fix your cart."

"I was born and bred in Algiers," I said angrily enough for her to realize that I would have no qualms about ditching her and the jalopy and walking home.

She calmed down, realized she had lost something, fumbled around on the seat and then rummaged in her bag grumbling, then she leaned back against the seat, exhausted and blasé. Further on, she switched on the light and started groping around on the floor again and riffling through her bag.

"Can I be of assistance, Madame?" I volunteered in a conciliatory tone.

"Yes, mind your own business."

Our eyes clashed in the rear-view mirror.

"You want my picture?" she shouted.

I looked away.

I could feel her rasping breath burning the back of my neck for the rest of the journey.

Hamid was looking out for us at the entrance to the residence. The minute he spotted the Mercedes, he ran and began opening the door, without waiting for the car to stop. The lady was fidgeting around in the back, in a vile temper. As she stepped out, I noticed she was stark naked under her fur coat. Junior joined us, casually embraced her and kissed her on the lips.

"Did you leave your smile in your powder compact, darling?"

"I had a little present for you but I can't think what I've done with it."

"Phew! I thought you weren't happy to see me." He pushed her in front of him and gave her a loud smack on the rump.

29

"We'll go and sort this problem out, precious. My way, of course."

They closed the French windows behind them.

"Do you know who she is?" Hamid asked me excitedly.

"No."

"Haven't you heard of Our Lady of Chenoua?"

"I'm not with you."

"Well, it's her: Leila Soccar. Even statues would turn to look at her. Daughter of a diplomat. They say that an emir of the Orient once gave up his titles simply because she asked him to."

"And of course, I'm supposed to believe these stories."

"Well I do. Even now, any big shot would give his eyeteeth to lick her toes. At forty, she's still the most sought-after piece of ass in Grand Algiers. When Junior met her for the first time, he nearly threw his clothes off there and then. Even though he has harems all over the place. But Leila is his trophy, his glory. Despite the age difference between them, the whole city's green with envy."

"I'm wiped," I said, to curb his wild fantasies. "May I leave?"

"No way, my friend. You're going to drive her home in an hour or so. Her husband comes home at dawn and she's got be there to greet him."

"Her husband comes home at dawn?"

"Oh yes! He's one of those ghosts who rest only on the risks they take. You haven't seen anything yet."

I drove the lady home around 3 A.M. We didn't exchange a single word during the journey. She stretched out on the back seat and stared at the ceiling smoking a cigarette and listening to the music on the radio. On reaching her house, she waited for me to open the door, then went inside without looking at me. Before driving off again, I noticed a box wedged between the cushions of the back seat. I went back and gave it to her.

"You forgot this, Madame."

Her ethereal gaze refused to take in the object I was holding in my hand, preferring to look deep into my eyes to find out what I was thinking. I felt her eyes bore deep into me, like a flow of lava, flooding my belly and troubling my soul. Her fingers languidly brushed my cheek, causing my flesh to tremble. Abruptly, she regained her composure.

"I never forget anything, dear."

Seeing I was at a loss, she added:

"You can keep it."

And with that, she gently closed the door between us.

Back in the car, I opened the box and found a splendid Rolex watch set in a gold bracelet.

"Nafa, my boy," I said to myself, "I don't know whether the steps you're climbing lead to glory or the scaffold; but one thing is certain: you're on your way."

Chapter three

The Rajas had been back from their trip for two weeks. Hamid had gone to pick them up from the airport and I hadn't managed to glimpse them even once. Mr. Fayçal had taken the precaution of locking the gate between my "walk" and the swimming pool terrace. From dawn to dusk, I moped in my room, inspecting my nails and flicking through the same magazines. Apart from being sent on a few errands by the "Butler", often personal ones, I found that my employers ignored me. Mr. Raja was always away. As for Madame, I had only heard her scathing tones striking fear into the servants and causing a general state of panic.

Junior had sent me on two missions, in the meantime. The first consisted of driving to Tizi Ouzou to deliver a gift to the widow of an industrialist. And the second was driving a prostitute back to Oran. Four hundred and thirty kilometers of storms, flooded roads and massive traffic jams. I telephoned Junior to request permission to spend the night at a hotel. I would be back on my feet after a bath and a good night's sleep. "No way," he yelled down the phone. "I want the car tomorrow, first thing." I just had time to grab a sandwich in a cheap eatery and I was on my way back. Night had fallen. The rain was bucketing down, and the lightning blinded me. Those four hundred and thirty kilometers nearly cost me my life. I fell asleep at the wheel and ended up in a ploughed field.

"You'd better pay for that out of your own pocket," warned Hamid when he saw the Mercedes' twisted bumper. "You haven't even been with us a month, it's not a good idea to mention the accident. If I were you I'd rush out and find a good panel-beater."

"Where's Junior? I thought he needed the car."

"He flew to Paris an hour after you phoned."

"So why the hell did he force me to come straight back in that foul weather?"

"That I can't tell you, my friend. The ways of the lord are strange."

So I had to ask Dahmane to lend me the money for the repair. After this setback, I started smoking again. Like crazy. Without even noticing. My days got me down, my nights came to an abrupt end. Despite the friendly atmosphere at Fouquet's, I realized I never stopped listening out for the telephone. Mr. Fayçal insisted on being kept informed of my whereabouts. I had to leave him my contact number wherever I was. He would often call at ridiculous times just to make sure I wasn't drunk or disorderly. When I rushed over, breathless, he would never fail to find some criticism to justify his persecution of me before dismissing me, thus ruining my rare moments of respite.

Then the Rajas' only daughter, Sonia, arrived. A venomous creature whose dangerous beauty hinted at hidden cruelty. When I went to pick her up from the airport, I immediately fell under her spell. She seemed so vulnerable amid all her luggage, a Bohemian headscarf knotted around her head, her legs imprisoned in tights that took your breath away. Tall, blonde and slim, she looked like a blade of corn greeting the splendor of summer. She had gratified me with a long look while I stowed her packages in the boot. In defiance of Mr.Fayçal's theories, she sat next to me and didn't take her eyes off my profile.

34

"Are you the new chap?"

"Yes, Miss."

She seemed to find my respectful "yes, Miss" funny. Suddenly, her clear eyes darkened.

"What's all this about the Islamic Salvation Front? Is it true that the fundamentalists have taken over the town halls at home?"

"It's true, Miss."

"And all the girls are wearing the *hijab*?"

"Not yet, Miss."

"In your opinion, will they take over the country?"

"It's possible, Miss."

"In Europe, that's all they're talking about. I wonder whether I did the right thing in coming home."

She leaned back against the seat and lifted up her hair with a weary gesture: "I was extremely happy in Geneva. Have you been there?"

"No, Miss."

"Haven't you ever been to Europe?"

"Only to France. I used to go there in the days when we were allowed to draw our wages in foreign currency."

"Do you have family there?"

"No, Miss."

Then, thinking that this might be an opportunity worth seizing:

"I wanted to be in the movies."

She stared at me for three interminable seconds:

"It's true, you have the looks."

"Thank you, Miss."

She stopped talking. To my great disappointment. I hoped she would dwell on the subject, tell me that she had connections in the movie world and would see what she could do for me, that sort of thing. Nothing. She turned on the radio and withdrew into an unassailable silence.

From the next morning, she had me driving her around. I took her to her club, to the golf club, and spent the whole morning in the car park, under a blazing sun. At lunchtime, I drove her to Bachjarah. And again, my hands perspired profusely on the wheel. Around 3 P.M., she returned to the club and stayed there until nightfall. I hadn't had a thing to eat since breakfast. I had to make do with a sandwich that I didn't even finish.

For seven days and seven nights, I had done nothing but fidget about in my seat and feverishly crumple up my cigarette packets, unable to move away from the car because Sonia hated having to run around after a servant. One evening, because I'd taken refuge in a snack bar on the opposite side of the street, she nearly killed me.

"And what next?" she shrieked as a crowd gathered. "Perhaps his lordship would like me to bring him breakfast in bed? Who on earth do you think you are? You are not allowed to leave the car without my permission. I demand you stay where I leave you. If you don't like it you can go back to your slum."

"Very good, Miss."

"Listen to that," protested an onlooker, literally sickened by my groveling.

I had never thought myself capable of hating somebody so much. I silently held the door open for her, and closed it again with a soft click. I had difficulty nosing my way through the indignant throng, then I drove towards the hills outside town. I parked the car under a carob tree, in a deserted spot. Sonia frowned:

"Where are we?"

I turned to face her. The look in my eyes sent a chill through her. I calmly placed my hand on her shoulder and pulled her violently towards me.

"Listen, Miss. It's true, I'm nothing but an ordinary driver, it's true, you can dispense with me whenever you please, but there's one thing you'd be wrong to lose sight of. I am a human being, and I have my pride. It's not enough to protect me from prejudice, but I have nothing else. If I were to lose that, I may as well lose my life."

She gulped when I released her.

I thought I'd had it, that my friend Dahmane would hold it

against me for the rest of his life. But I was wrong. The next day, a cleaning lady brought me a little parcel. Inside, there was a solid gold chain and a sheet of fragrant notepaper on which was written: "If you forgive me, wear this round your neck."

Sonia didn't shout at me again, but she continued to exploit me so relentlessly that her pendant around my neck became heavier than an iron collar.

One evening Mr. Fayçal summoned me in the middle of the night. Rigid behind his Victorian desk, he was nervously mopping his face with a handkerchief. His pallor and dripping brow made me fear the worst. He began by loosening his bow tie and frowning as if the reason for my being there had eluded him. Recovering his faculties, he wiped the back of his neck and his chin, and tried to concentrate:

"Madame is going out," he announced. "I'm warning you, she hates being jolted. And avoid the potholes and bumpy roads. Drive *carefully*. No speeding, no dangerous driving."

He fired off his instructions in one go, before he ran out of breath. Anyone would have thought his fate depended on my capabilities as a driver. Apparently he was absolutely terrified of Mrs. Raja. You would think she held him responsible for any domestic mishaps.

"Nafa," he added, running out into the corridor, "I can't say it too often: be cautious and pay attention."

"I promise."

Mrs. Raja must have had a string of rapt suitors in her youth. Her fine features retained a trace of true nobility. At fifty-five, she was already decaying, like a monument struck by lightning. Time had overtaken her when she was least expecting it. She was no longer able to stave it off. Mummified in her dusky shimmering sari, she sat regally on the back seat, a dying goddess at the entrance to her sarcophagus. Her huge eyes still followed the shooting stars, but her face, ravaged by illness, no longer believed in miracles. Its former beauty was stoically deteriorating, like an ancient legend that no longer has currency. It was a ghostly, bitter beauty, tempered by the powerlessness of wealth to grease the palm of erosion, despite the facelifts and luxury cosmetics.

She hadn't said a damned word since she had got into the car. Not even when a crack in the road filled with water escaped my vigilance. She merely readjusted a fold of her veil and carried on gazing at the lights of the city as quietly as a child in front of an aquarium.

We were driving through a sleeping residential district. It was after midnight, not a shadow stirred in the streets. From time to time, Mrs. Raja gave me whispered directions—"left", "right", "straight on"—until she asked me to pull up in front of a house with lighted windows.

"Come with me."

She alighted unaided and rang the bell. A young women opened the door, and stood aside as soon as she recognized the visitor. We entered a cozy living room: brocade-covered sofas, porcelain lamps and gleaming silverware. A man was ensconced in a deep sofa, his pipe within reach. His bald head gleamed under the crystal chandelier. He gave a start when we walked in, more irritated than surprised, stood up, picked up his jacket and went out into the street, without a word. Mrs. Raja refused to look at the young woman. She tried to be dignified. She had stepped slightly to one side to allow the man to pass, as if he aroused a feeling of repulsion in her.

The young woman leaned against the wall, raised a long cigarette to her bloodless lips and blew the smoke up at the ceiling with an air of annoyance.

The man climbed into the car. Mrs. Raja joined him, haughty and cold, and ordered me to drive them home. A silence heavy with resentment settled over the back seat, so pervasive that it absorbed the purring of the engine. The man let out a sigh and turned his face to the window. The fleeting stripes of light from the street lamps danced across his face. Mrs. Raja stared straight ahead, her lips sealed, her eyes impenetrable. I sensed she was battling to keep her dignity intact. After a few kilometers, she gave in and her fist came down on the seat:

"What are you playing at Salah?" she rasped. "That you are unfaithful to me with your army of secretaries, I can understand, but with my own sister..."

Mr. Raja did not reply. His face pressed to the glass, he stared obstinately at the Maqam, the monument to the martyrs of the War of Independence, on the top of the hill.

Five months at the Rajas and already my childhood dreams were shattered on the shores of lost causes. I had met celebrities, driven journalists, industrialists, *Aladdins*, and not once had their gaze alighted on that thing I carried inside me like a phantom pregnancy in the hope of giving birth to a constellation. They weren't even aware of my fevered obsequiousness, except to mention that a piece of luggage was particularly fragile, or to lambaste me for being a few wretched minutes late. My profile didn't strike them; my Adonis smile, my perfect build made no more impact on their arrogance than a sacred place on a vandal. I was nothing but a modern-day coach driver, a common porter who would do better to save himself the misery instead of struggling to break into an uncompromising elite. With the mounting disappointments, I had gained enough wisdom to allow myself to flirt with my status as untouchable without deluding myself. At the mercy of Sonia's mood swings and her brother's high jinks, I submitted to their tyranny with long-suffering patience. The previous week, Junior had dragged me out of bed at 2 A.M., to send me out to find him a bottle of whisky. He was at his second home, his latest conquest snuggled up to him in bed; they were giggling over a porno movie. Every single bar in town was closed, but there was no way I could return empty-handed. Junior would have taken it as a snub and would never have forgiven me for "humiliating" him in front of his date. I went to Sidi Fredj to avoid a misunderstanding. By the time I got back, Junior and his princess for a night had gone off to party somewhere else, leaving me, bottle in hand, exhausted, stumbling with sleep and rage, calling myself every name under the sun until I fell asleep. My inability to throw in the towel was a measure of my low self-esteem. It didn't take much. My pride had deserted me, no

39

doubt stunned at the number of concessions I had made. Instead of slamming the door behind me and marching out, I had chosen to crawl. Quite simply. Self-flagellation? Maybe. Having reached that point of servility, I reckoned people got what they deserved. So who was I, when it came to it? Nafa Walid, son of a retired railway worker; in other words a man who couldn't afford his own dignity. Slam the door behind me? And go where? Back to Bab El Oued and the stench of cracked drains, wandering aimlessly around all day among the winding alleys of the Casbah, pestering the schoolgirls of Soustara and going home to my bedroom with its closed shutters, cursing that tedious existence? Too late. There are curses that no exorcist can ward off. When you have shuddered under their spell, you find you are addicted to them. That was what had happened to me. Now that I had glimpsed the paradise of others, I strove to nibble at the edges, contenting myself with a crumb here, a splash there, convinced that the smell of money, even when it is whisked from under my nose, was worth all the charms of the working-class districts.

"Listen to you, talking to yourself," said Hamid, catching me unawares.

"I'm talking to my guardian angel."

"I don't see his hearing trumpet."

He burst out laughing, delighted with his own rejoinder, took down my jacket which was hanging from the coat rack and threw it in my face.

"I need you, my friend."

"Ask Fayçal."

"No need. Junior is in Sétif; Sonia's at the beach and Madame is unwell. In any case, we won't be long."

An hour later, we arrived at Dar Ez Rahma, an old people's home. The manager of the establishment, a tiny, lively woman with a severe bun and a mouth like an incision, received us in her office. She seemed harassed, and glared at Hamid.

"You should do something about your forgetfulness," she grumbled.

Then, after drawing a deep breath:

"Well, you're here. That's better than nothing. Follow me."

She led us across a courtyard surrounded by plane trees. Elderly people were loitering around the place, some sitting on benches, others in clusters on the steps of a dismal dormitory.

"We're forced to fit them in where we can," complained the manager. "We're short of beds and rooms. Subsidies are embezzled and charities are increasingly reluctant to help. The death rate this year is worrying."

She suddenly retraced her steps and walked towards an elderly lady on her own.

"Don't stay there, Mimouna. The sun's very strong this morning."

"I've only just sat down."

"Don't tell fibs, dear. I can see you from my office. I've been watching you for a while. Please go over and join the others."

The old woman nodded, but appeared unwilling to obey. She hunched her shoulders, withdrawing into herself.

"She's the oldest resident at the center," went on the manager, walking off. "Her companion died last week from terrible sunstroke. She's trying to follow her."

We came up to an emaciated eighty-year-old woman huddled in the shade of a shrub. The manager took her leave and left us alone. Hamid put down his basket of fruit on the ground, put his fist in front of his mouth and cleared his throat and said softly:

"*Hadja…*"

The old woman jumped. Her white eyes were confused. She stretched out a trembling hand, which Hamid gently intercepted.

"My child?"

"It's only Hamid, *Hadja.*"

She smiled. Her lined face crinkled. She was a pathetic, blind old lady in a faded but clean dress that was too big for her. I don't know why I was overcome with a feeling of pity and confusion. I had the impression that the home was growing dim, that the trees were suddenly turning their backs to us.

"He didn't come?"

"No, *Hadja*."

"It doesn't matter. I hope he's well."

"He's in good health."

"He's very involved. That's the way he is. When he was little, he was the last to go to bed. True, I miss him, but I understand. He's killing himself with work."

Her quavering voice wound itself around the shrub, like a shroud caught by the wind. Once again, her hand sought Hamid's face, found it and stroked it.

"Is there someone with you?"

"Yes, a charming young man. His name is Nafa."

"Does he have a relative here?"

"No, he came with me. He wanted to say hello to you."

"He must be a very nice boy then."

I kissed the top of her head. She liked that, took my wrist and held on to it.

"Hamid, my boy, people who live in the dark have no sense of time. Whether they're asleep or awake, it doesn't make much difference. Their blindness is exile. The only light that can reach them comes from the hearts of others. Do you understand?"

"I understand, *Hadja*."

"I still cling to life purely so that I can smell the scent of my child again. He's the only thing that keeps me here, on this island. No," she quickly pre-empted, "don't worry him. I'm fine. I just miss hearing his voice, feeling his breath against my face. He's all I've got left. I would feel less alone, afterwards. I'd be less cold in my grave if I could leave with the certainty that he is well. In my sleep, my stomach sometimes feels kicks just like the ones he used to give me when I was carrying him. I wake up in a sweat, and I tell myself that my child is in pain, that something awful has happened to him..."

"I assure you, he's well, *Hadja*."

"I believe you. You have no reason to lie to me. But a mother is like a child, she needs to touch in order to believe for herself. They brought the doctor to my bedside several times. He said I was finished. My mind has already departed, only my body refuses to follow. My heart isn't tranquil, you understand? A minute would be enough to make me happy. Then I would go without any regrets."

She turned her face away. To hide her tears. Hamid kissed her on the shoulder before backing away. We returned to the car in silence, he sullen and I dragging on a stubborn cigarette.

"Who is that woman?" I asked when we were far from the home.

"She's the mother of your employer, dear Nafa, the mother of the all-powerful Salah Raja. She's been rotting there for years, and not once has he deigned to visit her. It's not even he who asks me to go and see her."

Chapter four

Before becoming a nightclub, the Fennec had been a center for people with motor disabilities. Standing sleepily on its rock, it seemed uninterested in the prurient slums on the hillside. Huddled on its catafalque, closer to the sky than to the ghetto, it persisted in addressing the good Lord, the shadow of its age-old buildings barely disturbed by the intermittent squeaking of wheelchairs. Passers-by would surreptitiously cross themselves, praying to their patron saints to save them from such a place. But the city soon swallowed up the surrounding wasteland. Construction work obliterated the little copses under an avalanche of concrete, before unleashing the Hun-like bulldozers onto the rest of the site. Soon, in the place of the local inhabitants' pitiful vegetable gardens, opulent villas mushroomed over the hillside. In a twinkling, the former goat-path leading down to the shacks had been turned into a proud, neat avenue, twisting round by the water tower to hurtle down to the new town, which was festooned with neon signs, enticing shop windows and noisy discos. A number of developers had their eye on the old asylum. Its residents were re-housed on the pretext that it was being refurbished.

During the events of October 1988,* a fire of suspicious origin broke out, and thanks to the withdrawal of the charitable bodies and local authorities, the asylum was sold to a developer for peanuts. So it was with a certain relief that passers-by deciphered the eight multicolored letters usurping the pediment of the building, illuminating the night sky like an *aurora borealis*. This was the story behind the most exclusive private club of El Acima, a giant dance hall frequented by the Algiers jet set.

Unlike the Golf club, where I had to wait for Sonia in the car park, the Fennec had a little bar opposite the cloakrooms where the drivers could relax. They were entitled to a hamburger and drinks.

Perched on a high stool, I was nibbling my ration at the bar, my eyes riveted on the door concealing the dance floor. Every time someone came in or went out, it released a blast of wild music and allowed us to glimpse the light show sweeping over the heads of the frenzied dancers. Since I'd been sitting there, a man had been watching me all the time. Every time I turned around, I met his somber gaze, which seemed to belie his smile. He must have been around fifty, with white hair and a woolen jumper straining at the seams over his belly. At last, he got up and came and sat next to me.

"Don't you remember me?"

I gazed at him for a moment.

"Should I?"

"You don't have to, but I'd be pleased if you did. You are the guy who was in that TV movie?"

Realizing that I had no idea who he was, he gave me a clue.

"The musician, at Sid Ali, the poet's house."

I desperately tried to remember.

"We partied together," he insisted. "When *Hadj* Ghaouti's son got married, in Souk El Jemaa. You were with your friend Dahmane."

"It's true, I was there."

"Well the guy with the mandolin, that was me. Sid Ali said

* see Key Dates, p. 256

that if my instrument were a crystal ball, *houris* would spring from my fingertips."

"Sorry, I don't remember."

He nodded.

"It doesn't matter. I just came over for a chat. I've been hanging around for three hours. Have you been with the Rajas long? I saw you drop off their daughter."

"Six months. Why?"

"I used to know their previous driver. We don't see him around any more."

"He had an accident."

"Nothing serious, I hope."

"I don't know."

He proffered his hand.

"Yahia, the Bensoltanes' driver."

"I thought you were a musician."

"And I thought you were an actor. Nobody's interested in my traditional group. People want *Rai* bands. Times are changing, and so are attitudes."

He fished a coin from his pocket, rolled it on the bar, caught it and played with it between his extraordinarily deft fingers. He closed his fist, blew on it and opened his fingers. The coin had disappeared. He pretended to be confused, searched all around him, shot his arm out and pointed at my wrist and, with a snap, the coin reappeared between his thumb and forefinger.

"Are you a magician as well?"

He smiled.

"Sometimes. What time is it?"

I looked down at my watch to find it was no longer on my wrist.

"Shit, I've lost it."

"It's in the right pocket of your jacket."

And so it was.

"Impressive," I acknowledged.

"An old trick of a fallen magician. I can do anything with my hands. I've played every musical instrument, I've sculpted bronze, carved wood, produced hundreds of craft objects, but when it comes to earning a crust, my hands come down off their high horse and grip a steering wheel. In this predatory land, talent doesn't put food on the table. It barely helps, even when it tries to come to your rescue."

A sudden wistfulness clouded his expression. He gazed at his coin, made it disappear with an automatic gesture.

"Talent," he sighed.

His jaws worked gently up and down.

"Artists are the soul of a nation, poets its conscience, champions its strength. Maybe I'm wrong?"

His eyes flickered and hid behind a cup of coffee, and his cheeks filled with sorrow. He gently shook the left sleeve of his jacket and the coin inched its way out, clattering onto the bar.

His lips puckered:

"Subversion, that's what's considered clever nowadays. The source of harassment, absurdity and stupidity. A funfair attracts more admiration than an artist. When I pick up my mandolin, I sometimes feel ashamed. I tell myself that after all, music is a fool's profession; it's depraved, for faggots. It entertains the crowds but doesn't win their appreciation. You've seen how we're treated. People spend more time clapping their hands to call the masseur in the steam baths than applauding an artist. They laugh and scoff at you, and everyone's delighted when they get you. You thought you were a star. Poor fool! Now you're a laughing stock. Even the lowest porter in the Souk mocks you. And the kids, encouraged by the grownups, are jeering at your heels while you run to hide in the doorways like a leper."

I could feel his anger welling up from the depths of his being. Grief distorted his features, impulsive, tangible. I was embarrassed. I sensed, underneath his conjuring tricks, his shame at not being able to control this need to bare his soul to a stranger. He looked up at me and retreated behind his enigmatic smile, the prowess of his coin no longer sufficient to reassure him.

After a silence, which he seemed to find hard to cope with, he ran his tongue over his lips, cleared his throat and grumbled:

48

"I say our society is incompatible with art. In any case, that's how I feel when I play. People look at you with indifference. You're there to entertain, that's all. And I fantasize about grabbing my mandolin and smashing it down on someone's head, anybody's, lashing out at the crowd, because they're all the same. Do you realize? An artist, reduced to the status of a buffoon, forgotten about as soon as the show's over."

His breath came in gasps and white saliva began to foam at the corners of his mouth.

He nodded sorrowfully:

"But the truth is elsewhere, if you really want to know. It's not that people are ungrateful or uncultured. It's the system that does everything it can to separate them from the nobility of creatures and things. It teaches them to recognize themselves only in mediocrity."

His fist banged down on the bar. His embittered eyes gazed into mine as he cried:

"And I say, give me the Islamic Salvation Front, *kho.* Absolutely."

I shrugged. That irritated him. He clenched his fist, then relaxed it.

"At least the Islamists have a chance of shaking us up, of involving us in grand schemes. What I want is to do something with my wretched life. Be useful. Be part of something big, not necessarily an ambitious enterprise; just a serious, collective project with people who are proud of their little contribution, and others who share their enthusiasm. To serve without having the feeling that I'm crawling, licking boots and doormats. To do something, dammit! Not to stand here twiddling my thumbs, rotting away in the shadow of exclusion. Do you understand that? *Do something...* With the FLN, anything's allowed, for sure, but to be ignored. Ig-nored! You can conjure up houris with your guitar, nobody's interested. You might be consumed with the fire of a thousand geniuses, but they'll leave you to burn in your corner, to general indifference. Indifference is the worst enemy of talent. The Islamic Salvation Front may well declare that musical events are banned, along with disturbing the peace at night, but I'm sure they'll allow me to sing the praises of the prophet with respect and joy. What I'm waiting for is change, the proof that things are being dusted down, moving forward. In which direction, I don't care. But not stagnation. Please! Not stagnation. I can't bear it any more. So long live the FIS, *kho*. I'd happily grow a beard, even if I got tangled up in it, and I'd listen to their boring sermons all day long, because at least, at the mosque, I get the feeling they're talking to me, that they're concerned about my future, that I *exist*. With the FLN, I don't have that sense. Their system is corrupt, it's a hoodlum culture, antagonistic to art, learning and human genius which *they* consider to be a malign growth to be fought with chemotherapy. I refuse to be treated like a disease. I am an artist, a creator of beauty, sublimation, *kho*. I want to breathe, to be fulfilled. Is that too much to ask? So why must I spend my time feeling sorry for Dahmane El Harrachi, who died in exile and sorrow, or listening to the poems of Mahboub Bati and telling myself that the greatest wordsmith in the world has vanished, shrouded by profound silence, wondering whether Sid Ali is crazy to carrying on believing in the magic of words while he slowly kills himself smoking dope and drinking adulterated wine."

His eyebrows drew together around an incandescent fury. He jabbed at the bar and was almost shouting:

"I'm waiting to have my dignity restored, *kho*, my dignity and that of my idols, and my friends."

He fell silent suddenly. His feverish eyes looked away and his breath came out in a long sigh. I realized he resented having given vent to his feelings without the slightest restraint, and felt abashed at having confided in this way to the first person he came across. But I sensed he felt relieved of a heavy burden, like an unspoken, long wished-for vow.

He stroked the coin with the tip of his finger; it quivered, rose and began to roll unaided. He shook his head. His shoulders drooped. He was shrinking, melting under my gaze.

"I'm sorry, I think I got carried away. But we have to *do something*."

"I'm not an Islamist," I smiled at him.

"As long as you're an artist. Do you think I'm raving?" He regained his composure, suddenly wary. "Honestly, that's what you think, don't you? You're saying to yourself, what's got into the guy? Why is he going on at me like that? I didn't ask anything of him. I know that, *kho*. I'm not deranged. But I can't help it. The trouble with walls is that they have ears but absolutely no opinion. It ends up getting on your nerves. It's important to spew up what you can't stomach. I can feel myself getting sick."

"We live in a crazy country."

He looked up at me anxiously.

"You don't believe in the Islamists' promises?"

"I'm neutral."

"What does that mean, being neutral? You can't be neutral at the crossroads. You have to choose which direction to go in."

"You never choose."

"That's not true. You're responsible for your own destiny."

"In Algeria, there's no destiny. We're all at the end of the road."

"You're wrong. That's what they want you to think: renunciation. They're trying to clip your wings. Algeria is a Sleeping Beauty that a bunch of eunuchs is trying to *protect* from any prince likely to awaken her from her slumber, so as not to betray their own impotence. That's what Sid Ali said. And the poet never lies."

"It's possible," I said, wearily.

A couple walked past us, haughty, puffed up with disdain, exuding whiffs of expensive perfumes around the bar and the crushing shadow of their superiority over the servants who were suddenly petrified with meekness. The barman stiffened behind his barricade, and his arm froze in mid-air as he reached up to a shelf. The girl cooing in the depths of the cloakroom covered her mouth with a strangely guilty hand. The couple didn't even notice. The lady's nose was so high in the air that she looked as if she had a broken neck. Her translucent skin was set off by her midnight-blue silk dress inlaid with precious stones, and her eyes, two mysterious jewels, stared far into the distance as if letting them rove around the room would have compromised her. She was no prettier than a lurking moray eel, but her necklace was of pearls, and her diamonds authentic. The gentleman walked behind her, with a stiff, military gait in his shimmering dinner jacket, visibly exasperated at having to walk past us for a breath of fresh air. At once, an old man snoozing in a corner leapt up, scraping his chair, and ran ahead of them, groveling as he held open the door.

My companion gazed after them with a grim expression, his lips curled.

"The aristocraps!" he moaned. "Do you know them?"

"No."

"They're the Farainis, the textile barons. Apparently they don't have toilets in their place. I've met some constipated people in my time, but not like them. They're even worse than the British royal family. The guy crawling around in front of them has been their chauffeur forever. They still don't know his name. They think they're gods."

"Well, that's life!"

"I can see you don't know them. Not an ounce of humanity, I tell you, just a cast-iron pump instead of a heart. They have no more consideration for others than a one-armed bandit. Including for their own family. Their son killed himself when he was fifteen. He hanged himself in the garage. If their own child couldn't stand them, I ask you, who else could?"

"Their chauffeur."

My answer stopped him dead. He paused to think for a moment, disconcerted, understood what I was driving at and let out a strange laugh.

"You're a right character, you are."

"Vintage."

He laughed again, but his expression was still grim.

He resumed his serious air, and his hand toyed with the coin again:

"Long live the Islamic Salvation Front. At least with the Islamists, we'll all be equal."

"Relatively."

"Relatively maybe, but we only have one God."

The door swung abruptly open to reveal a pallid Sonia. I could feel her breath on me, reeking of wine and horrible. She nodded at me to rise. Behind her was a tall, thin young man with a parting down the center of his head, dabbing his brow with a handkerchief. He was embarrassed and didn't know what to do. He caught Sonia's elbow. She spun round and landed him a resounding slap. Nonplussed at first, he raised an arm which stayed in the air and, contrary to all expectations, raised his hand to his bruised cheek moaning:

"I didn't know she was here, darling."

Sonia's nostrils quivered unpleasantly.

"Bastard!"

He tried to grab her wrist, begging. She backed away.

"Don't touch me."

I got up from my stool and positioned myself in front of the man, my fists at the ready.

"The lady asked you to leave her alone."

He swept me aside and rushed out into the courtyard after Sonia. I ran after him, and restrained his shoulder. My gesture disgusted him. He was beside himself.

"Do you know how much this shirt cost? No, but you know where your filthy hand's been, don't you? And you're wiping it on Amar Bey's shirt, you little shit."

Matching his words with actions, he grabbed me by the throat and shoved me against the wall.

"You keep to cleaning your master's cars, flunkey. That's what you're paid for, isn't it. Keep your nose out of our business. This is a matter between my fiancée and me."

In the courtyard, Sonia was cursing. She pulled off her ring and threw it in his face.

"Take this piece of junk back, you bastard. I never want to see you again."

Amar Bey located the spot where the ring had landed, but did not pick it up.

"I swear there's nothing going on between her and me."

"Get out of my sight."

"For heaven's sake, I can't ban her from coming to the club!"

Sonia refused to listen. She climbed into the car, yelling at me:

"Get me away from that upstart."

I started up the engine. The fiancé grabbed the door handle, pounding frantically on the window.

"Drive, idiot!"

I reversed, nearly knocked the reckless fellow over, and sped towards the exit. The young man ran after us, one hand on the door handle, the other hammering on the bodywork.

"You're being unreasonable, Sonia. Think about it, please. It's absurd. We're not going to quarrel over a nobody. I didn't even look at her."

I had to accelerate to throw him off. After his frantic dash, I saw him slow down, sway, stop and finally kick a tree.

"The bastard, the bastard," fumed Sonia. "Little upstart. Doing that to me, the daughter of Salah Raja! For a cheap tart from the slums, the brat of a fortune-teller! He hasn't heard the last of it, believe you me. I'm going to shut him up once and for all. Nobody will ever want to look at him again. I'll make sure all doors are closed to him. It's thanks to me he's accepted, *I'm* the one who's made him who he is. He was nothing, nothing at all before. If he thinks he's already made it, he's very much mistaken. Turn right."

"Aren't we going home?"

"Don't you start being a pain as well. When I tell you to turn right, you do it, OK?"

"Very good, Miss."

"Bastard! Bastard! Bastard!"

She punched the seat in front of her furiously.

"He'll pay for it, the bastard! Turn down the little slip road on the left."

We left the main road. The houses became few and far between, and the countryside spread out before us with its orchards, fields and sleepy hillsides. From afar came the intermittent sound of dogs barking.

"Find us a quiet spot and come and help me get even with that opportunist bastard," she said suddenly, in a rough tone.

And she began to remove her clothes.

Chapter five

The festive mood of the streets had evaporated. The terraces lost their convivial atmosphere. The town was unrecognizable in its grayness. Farewell the beaches, idleness and showiness. Algiers, without its sunshine, is a sorry sight.

Mrs. Raja was sad, too, as she left her doctor's surgery. Shivering in her turquoise dress, she paused on the steps and looked up to the heavens.

I got out of the car to go and assist her.

She refused my proffered hand, but not unkindly.

"Take me to the beach."

Daylight was retreating. It was barely 6 P.M., and night was already stealing over the town.

Slumped on the back seat, Mrs. Raja read and re-read the results of her tests that the doctor had just given her. She sighed as she studied each sheet. Abruptly, she put the documents back in her bag and snapped it shut. After an interminable period of silence, she relaxed and unclasped her fingers.

"How old are you, Mr. Walid?" she asked in a broken voice.

"Twenty-six, Ma'am."

She nodded, and took an interest in the dilapidated apartment blocks streaming past the window.

We skirted the poor districts to reach the coast. The road was swollen with traffic chaos. A lorry had overturned shedding its load of mineral water all over the tarmac.

"Tell me about your family."

"My father is a retired railway worker, ma'am. We have lived in the Casbah for several generations."

"How many children are there?"

"Six; five of them girls."

"Are you the eldest?"

"The third."

She wiped her nose on a little handkerchief. Furtively. Her dark glasses hid her tears, but they were betrayed by her quivering chin. I could not get used to the idea that a lady of her station could cry, even less in front of a servant—this woman who fussed over the slightest crease in her dress, who refused to show any feelings.

Sensing my embarrassment, she took refuge in gazing at the countryside.

The police managed to clear a passage through. One of them waved me forward.

"Tell me about your mother."

I realized I didn't have much to say about my mother.

"Is she elderly?"

"She's illiterate, and with six children and never-ending house-work, she doesn't have time to count the years."

"What's your home like, how do you live?"

"It's an old three-roomed apartment. We stick together."

"Stick together," she said pensively.

She fell silent.

We reached an empty beach. The sea was dark, the furious waves pounded the rocks.

I turned off the engine.

Mrs. Raja huddled in her shawl.

"What's her name?"

"Who, ma'am?"

"Your mother."

"Wardia."

"Do you love her?"

"Of course I do."

She was taken aback by the spontaneity of my reply, which made her realize the stupidity of her question. She sighed and hunched over her milk-white hands.

"You are so young, so young... at your age I used to send my suitors off packing. I wasn't the sort of girl to stand by the window all day longing for her prince charming, thinking I saw his silhouette in the evening shadows. I thought I was immortal."

I didn't know whether she was talking to herself or whether I was expected to respond.

"Take care of your parents. A tiny little thing could break their hearts. Decent children still exist, I won't dispute that. I'd just like you to know that a mother, no matter how unpleasant she is, is sacred. Whoever hurts or neglects his mother is cursed. Heaven will turn its back on him forever."

Her hand came down on my shoulder.

"Do you hear me?"

"Yes, ma'am."

"I hope so."

She opened the door. The breeze whipped her face.

The air was cold, damp with spray. The smells of the Mediterranean were intoxicating.

"I don't remember the last time I went swimming. When I was a little girl, the minute I jumped into the water, I would cause a general panic. The lifeguards were tired of always having to battle against the elements to come and rescue me. My mother would scream, rousing the whole beach. But my father was proud of my daring. He used to call me his darling little mermaid."

A smile hovered on her lips, like a will-o'-the-wisp. Her eyes were nothing but painful evocations.

"We had the most beautiful family in the world. My fortune has brought me joyful moments but not true happiness. That I owe to my parents' love… money means a lot of compromises, Mr. Walid. It's just for show."

"Yes, ma'am."

"This is not just idle talk."

"I understand, ma'am."

"I doubt it, my boy."

She alighted from the car, walked over to a dune and sat down facing the sea. Night fell. The sky rumbled. A flash of lightning ripped through the clouds and huge drops of rain splattered onto my windscreen. Mrs. Raja seemed happy to huddle under her shawl and stay put. For a long time, she sat gazing out to sea.

"Get up in there. Hurry, go and get the car."

Hamid was in a lather. He yanked off my blankets and flung them on the floor, twisting my ankle as he dragged me out of bed. Stomping round the room in his boxer shorts, barefoot, he rushed over to the wardrobe, pulled out a suit and threw it at me.

"Get dressed fast. We haven't got a minute to lose."

He ran out into the corridor.

I rose, dazed. My watch showed 2 A.M. Without questioning why, I waited for my mind to clear and pulled on my clothes. Ten minutes later, I met Hamid at the gate by the mimosa. He clambered into the car beside me and ordered me to step on the gas.

"Can I ask what's going on?"

"Junior's in a spot of bother."

"Is it that serious?"

"He didn't say anything but from the tone of his voice, it sounds bad. He doesn't usually lose his cool."

The thunder shattered the night with a string of belches. Torrential rain poured down over the city. The road squelched furiously beneath the wheels, throwing up great sprays of mud either side of the car.

Junior's residence was plunged in darkness, which worried

Hamid even more. We entered the hall. An unnerving silence greeted us.

"Junior," Hamid called out.

A flash of lightning lit up the hall for a brief second. I found the light switch. The lounge was empty, but tidy. Hamid inspected the downstairs rooms, found nothing and motioned me to follow him upstairs. We climbed a spiral staircase. A dim light bled at the end of the corridor. Junior was there, in a kimono, slumped in a chair with his head in his hands, moaning.

A young girl was lying naked on the bed, one arm dangling against the side of the mattress. Her eyes were wide open, staring up at the ceiling, and her black hair was spread over the pale sheet.

"It's your fault," whined Junior. "Where the hell did you get that lousy coke from?"

"From our usual supplier," replied Hamid, going over to the girl.

He took her wrist, and swallowed: "Shit!" Then he let go of the arm, which flopped down again. I finally realized the extent of the damage. The girl, barely more than an adolescent, would not wake up again. Her puffy face had an unmistakable serenity. She was dead.

"I did everything I could to bring her back," raged Junior.

He leaped up and jumped on Hamid.

"It's your fault, you bastard! Idiot! Asshole! You let them rip you off."

"It's not possible. I checked, I promise. I tried it myself first. You know I don't let them get away with that sort of thing. I swear it was excellent quality."

"So why did she die on me? Look at those needle-marks on her arms. That proves she was a junkie. Why did her heart pack up this time?"

"Overdose?"

"No. I gave her half the amount. You were sold a load of shit, and that's it."

Hamid gently pushed Junior aside. He spread his hands, imploring his boss to keep calm.

"It's an accident. There's no point fighting. Let's keep our cool and think."

"I've got things to do. It's no longer my problem. You're the one who got ripped off, not me. I don't want to be mixed up in this. That kid copped it as a result of your idiocy, do you get it? I'm packing my bags and I'm out of here. When I get back, I want to find this place clean. As far as I'm concerned, this didn't happen."

"Calm down, boss."

"I'm perfectly calm. Get that shit out of here, and now. I'm already somewhere else, get it?"

He rushed over to his wardrobe, dressed quickly and left the room without a glance at the body.

Meanwhile, my heart was in my boots. The stiffness of the corpse terrified me. My Adam's apple scraped my parched throat. I grabbed something to stop my legs buckling. Shivers ran up my calves to the rest of me, making me quake all over. When the trembling reached my gut, I suddenly felt giddy. I found myself stumbling along the corridor groping for the bathroom, then, my head in the bidet, I began to vomit.

Hamid planted himself behind me.

"I always get the blame."

He was more vexed than concerned. His sang-froid made me feel ill again. I shoved my head under the tap and let the icy water cool me. My thumping heart pounded deafeningly against my temples.

"It's not the end of the world, Nafa. It's a stupid accident. We'll sort it out."

He grabbed my collar and hauled me to my feet.

"It's all right, I tell you. There's no need to panic."

"You're kidding!"

"I've seen worse."

"Not me. I'm handing in my notice."

"You're not going to let me down."

"I haven't seen a thing. I don't know anything about it. I never set foot here this evening."

I sponged myself with a towel. My hands trembled spasmodically.

Hamid crossed his arms over his chest, leaned against the wall with a grim smile, his eyes impassive. He allowed me to get my breath back, and said:

"This is what we're going to do…"

"We?…"

"I'm not asking for the moon, for fuck's sake. Just drive me out of the city."

"No way. Are you crazy or what? Since it's an accident, call the police."

He leaped at me as if he'd been electrocuted. His body hit me full on. I felt my vertebrae being crushed under his weight.

"Not that word, Nafa. It's not even part of the Rajas' vocabulary. It's not the tragedy that would upset them, but the scandal. So watch your mouth. Remember, you're as deep in this shit as I am. Where do you think you are my little fellow? When you're part of a dignitary's family, however lowly you may be, you have a duty to protect them from anything that might damage their reputation. If you haven't understood that yet, it's not too late to make up for it. Now calm down. This is what *we* are going to do. Whether you agree with it or not makes no difference. *We* are going to get that body out of the city. And now."

His fingers dug into my neck. I thought he was going to kill me. Overwhelmed by the turn of events, incapable of thinking straight, I gave in, hoping to gain time and recover my grip.

The rain was pelting down even harder, but even that didn't bring me to my senses. Hamid threw the corpse into the boot of the car. My chest nearly exploded when he slammed down the lid. I realized my legs had gone numb and I couldn't start up the engine.

"You wimp," shouted Hamid. "Give me the wheel."

After a few kilometers, the sight of a police roadblock made me panic. I fumbled for the door handle intending to make a bolt for it. Hamid's hand restrained me.

The police officer asked us to pull over. His shone his torch up and down the driver and then on me for a long time. My stomach was suddenly on fire.

"Your friend got a problem?"

"He's not well. Indigestion, probably."

The halo of light moved onto the back seat.

"So where are you two off to?"

"We're going home. We've just come back from a long trip, officer, and we're exhausted. We work for Salah Raja."

The cop nodded his dripping chin and withdrew.

We left the city without hindrance. An hour later, we drove deep into the forest of Bainem. Hamid had difficulty controlling the car on the slippery, rutted track that was virtually impassable. Caught by the wild gusts of wind, the trees writhed, their crazed branches banging against the bodywork of the Mercedes.

We stopped at the foot of a mound. Hamid took the body out of the boot and made for a copse, slithering in the mud. I trailed behind him, without understanding why, as if an evil power were sucking me into a nightmare.

Hamid dropped the body on the ground.

"Are you going to bury her here?"

"I'd have brought a shovel."

He rummaged in the surrounding bushes, brought back a large stone, raised it and brought it down on the girl's face with such violence that a lump of flesh hit my cheek. Caught unawares, I bent double and threw up.

Hamid struck again, and again, splattering me with blood and splinters of bone. Each one of his *aarghs* felt like a knife being thrust into me and bent me further. I couldn't take my eyes off the girl's face that was turning into a pulp. My urine cascaded down my trembling thighs. Drained, exhausted, I fell onto all fours, my face in my vomit, and began to howl and howl…

"There," said Hamid, straightening up, "even her own mother wouldn't recognize her."

I gave one last shudder and rose to my feet. I fled straight ahead into the shadows.

Hamid caught up with me in a ditch. I had tripped over a trunk, and my knee was bleeding.

"You've let me down, Nafa! I can't believe this. Just look at you! Even a whore wouldn't sink so low."

He kneeled down in front of me and sought my eyes.

"It's an accident. An unfortunate accident. You have nothing to fear. The girl was a runaway. She's not even from around here. Now it's finished. The worst is over."

"I want to go home."

"Of course."

"*My* home, in the Casbah."

"OK, so what's the problem? I'll drop you off at your place. And tomorrow, I'll take you to the Sun Center to fuck the prettiest chicks in Algiers."

"I'm not going anywhere with you. Our ways part here. I don't want to hear another word about you, or the Rajas…"

He grabbed my hair and twisted my neck, snarling. A flash of lightening lit up his features. His face was that of the devil.

"I hate ingratitude, Nafa. I can handle anything except that. Less than a year ago, you were down and out in Bab El Oued, your belly as empty as your mind. You came to us. You were raised to the ranks of the wealthy. Now you've been to the most select places, the trendiest joints, and you're used to the smell of money. You were a poor bastard who couldn't even stand up straight, do you remember? And now you wear expensive shirts, designer trainers, and you haven't dipped into your wages for months because you eat for free. And suddenly, because of a stupid fifteen-year old bitch, you disown your people and all you can think about is getting out. No way, Nafa. It's not fair. Too easy. But these things are predictable. And there's nothing to be done. I'm disappointed, sure, but no more. You want out? As you wish. But there are conditions, my lad. I won't ask you to pay anything back, that would be stupid. I demand that you keep that big mouth of yours buttoned up. What you've seen tonight you must erase from your mind in the same way you have just denied your benefactors. Because I swear to you over my mother's dead body that if you ever try even remembering this incident, I'll find you wherever you're hiding and I'll knock your teeth out through your ass, one by one. Right?"

His fist came down on my forehead.

"Right?"

He raised me up with one hand and landed an uppercut that doubled me up.

"Your predecessor also tried to be clever. Has anyone told you what happened to him? I bet they haven't. It's so horrible that nobody would want to talk about it. I won't let you ruin my life because of a stupid accident, Nafa, you sonofabitch. I won't even allow the good Lord to harm a hair of Junior's head. He's *my* Junior. He's mine, only mine. He's my fortune, my home—he's my entire reason for living. Do you understand, asshole, do you understand?"

Then in a frenzy, he shoved my face in the mud and went for me...

It was still dark when I came round. The rain was still pelting down and the wind howling. Lying in a puddle of water, my arms outstretched, it took me a long time to recognize the cracked façade of my father's house.

Chapter six

For days on end I remained cloistered in my room, deaf to my mother's continual laments, pushing away my food and keeping my door closed. My battered face and bruised body alarmed my family. My father gave up badgering me after our first argument. Faced with my refusal to answer his questions, he invoked the name of the Lord and spoke to me no more. My mother wouldn't be intimidated by my outbursts of anger. She wanted to know what had happened to me, and who had dared humiliate her only son in such a manner.

I heard my father shout at her in disgust: "That's what happens when you mix with hooligans. I have nothing to say about the beating he received. He won't admit what he's been up to. He must have put a foot wrong somewhere and slipped up. I warn you, I shan't lift a finger for him. He should have kept his nose clean."

To this my mother responded, indignant: "My son is a decent boy. He's always chosen his friends carefully. I refuse to believe he's been mixed up in anything bad."

And my father: "A simple driver can't suddenly afford luxury clothes and jewelry. His pockets were stuffed with banknotes. It's a dead give-away. That's why I wouldn't accept his presents."

I curled myself into a ball in a corner of my room, my ears pricked. An uproar in the street, a knock at the door, and I would huddle up. In my tormented mind, it was the police coming to get me.

I spent my days in a panic. My sleep was haunted by nightmare visions. The forest of Bainem howled like a chimera on heat, heightening my nocturnal terror. The girl's ghost stalked me through the mist. Her head kept popping up everywhere; amid the bushes, on the rocks, hanging from the trees like a gruesome fruit. The thumping of my heart mingled with Hamid's "aaargh"s, with the dull thud of the stone crushing the dead girl's face. I would wake up howling, my arms outstretched in the dark. My mother would call to me from the other side of the door. I felt she was persecuting me. I begged her to leave me alone.

One afternoon, Dahmane came to visit me. Recognizing his nasal voice, I rushed to open the door. I so desperately needed to talk to someone. Dahmane asked my parents to leave us alone. He could see how badly beaten I was, but acted as though nothing was amiss. He sat down on the foot of my bed and looked around at the mess in my room.

"I didn't know you had enemies among your own things," he said with a hint of irony. "Who started it, the wardrobe, the bedside table, the blankets or you?"

He rose and opened the shutters. The harsh daylight forced me to cover my eyes.

He came back and sat beside me.

"Now we can see properly and get some air into the room."

He opened a pack of Marlboro and held it out to me.

I realized I hadn't smoked for a week. My hand trembled as I took a cigarette. Dahmane offered me his lighter and waited quietly for me to take a few puffs before he inquired:

"Are you OK?"

My little sister brought us some coffee and disappeared.

"It was your father who called me. Apparently you're obsessed."

He raised my chin and felt my injuries.

"They've made a right mess of you, haven't they?"

"I'm in big trouble."

"I thought as much: dealer or jealous husband?"

"Worse."

"Tell me."

He listened without batting an eyelid, pursing his lips slightly. He did not seem in any way affected by my story, except when I told him about the horror of Bainem. Then he frowned.

"Unbearable," he acknowledged.

"Is that all you can say?"

"*Hélas*! I'm sorry."

"I can't sleep at night."

"I'm not surprised."

His terseness disarmed me, adding to my confusion.

"You should have seem him crushing the kid's face," I repeated, in the hope of making him realize how traumatic the whole thing had been for me. Strips of flesh stuck to me like leeches. And he just went on smashing, smashing... It was... it was..."

"What do you plan to do?" he broke in.

"I don't know. I'm out of my depth."

"I suggest you put it behind you."

"Do you think that's easy? We're talking about the death of a human being. If I'm arrested, I've had it. They'd ask me why I didn't report the crime to the police if I wasn't involved."

He shook his head.

"I wouldn't advise you to go to the cops. You'd be the only culprit."

"What? But I didn't do anything."

He became grave, his forehead furrowed.

"Think for a moment. Do you imagine the police would welcome a statement from you? We're talking about the Rajas, not your next-door neighbor. Just think how awkward that would be for the police. The law is for the small fry in our country. The big fish are above the law. Anybody who has a brush with them learns this to his cost. He'll never find another job. Where the hell do you think you are, Nafa? There are people who are out of reach. They're not going to let the death—and what's more, the accidental death—of a little hussy turn their wine sour. No police superintendent would touch it with a barge pole. Hamid acted absolutely naturally. His boss had a problem. He dealt with it. It's as simple as that.

All right, let's suppose you went to the cops. Hamid would deny the facts. He'll say that he was with Junior, at his residence. That nobody had heard of this girl. Junior will confirm his story. It'll be your word against theirs. You haven't got a hope. The police will conclude that it was you who killed the girl, and that you tried to implicate Junior so as to benefit from his family's reputation to get off the hook. There's no way out, Nafa. Everyone will be against you. It's happened before, you know. There have been dozens of "accidents" of this kind. Nobody gives a damn, if you want my opinion. The girl's body will be found—if it hasn't been already—and dumped in the morgue for a while. If nobody turns up to identify her, she'll be buried, and that's that."

"I don't believe it. This is a country of law and order."

Dahmane bared his pointed teeth in a bitter grimace. He seemed to despise me.

He said: "Yes absolutely. Algeria is a country of law and order. That is undeniable. But whose law is it? There is only one absolute law, *and that is the law of silence.*"

That night, a dream I couldn't shake off had me pressed against the wall. My pajamas were soaking, my throat raw from screaming. I crawled through the dark and huddled in a corner of my room, on the brink of madness. I clasped my hands behind my head and heard myself sob:

"Help me, God!"

Then the call of the muezzin echoed mine, suddenly soothing my spirit. It was a moment of incredible intensity. As if by magic, my anguish was appeased, and I was filled with a sensation of deliverance. I was convinced that it was a sign from Heaven. God was talking to me through the muezzin. There was no doubt about it. Salvation had knocked on my window. Prompted by an extraordinary force, I went out onto the patio, drew water from the barrel near the laundry room and, kneeling in front of my bowl, I carried out my ablutions. Ten minutes later, making my way through the dark, silent streets, I joined the faithful in prayer at the mosque. A few neighbors, pleasantly surprised to find me among them, nodded in greeting. A hand tapped me on the shoulder, another brushed mine. I was no longer *alone*. A world was coming to life around me, protecting me already, delivering me from my fears. The torments of the night faded as I felt surrounded by my people. I could at last stand up without faltering, prostrate myself without collapsing, and close my eyes without encountering the devastating horror of nightmares.

"You can't imagine how relieved I am to see you this morning," whispered Rachid, the shoemaker. "Welcome among your brothers."

Men at prayer greeted me.

"God be praised," said a distant school friend.

"God is great," added Nabil Ghalem.

The faithful dispersed in silence. Only a few penniless vagrants still remained outside the mosque, waiting for daybreak. I did not feel inclined to go home. I picked up a book from a shelf and sat down cross-legged near the library. The book was entitled *The Conduct of the Prophet*. At the end of the first chapter, the pages started swimming before my eyes and I fell asleep. It was a deep, dreamless sleep with no reverberations. I had just become reconciled with my soul.

I continued going to the mosque. A couple of weeks later, on seeing me alone, Imam Younes came to talk to me. He was about thirty, handsome as a prince, with clear eyes emphasized with kohl and a henna-dyed beard. The people of the Casbah valued his kindness and integrity. Always prepared to listen to the needy and to disaffected youths, he had succeeded in winning their trust. He had the gift of healing rifts, unraveling the tangles of discord as easily as a knotted string. His voice was imbued with ineffable goodness, and for ordinary people, his wisdom had the resonance of a prophecy.

He knelt before me with a radiant smile and a look of concern in his eye. A fascinating glow emanated from the drapes of his *kamis*.

"I've had my eye on you for a couple of weeks, brother Nafa. You are the first to arrive and the last to leave the sanctuary.

I would have been delighted if it weren't for a kind of unease in your attitude. Then it occurred to me that your solitude is burdened by a grave secret. I inferred, from the way you keep yourself to yourself, that you need to confide in someone, to relieve your conscience of the hidden anguish relentlessly consuming it."

His immaculate hand prevented me from speaking.

"All mortals are fallible, brother Nafa. The best sinner is the one who admits his wrongs, and learns from them never to repeat them."

"I have not sinned, Sheikh."

He gave a skeptical shrug.

"You're not in a court of law, but in the house of the Lord. He is clement and merciful. You can confess without fear. Your secret and your honor will be safe."

"I don't need to do that, Sheikh, I assure you. I think I can get through this alone. Because I've recovered my faith."

"That is wonderful, brother Nafa. I am pleased."

He didn't press me on the subject.

The next day, without being aware of it, I sought him out in his office, concealed behind a curtain, next to the *minbar*. He greeted me with deference, declaring that he was delighted; that Faith shared was better than all the asceticism in the world. Before allowing me to speak, he insisted in putting me at my ease. He recited *hadiths*, told me the story of Job and explained that pain was only suffering for the ungodly. Then he recited the Al Rahman *sura*. I was spellbound by his singsong voice. I wanted him to go on forever. Imam Younes had tears in his eyes when he was at last ready to listen to what I had to tell him. Not for a second did his angelic face betray any emotion.

"It was the best thing that could have happened to you, brother Nafa," he said, when I reached the end of my story. "Most of my flock have not had your luck. They are here because their parents were here before them. They were born Muslims and are merely perpetuating the tradition. But you went looking for other things, beneath different skies. You had dreams, ambitions. You had a lust for life. And God led you where you wanted to go. To enlighten you. You have seen wealth, power and complacency. Now you *know* that this extravagance, this flashy ostentation serves only to conceal the ugliness of vanity and the moral bankruptcy of those who refuse to admit that ill-gotten gains never bring good fortune. Now you *know* what is right, and what is not. You have been among the fat cats. They are vile, unscrupulous and ruthless people. They mingle so as not to lose sight of each other, and loathe each other cordially. Rather like wolves, they operate in packs to boost their spirits, but have no hesitation in eating a fellow wolf alive if he is weak. There is no substance behind the imposing façades of their palaces or their hypocritical words. You must thank the Lord for this invaluable experience. You have been at the gates of Hell, but you did not fall. On the contrary, you became aware of the Truth. You can look into a mirror without turning around, or turning away; truth helps you take responsibility for yourself in adversity. You have been resuscitated, Nafa, my brother. Do you realize how lucky you are? We always lose our way when we seek elsewhere the very thing that is within our grasp. Now, you know that. You know where you belong. It is not the death of a little birdbrain that upsets you. In a way, she deserved it. You are unhappy because your country infuriates you. You despair of everything in it. You refuse to be what *others* want you to be, the shadow of yourself, a sinner in spite of yourself. Like all the young people of this country, you have been seduced and abandoned. But you are no longer alone. You have bearings, and thousands of reasons to hope. When there is nothing left in the world, when the Earth is reduced to dust, *everything will perish except the face of Allah.* And, on the Day of Judgment, you will be asked, without indulgence: "What have you done with your life, Nafa Walid?" And you should begin preparing your reply now. For there is still time. Do you really want to make something of your life, brother Nafa? So much the better! You wanted to be an actor, land the parts that would put you up among the stars. Well, these I grant you: I offer you the sky as your screen, and God as audience. Now show me your talent."

I still don't know exactly what happened to me that day.

I left the mosque and strolled around the Casbah, seeing it with new eyes. Then I climbed the hill.

As a child, I loved to go up to the top of Notre-Dame at dusk to contemplate the bay and boats in the harbor. The squeals of the street urchins fluttered around me like veiled birds. It felt as if my gaze flew beyond my thoughts, that the world at my feet could still give me so many things to dream about. I was in a hurry to grow up and gather the laurels which, if heaped on the town, would mask it completely. Sitting on the low stone wall beside the road, I breathed eagerly, happy to be alone and not disturbing anyone. Once I had drunk my fill of multicolored horizons, I returned to the ancient Casbah nestling below.

With its rolling foothills like a mangle and its jumble of garrets like bundles of washing, it reminded me of my mother, on the banks of the wadi, scrubbing away at old rags to give them a silky sheen.

I loved my mother deeply.

But God, I pitied her...

My head in my hands, my heart like a fist in my chest, I was lost in thought. There was a choice to be made. Once and for all. The pestilential heat rising from the rock distracted me. Something inside me was not responding. For a moment, I wished I could be made to disappear with the wave of a magic wand. To vanish, suddenly, like a reflection engulfed by creeping shadows.

Behind me, huddled in a doorway, a group of youths were singing a song by *Hadj* M'rizek. The poorest of them, recognizable by his talent, plucked inconsolably at his guitar. When his tormented gaze met mine, he gathered his thoughts for a moment, cleared his throat and without warning, launched at the top of his voice into a poem by Sid Ali accompanied by emphatic chords on the guitar:

74

When dreams fly away
When all hope melts
When the sky loses its stars
When all becomes meaningless

Then is the beginning
for you and me, my brother
of the descent into hell.

I walked down towards the shore to watch the sun retreat. When I reached the creek, the day was being consumed in its own flames and the distant waves resembled huge gashes.

Sonia's gold chain felt heavy, suddenly weighing on my conscience. I ripped it off in anger and flung it into the water in a gesture of renunciation.

I don't know how many hours I stood there. I felt cold in body and in spirit. And yet, I was convinced: a dream is seductive, persuasive and a companion, but, in most cases, it is no friend.

Who has not dreamed of reaching the stars? But once you do, they crumble between your fingers like decayed old relics.

Part two:
The Casbah

If I were to seek a comparison among the stars
the sun itself would not eclipse
the light of the word that you conceal.
No sacred place, no capital
could contain that which each morning
dawn offers you as a garland.

Mienne, ma Casbah
Himoud Brahimi, known as "Momo"

*T*here are moments when gurus supplant demons. Then the scorching heat is inspired by the flames of hell to melt spirits. And men, unwittingly, join the carnival of the damned. Algiers was aglow with the orgasm of the 'enlightened' who had raped her. Pregnant from their hatred, she made an exhibition of herself in the place where she had been violated, in the middle of her bay, forever cursed.

Algiers was sick. Wallowing in purulent filth, she puked and defecated continuously. The slums disgorged dysenteric crowds in chaotic eruptions. Rats bent on destruction poured out of the sewers, swarming through the sweltering streets.

Amid pain and nausea, Algiers was giving birth. Amid horror, naturally. Her pulse throbbed to the slogans of the fundamentalists who paraded triumphantly up and down the boulevards. She clung to her hillsides, her skirts hitched up above her swollen genitals, wailing diatribes from the minarets, heaving, groaning... With bated breath, the people watched her bring the incestuous monster into the world. And she gave birth without restraint, but with the rage of a mother who realizes too late that the father of her child is her own son.

An emblematic figure from the Islamist movement climbed onto the roof of a bus. A megaphone in his hand, he demanded silence. The crowd refused to calm down.

"As long as Algerians are deprived of their right to full citizenship, as long as they treat us as mere onlookers, as long as they continue to shout 'Move on, there's nothing to see,' just to make sure we are still alive, we won't budge from here."

The crowd rose amid a thunderous clamor.

"We won't go anywhere. We will stay here, in the street, day and night. They can surround us with their damned riot police, threaten us with their guns and their ridiculous Armada, we won't budge from here. We'll tell them that we've had enough of their nonsense, that we won't play their game. We won't go back to our jobs until they realize, once and for all, that we don't want them any more, that we're tough enough to take our fate in our own hands, without their help. The sinful age is over, our land has become holy again. Their place is no longer among us. Since they refuse to follow the way of the Lord, let them go to hell."

The Islamic Salvation Front had just declared civil disobedience.

Chapter seven

Sid Ali tossed a pinch of fragrant benzoin into the brazier and inhaled the wisps of smoke that rose from the embers with relish. The acrid smell of the resin immediately dispelled the musty smell of the room, making Nafa Walid rub his nose, discreetly.

The poet's house was like a prison cell. The walls were bare, rough to the touch. They hadn't seen a coat of paint for a very long time. The ancient stone gleamed in the half dark. The ceiling was high, discolored with saltpeter. Sheepskins were scattered over the tiled floor concealing the cracks. A wan light filtered through a skylight, sharp as a blade, picking out rugs in the recesses, a mandolin, an earthenware jar, manuscripts and a giant tortoise shell. Sid Ali was content with this mystical poverty. He spent most of his time lying on his straw mattress protected by mosquito nets, sucking on his opium pipe and composing *qacidas* inspired by his muse.

For Sidi Abderrahmane's men, chauvinistic to the roots of their hair, he was the greatest poet after El-Moutanabbi. The old men were proud of him, the young worshipped him; they merely had to meditate on his words and they were prepared to forgive anything.

When Sid Ali recited, the peacocks fanned their tails and the angels laid down their flutes. More than a legend, he was a healer.

Nafa Walid nibbled a few peanuts. Sitting cross-legged on a mat, he waited for his host to deign to take notice of him.

Sid Ali was in no hurry. He allowed his ankles to be massaged by a young woman with dark eyes, and sighed with pleasure at her touch.

"It's nearly time for the *Al Asr* call," remarked Nafa.

Sidi Ali came back down to earth. With a lordly gesture, he dismissed the woman and sat up.

"Time has no meaning in my house."

"Someone's waiting for me outside."

"You didn't come alone?"

"I'm with someone."

"You shouldn't have left your friend in the street. In my house, everyone's welcome."

"I thought you wanted to speak to me."

Sid Ali scratched the tip of his nose.

"Finish your tea first."

"I have a stomach ache."

Sid Ali smiled. His face, distorted by opium and the long nights of meditation, was creased with gray wrinkles that ran from the corners of his mouth to his temples in a spiral movement like the ripples of a pebble on the surface of the water.

"Come with me."

Reluctantly, Nafa Walid rose and followed the poet onto the patio.

Sid Ali dusted down his Saharan robe, whose embroidery was fraying around the neck, smoothed his beard and leaned over the balustrade to gaze at the sea, pretending to ignore the seditious clamor all around and his guest's growing impatience.

He said:

"I may be merely a passionate story-teller, a *griot* dazzled by his own genius, but however wild it may seem, I cannot abandon the idea that in the beginning, the Mediterranean was a fountain. A spring not much wider than the shadow of a carob tree, before Eve bathed in it and Adam slaked his thirst. It is here, somewhere before us, that they were reunited after being banished from Eden and wandering in search of each other for many years."

He straightened up and stretched out his arms to embrace the horizon:

"For everything was born here, somewhere in front of us. The spring grew bolder, became a sea, gave birth to the oceans…"

"Was it to talk to me of the sea that you *summoned* me?"

Sid Ali tapped the balustrade, irritated at being interrupted.

"Yes, to talk to you of the sea. I'd like to tell you about the sky, too, but others got there first."

He stood squarely in front of Nafa, his eyes blazing. Anger made his beard quiver. His forefinger shot out, rigid.

"What were you seeking at the mosque, Nafa Walid?"

"Peace."

"Peace? I didn't know peace was so chaotic." He pointed to the town, swollen with bile. "It's war they're after down there."

"Not war, dignity."

Sid Ali stiffened.

His voice dropped like a fever:

"When I was little, I used to go to the railway station every day to listen to the trains whistling. I loved watching them steaming past, polishing the rails with their great wheels. Those were wonderful moments. Just picturing myself in one of the carriages was enough to make me happy. I wasn't a demanding child. I told myself that one day, I too would leave. I believed that knowledge of the world was a question of travel. Then, for no reason, I never set foot in a station again."

Nafa remained on his guard. Sid Ali was cryptic. It was impossible to stand up to him.

"It was at the station that I met your father," he went on. "I had no parents. Surname unknown, that was me. Your father didn't have a penny, but he always had a candy for me. Sometimes, he would give me his whole sandwich. He was a good man. Now, I'm famous,

85

but I haven't changed. I'm as poor as ever. I only have a cup of tea to offer you, and a little of my time."

He placed his hand on Nafa's shoulders, and looked into his eyes.

"I don't want you to hurt him."

"I don't see how, now that I've fallen back into line."

"Yes, with the mutants."

Nafa pushed away the poet's hands. His face reddened.

"You have no right to call ordinary Muslims names."

"Listen."

"No, you listen. They aren't monsters. They are as human as you are. They're fighting for a noble cause."

So saying, he spun round and made to leave.

"Nafa!"

Nafa stopped in the doorway. Without turning round.

Sid Ali made no move either. He said:

"Beware of those who come and talk to you about things that are more important than your life. Those people are lying. They want to use you. They speak of great ideals, supreme sacrifices, and they promise you eternal glory for a few drops of your blood. Don't listen to them. Always remember this: there is *nothing, absolutely nothing* that is more important than your life. It is the only thing that should matter to you, for it is the *only* thing that truly belongs to you."

Nafa crossed the room, seething, and went out into the street.

Crouching at the foot of a wall, opposite the poet's house, Nabil Ghalem was drawing arabesques on the ground with a piece of scrap metal. Looking up, he saw Nafa Walid coming out of the hovel. From his furious expression, he gathered that the conversation had not gone well. He dropped the piece of metal, wiped his fingers on his *kamis*, and hurried to intercept the Rajas' former chauffeur.

"What did he want with you?"

"Nothing," said Nafa, sickened.

It was more his attitude than his curt 'nothing' that annoyed Nabil.

"What do you mean, nothing?"

"Nothing worth mentioning."

Nabil repressed a burst of anger. He hated being spoken to in this manner. His flashing eyes turned towards the poet's house, rested on it with the spite of a curse, and sought, in vain, for a silhouette behind the wide-open windows.

"I bet he's still got that filthy pipe."

"Can a man get rid of his shadow?"

"You found him in a stupor, didn't you?" pried Nabil. "I bet he was rambling. What on earth did he say to you to upset you like that?"

Nafa preferred to say nothing, and disappeared into the narrow winding street whose cracked steps, streaming with sewage, ran down towards the bedrock. The mounds of garbage, baking in the sun and covered in incredible clouds of flies, filled the air with their stench. Unperturbed by the odor, kids were tormenting a dying puppy, its mouth gaping hideously and its nostrils crawling with slugs. Dogs and cats were an increasingly rare sight in the city. With no playground to kick a ball around, children were discovering a vocation for torture. Sometimes the spectacle was horrific. Standing neglected in a doorway, two infants were jumping up and down in a puddle of dishwater, splashing and laughing. They were filthy, their legs covered in bruises, their faces faun-like. A third, bare-bottomed, his scalp covered in whitish sores, was clambering up to a fanlight with broken panes, as people walked past, indifferent.

"We know all about his little game," went on Nabil Ghalem. "Here, we're in control of everything. We know he's tried to corrupt some of our members. I'm glad it didn't work with you either."

Nafa shrugged.

A girl was walking up the street, clutching a bag to her chest. Nabil disapproved of her short skirt and waited for her to draw level with him to shout at her.

"Aren't you ashamed? Walking around the streets half naked?"

The girl ignored him. Visibly weary of being subjected to this type of reprimand, she continued on her way, keeping close to the wall.

"Slut!" yelled Nabil. "Go and put some clothes on."

With stoic steps, her head bowed, the girl silently ascended the steps and vanished.

"If it were up to me, I'd take a blowtorch to her legs, the filthy bitch."

"That's enough," shouted Nafa, shocked. "There are children."

Nabil groaned and calmed down.

In the Casbah, many people found it hard to understand what two such different men could have in common. Nafa was considered polite, slightly reserved but amiable, well groomed, jealous of his reputation as a heart-throb. He was one of the few faithful not to wear the *kamis* or to let his beard grow. On Fridays, at the mosque, he didn't mind not being at the front. When there were protest marches, he didn't parade in formation, nor did he take part in any secret meetings. In the evenings, he would either go into the city to see a blockbuster movie or drink coffee at one of the pavement cafés on the boulevards, otherwise he would shut himself away at home.

As for Nabil Ghalem, he couldn't keep still. He was everywhere, in the mosque, at meetings, on the roofs, taking down satellite dishes, in the slums, trying to convert women of easy virtue and their pimps, ready to do battle with everyone over everything. He was a person of excesses, unpleasant and invasive. The perfect temple guard. Nothing escaped his vigilance. At twenty, he had managed to convince his party leaders of his determination to cleanse the city of drunkards and delinquents. Barely appointed head of the district committee of young Islamists, he instilled in his group an iron discipline and succeeded in recruiting large numbers of disaffected youths. He was in charge of ten volunteer militiamen, a fundraising team and another team, made up of keen girl volunteers, that looked after families in need and the elderly. The fundamentalists were delighted with his efficiency and his ability to bring in money. Imam Younes frequently boasted of him to the dignitaries of the Majlis Echoura—the advisory council. Thanks to his heavy-handed methods, the bars had been converted to shops, the sole gaming room had now become a Koranic library, and the young delinquents who troubled the peace of the night like spirit rappers, were forced to seek new pastures. The streets were quiet again, and night owls no longer bothered to look behind them as they made their way home.

Nafa Walid did not like Nabil very much. He was even a little afraid of him, now that he spent a lot of time with him. He didn't like his coarse language, or his habit of prying into other people's business. But he was crucial to the plans Nafa had been hatching since his return to the fold. The fact was, Nafa thought only of taking a wife and turning over a new leaf. He had found a two-roomed flat in Souk El Jemaa, and planned to move in before the end of the year. The apartment was on the ground floor of a decrepit building, without running water and with no lighting on the stairs, but the rent was reasonable and the neighborhood respectable. As for his future wife, he had glimpsed her one evening, at the bus stop, and had immediately been smitten. She was a local girl whom he had somehow never noticed when they were younger. Her grace and humility had surprised him.

Her name was Hanane. She was Nabil's elder sister.

Every day, at 5 P.M., Nafa hung around the bus stop, anxious, impatient, his eyes glued to his watch, cursing every time the wrong bus came. When she finally alighted, he swallowed convulsively, completely at a loss. First of all, he was careful not to be seen, either by her or by the neighbors who loved gossip, at the risk of unleashing the fury of the heavens. This type of amorous behavior aroused their indignation as much as treachery or desecration.

Hidden behind the remains of a kiosk, he watched her from a distance, with the timid fascination of a schoolboy with a crush on his teacher.

Without ever having spoken to her, and without being certain of ever being able to approach her, he was convinced that *she* was the woman he wanted to spend his life with. And at night, in his room, unable to sleep, he would picture her over and over again; his profound solitude haunted by her lovely, huge, dark eyes. He visualized her hurrying down the narrow street, radiant beneath her *hijab*, like a *houri* in the meadow, impervious to the taunts of the idiots in her path, majestic and serene, her gaze modestly lowered as befits a girl of a good family. In the morning, he would awaken and realize that she was no longer there, that his room was empty, and that he was going to have to yearn for her all day during the cruel hours of idleness that separated him from the sublime moment when she would appear in the square, in the evening, shortly before the call to evening prayer.

But, for the last few days, Hanane had not returned home.

"You should talk to Nabil about it," suggested my mother.

"It's not easy. He's so unpredictable."

My mother frowned. She disapproved of my indecision. Patiently, she let me finish my dinner, removed the tray that I had barely touched, scolding me for eating so little, and followed me to my room to argue with me. She sat down, rested her chin on her clasped little hands roughened by the household chores, and thought.

My little sister appeared in the doorway.

"You promised you'd help me," she pleaded, brandishing her school exercise book.

"Nora, please," my mother scolded. "You can see your brother and I have other things to worry about."

"Yes, but we've got composition tomorrow."

"Later, darling."

Nora pulled a helpless face and went back into the next room.

My mother leaned over the coffee table.

"You're not hoping that someone else will do it for you, are you? In my view, you should go and talk to him about it. There's nothing wrong in asking for a girl's hand."

"He's a suspicious character, I tell you. He might think that

I've been going out with his sister for ages. I'm afraid of his reaction. Nabil always sees the bad side of things. I've been toeing the line for months. I go to prayer; I've kept my nose clean. But he'll use any excuse to bring up my past. I try to placate him, but it's useless. He's blinkered and only thinks about fighting. And then with all the agitation, he's so busy, I daren't broach the subject."

"I think you're the one who's making things difficult. This is about a marriage proposal. It's serious. And the events in the street won't change anything. My mother got married in the middle of the First World War. Bab El Oued was swarming with Americans. The sky was rumbling with bombers and the sirens wailed all night. But we celebrated our wedding. And me in '62. The OAS was blowing up the district. Submachine guns were firing on every street corner. Every day there were attacks on strangers. That didn't stop the wedding procession parading down the boulevards. The *zorna* played till dawn. That's life, my boy. The world goes on regardless. People get married despite everything. Otherwise, the world would have no reason to go on. I remember, on my wedding night, while your father was being pushed in the bridal chamber by his friends, bursts of gunfire could be heard a stone's throw from the house. And your father said to me..."

"I didn't say anything," shouted my father's husky voice from the depths of the living room. "And I needed no pushing that night. Watch what you say, wife. In my day, I didn't need shoving, especially not in front of a fifteen-year-old virgin."

My sisters, who were eavesdropping in the kitchen, burst out laughing. My mother covered her mouth guiltily with her hand and hunched her shoulders. With the other hand she waved an invisible fan over her gaffe which, failing a miracle, the old man was unlikely to forgive her.

I, too, began to laugh.

Chapter eight

Before the outbreak of national hysteria in October '88, Omar Ziri had been a hoodlum who was very proud of the blue-green anchors tattooed on his biceps. He sported a Basque beret set jauntily over his ear, and a flick-knife in his belt. All year round he wore blue overalls, frayed at the knees, and a threadbare marine sweater stretched over his grotesque paunch. Sullen-faced, cigarette butt hanging from his mouth, he never said thank you and considered saying sorry as the worst cop-out. He ran Le Nef, a seedy eating-house next to the mosque—a rat hole cluttered with worm-eaten tables and benches that wore out pants seats faster than sliding down the banisters.

From midday until nightfall, soothed by the lyrics of the dying Dahmane El Harrachi, he snoozed behind his ancient till, as old as a gas lamp, which would obstinately jam when he had to give someone change. His customers were a motley crew of foul-smelling refuse collectors and day laborers who ate like animals and whose filthy hands left grimy imprints on the thick slices of bread. There was a twenty-dinar fixed-price menu. The same dishes were served for lunch and dinner: *chorba*—a meatless stew, dubious-looking chips, a bowl of curd and shriveled biscuits.

After October '88, Omar Ziri was caught up in the Islamist wave. He sniffed out the imminence of a revolution that would forgive nothing of those who did not leap onto the bandwagon. The message was clear and the threat blatant. So when Imam Younes asked him to transform his eatery into an Islamic Salvation Front-style soup kitchen, Omar declared that he was extremely honored to do so. Overnight, the till vanished, and the pernicious songs of Dahmane El Harrachi were supplanted by religious music. Beggars joined the former clientele for a free meal, and, moved by their pathetic appetite, Omar the philanthropist would ostensibly brush away a tear, thanking the heavens for placing him among the men of good will. He exchanged his overalls for a *kamis* more reminiscent of Medina, and, instead of his Basque beret, he wore a headdress like that of the FIS leader Ali Belhadj, beneath which he quietly hatched his big plans.

Every day, cohorts of beggars gathered in front of the eating-house, and Omar feigned embarrassment at their effusive expressions of gratitude, for, as he kept repeating, there was nothing more disagreeable than a thank you for a simple charitable duty.

The poor were entitled to the same menu as the former clientele with, depending on his generosity, a piece of chicken, a slice of melon or a pot of yogurt. If they were still hungry, they were given double rations, with good grace. With their bellies full, the needy were more inclined to listen to the strange migratory birds that had set off for the Orient to spread the good word and had come home with messages of hope and a program for salvation. These were well-brought-up fellows, as neatly groomed as marabou storks, slightly odd due to their Afghan dress, but sober and touchingly indulgent. They were called sheikhs. Between two mouthfuls, they would take it in turns to speak, telling the poor how deeply they sympathized with their misfortune. Even though their beards gave their faces an unfathomable look, their voices were filled with compassion, and their sincerity was as visible as the Holy Book, which they brandished. They seemed to know all about the misery of ordinary people, and it pained them. They talked about the village, overrun by dogs and layabouts, the corruption rife in ruling circles, the paradox that did not explain why, in a country as rich as Algeria, fully-fledged citizens should languish in the most ignominious poverty. They said: "Before '62, our country was the granary of Europe. Now, it is in ruins. Before '62, an Algerian would have preferred to cut off his hand rather than hold it out to beg. Today, he holds out both hands." They said: "Why are you here, in this tavern, dependent solely on the charity of a few good souls? Why should you be content with a soup kitchen while they are throwing *your* money out of the window, pumping *your* oil under your noses, trampling your dignity and your future?"

Simple questions, but which elicited only muffled indignation and confusion in reply. The sheikhs did not hope for more. They pointed heavenwards declaring that the angels had abandoned Algeria, and that God was angry with a people so profoundly religious but so forgetful of His teachings and heedless of its own decay when the way to liberate them from the clutches of Satan and lead them towards the Light was clear.

The sheikhs spoke so eloquently that the poor did not even notice that a sign proclaiming Islamist slogans had replaced that of the eating house, that the hostel for the poor was being turned into an information and propaganda center, that in place of the counter, the worm-eaten tables and the kitchens, there were now offices, and on the wall, that had at last been distempered, heart-rending photos bore witness to the excesses of the security forces during the October riots. These images had not been tampered with, they swore. The photos were a reminder of the teargas-filled streets, the burned-out vehicles and buildings, the riot police beating up demonstrators with their bludgeons, the stretcher bearers ferrying the wounded, women sobbing, traumatized children… and, above all, the bodies lying in the street in pools of blood, mutilated, devastated, their eyes wild, their fingers pointing to the heavens, seemingly saying to the survivors, according to the sheikhs, "We died for you. Don't forget us."

Of course, in a society where about-turns and hypocrisy are commonplace, neither Omar Ziri nor his eating house were worth dwelling on, but this anecdote illustrates with disarming simplicity how, without conflict and without a fuss, almost unwittingly, the Casbah of the poets was transformed into a fundamentalist citadel.

That morning, there were a lot of people milling around the mosque and in the adjacent streets. Hundreds of the faithful, militants and sympathizers, thronged the pavements, some standing under awnings, others under umbrellas, sheltering from the sun. They were all waiting for news from the *Majlis*. Civil disobedience was spreading, taking hold. The country was paralyzed. The megaphones blared out their harsh sermons across the city. Young militiamen sporting arm-bands and green bandannas around their foreheads handed out water and biscuits, and disciplined new arrivals continued to flock from all four corners of the city. From time to time, a sheikh climbed up onto a soapbox to read messages from the national bureau, punctu-ated with the inevitable "the government will fall," which the faithful greeted with sound and fury. Nafa Walid took advantage of a passing delegation to elbow his way through to Omar Ziri's eatery. Nabil Ghalem was stacking cardboard boxes in the former kitchen, which had been converted into an archive room. He was not alone. Nafa recognized, crammed together on metal chairs, the Chaouch broth-ers, two eminent academics, Hamza Youb, a house painter, Rachid Abbas, a relative of Imam Younes, and three "Afghans," militiamen at the Kabul Mosque of Kouba who sometimes came to supervise the organization of the strike and give Nabil Ghalem a hand. The tallest was called Hassan. He had lost an arm in Peshawar, learning how to make explosive devices. The other two had the fanciful nicknames of Abou Mariem and Ibrahim El Khalil. The stories of their feats in Afghanistan were so far-fetched that they themselves no longer believed in them.

"And then what happened?" asked Omar Ziri, quivering with excitement.

"Well," continued Ibrahim El Khalil in a detached tone, "the inevitable. I asked the fellow what he was doing in the woods with a girl in an old banger at that hour. He was scared out of his wits. He said he was discussing serious problems with his wife. I said: Let's see your family allowance book. He said: I've left it at home. I asked the woman if the man was her husband. She said: Yes. I said: What's his name? She said: Kader. I said: Kader what? And she nearly swallowed her saliva glands. Then she fell apart and started gibbering, saying she was a widow and jobless, that she had kids, disabled parents, and nobody to rely on, that she had to do *that* to feed her family. I said to the man: you filthy liar, show me your hands. His mustache trembled. He showed his hands, like a school kid. I rapped his fingers with my belt. Thwack! Thwack! With each stroke he knelt on the ground on one knee, wincing with pain, and stuck his hands under his buttocks. Anyone could see he was putting it on. So I got angry. I always get angry when people go too far. I told the brothers to strip him and I gave him a *falaqa* that he won't forget in a hurry. He was unable to stand up afterwards. He crawled away on all fours."

Omar Ziri laughed heartily. His belly wobbled on his knees.

"There's nothing better than a good thrashing," declared Abou Mariem sententiously.

"What about the woman?" chuckled Omar Ziri, lustfully.

"That you'll never know, you pig," replied Ibrahim.

"And what were you doing in the woods at that hour?"

"That you'll never know either."

Nabil Ghalem stepped back to contemplate the shelves.

"What do you think of them, boys? Aren't they lovely?"

"Lovely," approved Rachid. "I'll have to invite you over to my place some time to sort it out."

"I'm not your maid."

Omar Ziri leaned towards Ibrahim:

"Really, you won't tell me, about the girl?"

Nabil ran a duster over the cupboard, rearranged a couple of boxes and stood back again to admire his work. He was satisfied.

"Have you got a minute?" Nafa asked him.

"He hasn't even got a watch," retorted Omar with a cackle.

Nabil wiped his hands on his knees.

"A problem?"

"Not really."

97

Nafa tried to take his arm to steer him away from the others. Nabil resisted.

"The government's going to abdicate any minute," he announced. "The strike was an all-out success. Brothers are coming back from all over the place. They're unanimous: those bastards have only got a few days to pack their suitcases and get out. Do you realize?"

Nafa was relieved. Nabil was in a good mood, therefore predisposed to listen to him, at last.

"Yes?"

Nafa scratched his cheek, moistened his lips and took his courage in both hands, but the words wouldn't come.

"Well, you see…" he stammered, "I wanted to talk to you about this ages ago, only you didn't seem… I mean you were so busy. Now… Could we go somewhere else? It won't take long."

"We're among brothers. There are no secrets here. It's not serious, I hope?"

Nafa suddenly realized what he had started. But already Nabil was embracing him, kissing him and hugging him tight:

"I knew it, I knew it…"

And turning towards the others:

"What did I tell you? Nafa's made a wonderful choice. He's finally decided to join our movement."

"That'll be a lot of use to us!" said Omar, snidely.

Nafa was caught off-guard. It took the wind out of his sails. He was choked with humiliation. Swept up in his companion's enthusiasm, he bitterly regretted having to defer his marriage request.

At 5 P.M. that evening, he went back to count buses in the square. Thirty minutes later, there was no Hanane, and he spat on the ground and went home.

"Go and see who's at the door, Ikrame," shouted mother Ghalem from the kitchen.

The little girl fearfully slid her magazine under a cushion and ran into the hall. Suddenly, she froze. Supposing it was Nabil? No, Nabil had a key. Besides, he never knocked. Ikrame raised herself up onto tiptoes and drew back the bolt. A lady was standing on the landing, tall and beautiful, wearing a tight-belted raincoat. Her western-style dress fascinated the little girl, who glanced apprehensively at the staircase. She shuddered: What if Nabil were to see that!

"You must be Ikrame, Hanane's little sister?"

"Yes, madame."

"Is your sister there?"

Ikrame raised her fingers to her lips, uncertain.

"Nabil hates women who dress like that," she said awkwardly.

"Really, why's that?"

"Nabil says that women who don't wear the *hijab* are bad. When they die they'll be covered in flames and will burn for all eternity."

The lady stroked her cheek.

"Go and tell Hanane that Madame Rais is here."

Ikrame nodded and ran to her sister's room. She found her staring at herself in the mirror. Her lips were swollen and she had a black eye.

"Madame Rais is here."

"Tell her I've gone out."

"Nabil says that liars will be hung over the flames by their tongues and will roast in hell until the end of time."

Hanane dropped the mirror and rose reluctantly.

Madame Rais heaved a sigh of relief that turned into a gasp: "Oh my God!"

Hanane invited the visitor into the sitting room and indicated an upholstered bench.

"You poor thing," protested Madame Rais. "What happened to you?"

Hanane sent her little sister to fetch some coffee before blurting out angrily:

"Why did you come here?"

"You don't normally take time off without telling anyone. At the office people were beginning to get worried. The boss sent me to find out what had happened."

"It's finished."

"What's finished?"

"The office," groaned Hanane, a lump in her throat.

"What do you mean?"

"It's obvious, isn't it? I won't be coming back to work."

"That I've understood. But why? Because of Redouane? He loves teasing girls, but he doesn't mean any harm."

Hanane crumpled onto a cushion, and began to sob. Madame Rais sat beside her and put an arm around her shoulders.

"My poor darling, what's the matter?"

"You're wasting your time," said the mother, bringing in a tray.

Madame Rais rose to embrace the elderly woman.

"I am a colleague of your daughter's. As we haven't seen or heard from her for two weeks, our manager asked me to come and find out if anything is wrong. What happened to your daughter, *Hadja*?"

"The same thing that happens to Algerian girls every day," sighed the mother.

Hanane frowned at her to make her shut up. The old woman shrugged, placed the tray on a pedestal table and started pouring coffee into the three cups.

"I spent a fortune on her education," she went on, vexed. "I worked my fingers to the bone so that she could carry on studying. And the minute she's got her diplomas and found a good job in a respectable company, she gives it up."

"Mother…"

"You be quiet. I've sacrificed the best years of my life for you. I feel you don't have the right to let me down. Your job is all you have. One day, I'll close my eyes forever. Nabil will take a wife, have children and will want the house for himself. He will begin to make your life a misery, accuse you of all sorts of things, call you an interloper and will end up throwing you out into the street. Only then will you wish you hadn't given up the job you're about to leave."

"Mother…"

"What? Don't think you can stop me complaining."

Madame Rais realized that something serious had happened. The mother told her the whole story.

"Her monster of a brother is persecuting her. The sheikhs have corrupted his mind. He only talks about bans and sacrilege. In truth, he's jealous at seeing her succeed where he has always failed. He's jealous of her education, her job, and her paycheck. And that is why he beats her. As soon as her scars heal, he beats her up again. It's his way of locking her up, of stopping her from 'flirting' with men."

Madame Rais turned to Hanane:

"Is that what your problem is?"

"Her nightmare."

"Aren't you being a bit pessimistic, dear? You want us to believe that you're *still* being persecuted, at your age?"

"He swore he'd slit my throat," exploded Hanane.

"So? That's what they all say. We're not animals, you know."

"He's a monster. He's capable of anything."

Madame Rais stretched out a finger towards Hanane's bruised face, and raised her chin:

"Nonsense! I've been there. Like all women. I staggered under the blows, cringed at the insults, trembled without knowing why. Sometimes I didn't sleep a wink all night for some trifling misdemeanor. But in the end I fought back. I took responsibility for myself. The result: I'm *free*. The things I own are all the result of my own efforts. I choose my own path. I go where I *want*, my head held high. And I married the man I love. The days of the beast of burden are over. We won't put up with it any more. We won't let *them* trample us any more. We should only have one goal: to *oppose* them, and say to them: *Nyet,* that's enough!"

"It's obvious you don't know Nabil."

"Nabil, Antar, Ayatollah or Bluebeard, I don't give a damn. Wake up, my dear. We're living in the age of the computer, the scanner, and artificial intelligence. Space probes are exploring the universe. And you, you continue to put up with the ravings of a madman. You're a manager for goodness sake! You deserve respect. You have proved what you're capable of, that you are *free*. Besides, it's good timing—on Thursday the women's association is organizing a protest march against the machismo and the demands of the fundamentalists. Join us. We'll go and scream our discontent in the face of society."

"You're crazy."

"No, I'm only a woman who has thrown off her chains. I said: Stop! I want to be *me*, not to be ashamed of my curves, but to be who I am: a human being in my own right, with everything that means, with a heart—with *courage*—ambitions and millions of desires."

Hanane curled up.

Her mother left the room, muttering furiously.

"Go away," sobbed Hanane, addressing her colleague.

"Out of the question."

"Yes, you're leaving. And now. You don't know what you're talking about. You've been lucky, I haven't. I'm not giving it all up. I never had anything in the first place…"

"That's defeatist. That's what they've been trying to get into your head. Sharpen your nails into claws and scratch their eyes out. Bite, punch, yell. If their arms are stronger and their blows more vicious, fight with your heart. Remember how many times you've kow-towed to them and suffered their abuse, what the washing up has done to your pretty hands, what their insults have done to your ears. You are a Woman, Hanane. Do you realize what that means? *Woman*. You are everything, the mistress, the sister, the brains, the warmth of the earth and the mother, have you forgotten? The mother who bore *Man* in her belly, who brought him into the world in pain, suckled him, gave him love, confidence, taught him to speak, to walk… you, the great mother, the first smile, the first word, man's *first love*."

Nabil was beside himself. His rasping breath rebounded off the walls. The look he shot Ikrame, who stood dumbstruck in the hall, was inhuman.

"Where is she?" he growled, grabbing his mother's arm.

"Cursed be the day you were born, wretch. How dare you raise your hand to your own mother?"

Nabil pushed her away. His jaws rotated in his hate-filled face when he caught sight of Hanane's *hijab* lying crumpled in the corner.

"She's gone to the women's demonstration. Yes, that's it. I bet she's gone to make an exhibition of herself with those hussies."

His mother averted her eyes and he knew he was right. He let out a roar and rushed outside. The children, who were playing around in the street, scattered at the sight of him. His nostrils quivering with rage, he sought a friend's car, or a taxi, hailed a young motorcyclist, clambered on behind him and ordered him to take him to Place des Martyrs.

A hundred or so women, waving banners, were clustered on the esplanade, under the bemused gaze of the passers-by. Nabil plunged into the crowd, aggressively pushing his way through. His temples pounded with the thought: *That she-devil! Disobey you? That bitch dared flout your authority...* He cleaved through the group of women like an icebreaker, searching, searching. For a second, he pictured himself holding a flame-thrower and burning this gang of bitches, these witches... *Whores! Whores...* He pushed over a woman, jostled some nurses and thrashed about, generally causing alarm.

As he rounded a group of demonstrators, he saw *her*. Hanane was there, standing before him, in a tight skirt that he loathed. She watched him coming. He thrust his hand into the opening of his *kamis*. His hand closed over the handle of the knife... *bitch, bitch...* he stabbed her beneath her breast, there where her perverse soul lodged, then her side, then her stomach...

The day was fading. Hanane could see it no longer. She was caught up in a murky, freezing, soundless maelstrom. A voice called her. Was it a seducer, or was she talking to herself? It didn't matter. The square melted into a river of shadows. Hanane sank like a stone in a pond. She was dying. *Dying?* If only she had lived, kissed the lips of a beloved, thrilled to a loving caress. But instead, she was a virgin being snuffed out like a candle in a funeral chamber. With a final convulsion, she turned towards the elusive past, which melted like an illusion. School and university had all been for nothing. Her diplomas had not protected her from her brother's murderous blade, which burst her dream like an abscess.

Chapter nine

Hanane's death had given me a shock. It was as if she had rejected me, after leading me on for a long time. But I did not mourn her. What was the use? For me, it was no more than a wish that would never be fulfilled. I was beginning to get used to that.

I felt anger, but above all pain, when I realized to what absurd extremes people were capable of going, and yet, I do not remember feeling hatred for Nabil. He was not worthy of it, in my view. His action was one of madness. He had wounded my flesh without even touching my spirit. I remained clear-headed. I managed to take a philosophical view of tragedy. Beyond the sad death of the woman I had wanted for my wife, I was convinced that this was no mere combination of circumstances, but a divine sign, that God was putting me to the test.

I did not even attend the funeral.

I stayed at home and prayed.

Of course, sometimes I still rebelled against fate, which insisted on thwarting all my aspirations with a particular vengeance; then, like a good believer, I regained my grip. I was saddened by the loss of the radiant, calm, discreet girl, but I would not allow myself to enter into speculations that would mire me in pointless confusion. I didn't have the energy. I had been weakened by the string of disappointments and shattered dreams. I felt as vulnerable as a fly within reach of a chameleon. I needed, at all costs, to build up my strength again. First of all, I gave up on my two-roomed flat in Souk El Jamaa; then, after a good deal of reflection, I decided not to get married before gauging the full measure of the tide that was about to engulf the country in what threatened to be a disaster.

Now that Nabil had been arrested, there was no need for me to keep in with the militant Islamists and pretend to be interested in the lessons given to us by the sheikhs. Once I had finished my prayers, I was the first to leave the mosque. Then I hung around the streets, my hands behind my back and my lips heavy. I was bored.

In the Casbah, it was impossible to find someone to console you without giving him a chance to indoctrinate you. They abused the confusion of "lost souls" and took advantage of their weakness to rope them into the movement. At that point, just about everyone discovered a vocation for being a guru. Everywhere, young imams went sniffing out resentment, invading people's consciousness and forging minds to suit their purpose. They could be seen in the cafés, schools and health clinics, and even on staircases. Impossible to grin and bear it. A mere whimper and the followers heaped their sympathy on you then, without warning, you found yourself in the hands of the architects of Salvation. No more privacy, no running away. Unless you closed the shutters and locked yourself in your room. Life was becoming intolerable.

To escape the tension, I went to see Dahmane, in the city center. There, despite the omnipresence of the *kamis*, the sound of the fury was less aggressive. People were going about their business, the shop windows glittered and the pavement cafés were crowded. Jokes and bursts of laughter erupted here and there, probably exaggerated to conceal anxiety and anguish. What did it matter! All Dahmane had to do was close his door to shut out the street. His apartment was spacious and charming, decorated with fine pictures, comfy armchairs and silky curtains. Dahmane lacked for nothing. He seemed fulfilled. He had a delightful little daughter and an attentive wife whose smile sparkled like the snows of Tikijda. They welcomed me with open arms, and often insisted I stay for dinner. Eventually, I realized that I was spoiling their happiness with my endless tales of woe. I never stopped complaining, without knowing exactly what I was complaining about. My visits grew further apart, then I stopped going there altogether. In truth, I was envious of their comfort, of the bliss in which they basked, far from the vengeful clamor and bloodshot eyes; I was envious of my childhood friend's good fortune. He had started with nothing and become successful. I envied him his beautiful wife, who had brains too—she taught psychology at the university. I envied their steadfast purity.

My jealousy sometimes bordered on aversion when, returning home, I was once again subjected to the ill humor of my father, sitting in his corner like an evil spirit, waiting for the slightest pretext to start berating his family. I hated him, hated his dentures moldering in their glass, his hypochondriac's smell. I hated our miserable apartment that was suffocating my sisters. Our family's poverty deterred any potential suitors despite the girls' beauty and their reputation as excellent housekeepers. I hated the squalor of my room; it reflected that of my soul, and I hated the miserable food my mother improvised and served with an apologetic smile, and her sad eyes that dragged me down a little further each time her gaze rested on me...

I couldn't bear it any longer.

Outside, it was worse. There were more and more Islamist rallies. Fanatical with their bristly beards and fiery eyes, the demonstrators occupied the squares, the sanctuaries and the few parks, haranguing passers-by and provoking the police. The streets were closed to traffic. The Islamists shouted abuse and sometimes rocked the cars of irritated motorists. The militiamen had a whale of a time. The slightest thing served as a pretext. Woe to anyone who complained. Girls not wearing a veil were attacked by over-excited kids who threw stones at them, splattered them with wastewater and yelled filthy words, which in the mouths of children rang out like blasphemies.

Graffiti on the peeling walls read like declarations of war. The sermons turned into calls to arms, and intimidation led to skirmishes. Between protest marches, news items brought home the reality: the first victims of fundamentalism were beginning to pay the price: a prostitute, a drunkard, a "shady" establishment. Not enough for the nation to go into mourning, but sufficient to arouse speculation. Fear gradually set in. They're being too soft on them, protested the secular elements. No compromise, retorted the extremists. Amid the uncertainty, splinter groups of the Islamic Salvation Front emerged. The *Hijra wa Takfir*, the most radical wing of the movement, was gaining a sinister reputation. Its henchmen infiltrated the deprived milieus, recruiting among the wretched and the frustrated, striking fear with their zeal and fierce determination. Everywhere they were described in the same way: aggressive and ignorant with their shaven heads, expressionless eyes and ill-kempt beards. They were hot-tempered, violent hard-liners. They assembled under cover of night to train on wastelands or in the woods. Tongues wagged. People talked of sabers, machetes, an arsenal, and shadowy squadrons.

Suddenly, the sword of *Da Mokhkess* came down like a guillotine. Civil disobedience was outlawed, and the leaders Abassi Madani and Ali Belhadj were thrown into prison. The giants revealed they had feet of clay. People could not believe it.

After the government's show of strength, the Casbah woke up in a state of grogginess, disoriented. The mosques were silent, the streets traumatized, and the cheated militants wandered around in a daze; dumbfounded, incredulous, ready to make a run for it at the wail of a siren.

Despite the neutralization of its figureheads, the *Majlis* regained control and reorganized, spurred on by an energy born of despair—the despair that rekindles causes that have been subdued but not lost. New, Christ-like leaders appeared. Student *mufti* soon proved more efficient than their teachers. Local Islamist cells opened their doors again, brought out their loud hailers and their archives. Their resolve had not been dented. People invoked the lessons to be learned from the mistakes of yesterday. They opted for a softer, more persuasive approach. Passionate diatribes, provocation and all the excesses that frightened off the masses, were banned. The government had erred. It was essential to maintain the image of a tyrant censured by the saints and by other nations. From now, they would play the ballot box game to the end, taking care not to put a foot wrong or indulge in crude condemnation, as the polls were largely on the side of the "wronged".

I was regularly stopped by all sorts of cranks, and so I ventured into the narrow streets of the Casbah as seldom as possible. Early in the morning, I slipped on my jeans and trainers, and went out to stretch my legs, either in Soustara, or in Rue Larbi Ben M'hidi. With the money I'd saved at the Rajas, I could afford to treat myself to a grilled lunch and a trip to the coast where life followed its course, blithely ignoring the alarmists. Although summer was drawing to a close, the beaches were swarming; the sand couldn't be seen for beach umbrellas, and carefree girls wriggled into swimsuits that were barely visible against their golden skin. I would find a café terrace and sit for hours on end with a glass of lemonade, listening to Raï music and watching the sunlight dance on the ocean.

That was how I met Mourad Brik. I didn't recognize him because of his obesity. His face was podgy and his eyes engulfed by rolls of fat. But his gurgling laugh, like a teapot left on the brazier, immediately jogged my memory. Mourad Brik had shared my room in a sleazy hotel in the suburbs for the two months we had been shooting Children of the Dawn. At that time, his belt was on the tightest hole. Broke and starving, he was always cadging cigarettes from technicians on the set. We were two young, ambitious actors, lured by the limelight, who were absolutely convinced that one day we'd tread the red carpet at Cannes. In the movie, he plays a cousin who goes off the rails, and I try to get him back on the straight and narrow. He ends up destitute, a junkie, who throws himself dramatically under the wheels of a train, hammering home the message to the audience—grown-ups and kids alike—that no good can come of sloth and keeping bad company. The public appreciated the moral, and the press, convinced that this was the best way of making young people aware of the dangers, had generously devoted a paragraph to him on the center page, which was more than I received. Later, when I was chasing rainbows at the Lebanon, Mourad Brik leapt at the smallest part on offer. From time to time he would appear in a dreary TV series, then in a bit part in a play, and then in a feature film that was relatively successful and won him, to my great annoyance, a prize at an African film festival.

I lost touch with him.

After the customary embrace, he sank onto a chair and patted his curly locks to flatten them. His Hawaiian shirt gaped over his paunch. He ordered an ice cream and began by asking me what I was up to. He gave me a good grilling before he was prepared to talk about himself:

"I'm leaving for Paris, in December. A one-way ticket, I make no secret of it. Some friends of mine applied to the French Cultural Center and they've given me a grant. I'm going to train at a professional theatre."

To corroborate his story, he pushed a paperback towards me. It was Corneille's Le Cid.

"At night, in my room, I stand in front of the mirror and rehearse my lines. Impressive. But I'm sure that my time at the institute will be a mere formality. I'm gong to make loads of friends in theatre circles and land a big part within a year. Otherwise, what's the point of shouting myself hoarse every night in front of the mirror? The poor neighbors have bruised hands from banging on the wall to shut me up. The award I won in Ouagadougou will open a lot of doors for me. It'll be great—galas, fashionable dinner parties, press conferences, photo shoots, TV appearances, money and women. I'm going to make up for lost time in a flash, trust me. Do you know that Madame Simone Fleuret wrote to me?"

"How would I know that?"

"I bet you don't even have any idea who she is. Madame Fleuret, one of the top casting agents. Her office is bigger than a public library. She's the key to fame and glory. Well, just think—she wrote to me. Of her own accord. That's something. I most likely won't even take the course I'm supposed to be doing if she's got plans for me. It's the beginning, Nafa. I'll never set foot again in this dump where even the flowers stink."

He was getting carried away, gesticulating wildly, almost in a trance. His ice cream was melting, trickling down the side of the goblet and forming a tiny milky puddle on the table. Mourad was oblivious. His laughter and exclamations were getting on my nerves, and he'd prod me whenever my attention flagged.

"Do you think I've got a chance with the French Cultural Center?"

He nearly swallowed his tongue and choked. His expression became evasive and he replied:

"It's a bit late, in my view."

"Why?"

"Well, it's past the closing date for applications."

"I want to try my luck."

He looked peeved, and retracted his neck into his flabby shoulders.

"I don't want to disappoint you."

"I'll take the risk."

"It won't be easy, I warn you."

"I'll be indebted to you for the rest of my life," I begged him.

"It's not up to me... you've only made one movie, Nafa. Have you even got a press book? It hasn't been easy for me, despite my press clippings and my African prize. I had to get friends to pull strings and grease a few palms."

"Ask them to do it again. Think about it, the two of us in Paris. We'll help each other."

Mourad finally plunged his spoon into the melting ice cream.

III

He took his time, scraped the bottom of the goblet, and licked his lips thoughtfully.

"To be honest, you've caught me on the hop. I didn't think you'd force me to tell you everything. My track record as an actor wasn't enough. To get the grant, I had to cough up."

"How much?"

He pushed the goblet away and folded his hands over his paunch. His mean eyes held me at bay. He stared at me in silence, then nodded painfully:

"Drop it, Nafa. It's not for you."

"I don't intend to spend another minute moldering here."

"You really want to launch yourself?"

"Absolutely."

My determination seemed to worry him. He gazed at the heavens seeking a way out, but found none. His cheeks quivered.

"Let's agree on one thing, Nafa. I hate this messy business. And you are absolutely not to think that I expect any kind of reward for my trouble. I'm an artist. Wheeler dealing isn't my bag. It's important you remember that. It's a question of my dignity. And it matters to me."

"I don't give a damn. What I want is my passport so I can try my luck. How much?"

"Twenty thousand dinars, cash. And three thousand French francs on embarkation," he retorted curtly.

I didn't hesitate for a moment. I had saved up enough at the Rajas to be able to negotiate two or three operations of this kind. I realized I hadn't yet said goodbye to my dreams of the past and that they had been rekindled by the picture Mourad had drawn that day, sitting under a faded sunshade. I could already see myself doing the rounds of the Paris movie studios, a film script under my arm and my eyes wider than a screen, far from the alleys of the Casbah, from the musty odor of my solitude and the torment of idleness. Paris filled my mind. I understood then, that if I did not take advantage of his generosity, I'd be better off dead. From that day, I was obsessed with a single urge: to leave. Leap onto a plane and stand on my own two feet.

The financial problem resolved, Mourad asked me to put together, before the end of the week, a complete application, with a hand-written letter addressed to the director of the French Cultural Center, my CV, a visa application and passport, and the usual documents: birth certificate, twelve passport-size photos, certificate of residence etc.

Then he arranged to meet me at the Hammamet, a classy restaurant where I would never have dared venture alone, even when I was working for the Rajas.

Mourad had already ordered his food and was on the main course when I arrived. He wiped the corners of his mouth with the tip of his napkin and invited me to sit opposite him. I proffered the envelope containing the requisite documents. He merely counted the money and carried on eating.

"Order something."

"No, thank you."

"The roast lamb and mushrooms is delicious."

"I'm not hungry. Besides, I've had no appetite since the other day. I can't sleep, and all I can think of is the grant."

"It'll be a sweat, but we'll get you that wretched grant," he reassured me. "I've already made contact with someone who's influential at the French Cultural Center."

He ate enough for four, wolfed down his dessert and glanced at his watch.

"I'm late," he said, rising.

"When do we meet again?"

"I'll contact you."

"You don't know where I live."

"I'll ask."

"I'd rather you took down my phone number."

He forced himself to sit down again and irritably wrote down my phone number on the envelope I had handed to him.

"Will it take long?"

"Nafa, my friend, don't be in a hurry. In any case, the course doesn't start until December. We've got two months ahead of us."

"Isn't there somewhere I can get hold of you?"

"Relax, kho. It's not your problem any more. As soon as I have some news, I'll call you."

He shook my hand and vanished, leaving me to pay the bill.

Chapter ten

That's enough," protested Nafa's father. "It's not a switchboard here. 'Has Mourad phoned, has Mourad phoned?' Nobody's phoned. Do you want to drive us round the bend? From dawn till dusk, it's always the same refrain. We've got other things to do, you know. Besides," he added, making a pretence of tearing his son away from the phone, "I'm going to smash that wretched contraption to smithereens."

Nafa grabbed his arm and pinned him to the wall. He gripped him so hard that the old man thought he heard his arm snap. With his mouth contorted by pain and his legs buckling under him, he had only his eyes left to register his fury. The son held his ground. His flushed face twisted into an animal snarl and he shouted:

"Don't you dare touch that phone…"

The father stared incredulously at the hand that was crushing his flesh. Suddenly, the enormity of his son's betrayal dawned on him. Mustering his shattered strength, he rose to his feet amid a string of curses.

"Filthy bastard! You think you can intimidate me, you filth?!

You're a bad lot! You dare raise your hand to me, you, the fruit of my loins. I may be old, but I'm not finished. I will not allow you to lay down the law under my roof. You're nothing but a fool. You think you're big? I need a microscope to see you, you sonofabitch. I curse you."

The full gravity of his action dawned on Nafa. He released his father's arm, stepped back, unable to understand what had possessed him.

Nafa's father refused to rub his bruised wrist. For him, a thousand years of taboos had just been shattered. Did this signal the advent of the Apocalypse? It had always been said, as far back as human memory goes, that the day a son raises his hand to his father, that day would be the beginning of the final reckoning. Red as a poppy, he spat on the ground and staggered over to the mattress, wishing he could die before he reached it.

The four women, huddled motionless in a corner of the room, held their heads in their hands. Little Nora stared at her brother in horror. His mother's face was like an overripe quince. She refused to admit what she had just seen, there, in *her* house.

"I was prepared for anything," she said with a tremor in her voice, "except that."

Nafa spun round, then banged the wall, letting out an animal howl before he went out into the street. The mother ordered the girls to go to their rooms, murmured a prayer and went over to the offended father.

"Stay where you are," he shouted. "You're no better than he is. A respectable mother is not capable of producing such a child. Now I know you must have deceived me."

Nafa felt as if he were going mad. Already it was the end of December and there was no trace of Mourad Brik. Each time the phone rang, he leapt to the ceiling before banging the phone down when he did not hear the actor's voice on the other end. His sisters feared his presence in the house. If there was no message for him, he'd curse them,

Yasmina Khadra

sometimes hit them. Now they ran to their room for cover as soon as they heard his tread on the landing.

Nafa spent most of his time in taxis and buses, tossed about from one end of the city to the other, looking for former movie extras who might be able to help him find Mourad Brik. Their shrugged "no" stung. He returned to the Hammamet several times, went frequently to the airport: Mourad had vanished into thin air. At night, on returning home depressed as a result of his fruitless search, he could do nothing but howl until morning. He had grown thin, and neglected his appearance. His unkempt beard and glassy stare gave him a demented look. The longer Mourad took to resurface, the more determined he became to leave. Paris had become an obsession, rooted in his innermost being, and he was consumed by it.

The elections found him in an office of the French Cultural Center.

The secretary flung up her arms apologetically:

"We haven't awarded a grant to anyone called Mourad Brik."

"It isn't possible."

"We've checked. Our files are accurate."

Nafa stifled an expletive. He wandered through the city like a ghost.

He saw neither the people hurrying around him, not the army tanks that had taken up positions in the streets during the night.

There was not going to be a second round of voting.

The parliamentary election was cancelled.

The Islamist rallies were met with police raids, round-ups, and witch-hunts.

Algeria was plunging headlong into the irrevocable.

In next to no time, the clamor of the fundamentalists was drowned out by the din of sirens. Police cars combed the territory of the gurus, desecrating their sanctuaries. Doors were smashed down. Awoken at all hours, families succumbed to panic. Women's hands tried to release a brother, a father, a son-in-law. To no avail. Handcuffs

117

deterred any pleas for clemency. The sheikhs promised to return, one way or another, to avenge the affront. Some left their families with their heads held high, glowing, convinced that the future would prove them right, that oppression would consolidate their ranks and strengthen their resolve. Others clung to their parents' arms, swearing they would shave their beards to the roots so that they would never grow again.

Police batons were a powerful weapon of dissuasion. The police vans disappeared into the night.

Leaning against the French window, Rachid Derrag watched the riot police charging gangs of youths in the main streets of the district. Tires were burning in the middle of the road, and the buildings were shrouded in a pall of blackish smoke. Bursts of gunfire echoed off the walls, melting into the clamor, like the cries of a frenzied hydra. The demonstrators rushed to pick up the tear-gas grenades before they exploded and threw them back at the police, or submerged them in buckets of water. Iron bars crashed down on cars, smashing the windows and denting the bodywork. Thugs attacked storefronts, shattering the windows and pouring in to loot. A police squad arrived in the square, but beat a hasty retreat under the hail of stones. Hit on the head, an officer crumpled at the foot of a lamppost. Two bearded men leapt on him, divested him of his gun and vanished into the fray.

At a street corner, there was a police vehicle, its windscreen crazed and its tires blown out. A petrol bomb hit it full on. The fire spread to the inside of the vehicle, from which a shrieking human torch was thrown. Some police officers braved the missiles to run to his aid.

Further off, a military convoy was on the way to provide backup, and the crowd withdrew. Once again, the sound of machine-gun fire could be heard, at first sporadic and then continuous.

"It makes you sick," sighed the moviemaker, taking his hands out of his pockets.

Nafa Walid sat kneading his hands and gazing at the cupboard facing him. Rachid Derrag's cramped office was no more than a foul-smelling storage room with metal drawers stacked on top of each other, two flaking imitation-leather chairs, a scratched table and shelves laden with dog-eared notebooks. Shoes left a clear imprint on the dusty floorboards. On the wall was a yellowing poster of the *Chronicle of the Years of Fire*. In places, the credits had been erased and satanic horns had been drawn, using a heavy felt-tip pen on the close-up shot of the face.

Originally from a remote village near Tadmait in northeast Kabylia, Rachid had come in the '70s to roam around the outlying districts of Algiers in pursuit of a childhood dream. An open-air screening of *The Ten Commandments* had kindled in him a strange but compulsive ambition. He had made a few documentaries for television before leaving to study cinema in Moscow. Top of his year, he returned home to sit twiddling his thumbs. Budgets were negligible; he had cobbled together a couple of movies about discontented youth, including *Children of the Dawn*, which had been Nafa Walid's début, and learned to wait, like so many other directors, until the government's decision-makers deigned to whistle for him. Although he had never had the resources equal to his talents, Rachid had had the consolation of discovering many young actors. Some had managed to survive the rigors of the profession and climb the steep path to glory, achieving success in France. They never came back to tell the tale of their exciting struggle. Others, less fortunate, had become junkies or alcoholics, and sunk so low that they were beyond reach, even with diving equipment.

Rachid Derrag sank into the chair behind his desk, grabbed an empty cigarette packet, threw it over his shoulder, plunked his elbows on a blotter and pressed his thumbs to his temples. His baldness was emphasized by his few strips of long, wispy hair. He had aged. His condition was deteriorating like that of his only suit, which in itself betrayed the decline of a generation of artists whom the regime had impoverished so as to subjugate them.

"I don't like the look of that, I don't like it at all."

He was talking about the streets.

Nafa had other worries:

"You must have his address in your records."

"Whose address?"

"Mourad Brik's. Otherwise how would you get hold of him?"

The movie director remembered the purpose of Nafa's visit. He said "ah" and went on:

"We didn't need to. Mourad used to hang around every morning. As soon as someone handed me a script, he would appear before I'd even had time to read the title."

"Just let him give me back my passport. Never mind about the money, I want my passport back. Otherwise I'm condemned to fester here."

Rachid Derrag puffed out his cheeks.

"What upsets me most is to see an artist change course so radically. Mourad Brik—a swindler?... A talented actor reduced to such outrageous scheming? I'm ashamed, for him and for the whole movie profession. It's grotesque, grotesque..."

"Apparently he's ripped off other colleagues..."

"I know..."

"I've got to find him. It's absolutely essential."

"What are you on about now?" exploded the exasperated moviemaker. "Are you trying to make me feel guilty, or do you take me for a detective? The country is falling apart, and you come and pester me with your story about being swindled. You were ripped off, and that's that. You only have yourself to blame. Do you think you're the only one who wants to get out? We *all* want to be shot of this place. There are some rather unorthodox things going on out there. The President has been ousted. The streets are being ripped up by tanks. There are vigilantes under our beds, and the sirens keep us awake all night. And you, because a bastard took advantage of your stupidity, you come here and you think the world revolves around you... This is not a remake of October '88, a 'regrettable student riot.' This is war. We're done for. Now, get going. Please leave. I need to be alone."

Nafa left Rachid Derrag with a lump in his throat. It wasn't yet midday but it felt like night. Two cars were burning in a courtyard, the flames leaping up to lick the branches of a deformed tree. Stones, broken bottles, scraps of iron and the remains of burnt-out tires lay scattered over the road. On the grimy walls, blackened by the smoke, tattered election posters flapped like winged creatures trapped in the fabric of the walls.

People shut themselves up indoors, overwhelmed by the turn of events.

At the end of the street, a gang of ragamuffins raced past with the police at their heels.

In the distance, gunfire rang out, sometimes in sustained rounds, sometimes in fleeting bursts. In places, the denseness of the smoke masked the sky, engulfing the houses in a suffocating blanket. Military trucks roared in all directions, crushing the crude barriers that had been hastily erected on the tarmac. Processions of ambulances sped past in a deafening chorus, weaving in and out of the barricades and vanishing into the mists of the disaster.

The riot overtook Nafa as he turned into a square, dragging him along towards a seething arena. Someone slipped an iron bar into his hands and pointed at a powerful car with its doors wide open.

"It probably belongs to a filthy bourgeois bastard. Go for it!"

His wild eyes echoed his words. Without thinking, Nafa raced over to the car and started smashing it up as if Mourad Brik were inside. Then nothing. Just a long tunnel of noise, turbulence and darkness.

Nafa woke up in a police van, his jacket ripped, blood on his shirt and handcuffs on his wrists. He was locked up for two days in a nauseating cell, with a collection of overexcited vandals chanting fundamentalist slogans non-stop at the tops of their voices as they tried to prise out the bars. They shouted themselves hoarse on the first day, prayed the first night and only began to run out of steam the next day. In the afternoon, a police officer ordered Nafa to follow him. He shoved him into an office where an inspector was drawing up lists from a pile of identity cards on the desk.

"Are you Nafa Walid?"

"Yes."

He put down his pen to scrutinize him.

"A friend certifies that you had nothing to do with these crazy animals. I was good enough to believe him. Do you think I made a mistake?"

He motioned to the exit.

"You are free."

Before dismissing him, he tapped a register:

"I warn you, your name is in here. You've got a record and that'll stick. In other words, you've got a suspended sentence. One false move, and I'll take pleasure in nailing you myself."

Nafa Walid gathered up his personal belongings from the counter and went out into the street. The sky was gray. A wan sun filtered through the clouds without managing to tickle the streets. Dahmane was getting out of a car. His hand on the door, he improvised an appropriate smile.

"I didn't ask you for anything," fumed Nafa, furious at finding him there.

"But your father did. His heart won't hold out if you carry on being such a fool. When are you going to calm down?"

"When you get off my back."

"Show me first of all that you can stand on your own feet."

Nafa wagged a threatening finger at his friend:

"Watch what you're insinuating. I'm big enough to fend for myself."

"You wouldn't have to, if you toed the line."

"It's none of your business. We're not on the same ship. You're on a cruise liner, and I'm a galley slave."

"And whose fault is that, in your opinion?"

"You can't understand, Dahmane. We don't see things in the same light. You move in high-up circles, you've got a luxury apartment, a bank account and no worries. I'm not in your league."

Dahmane felt his heart contract. He said, in a conciliatory tone:

"Come on, let's go for a drive."

He got back into the car, and reached across the front seat to open the passenger door.

Nafa Walid spun on his heels and walked off.

Dahmane did not run after him. Something told him that his childhood friend had irrevocably chosen a different path.

Chapter eleven

The Café Bahja was swarming with people. The din drowned out the noise from the street. Everybody was giving their own commentary on the events, but they all concurred in justifying them. The other districts were venting their anger in an equally destructive frenzy, and it was not advisable to set foot there: more round-ups and deportations, new skirmishes breaking out. The café was the only place where the people of the Casbah could take refuge.

Zawech pitched up at the Bahja in a sorry state. His *kamis* ripped down one side, a crutch under his arm, he proudly showed off his head turbaned in a grotesque bandage splattered with stains of bright red disinfectant.

Zawech fulfilled the role of the village idiot. Not that he was simple-minded, but the position was vacant and Zawech wasn't very particular. With his long, spindly legs, his squat torso and humped back, he had the profile of a wader bird, a heron, hence his nickname, *Zawech*. Nobody knew his age. Around forty, maybe more, no matter—nothing would shield him from the taunts and the children's pranks. Rejected by the brotherhood of elders, he found a semblance of warmth among the young people, which he struggled to preserve by playing to the gallery. His status as a clown relegated him to the rank of untouchable. When he eventually took his courage in both hands to go and ask for the hand of a spinster, the woman's family was deeply offended. Doomed to celibacy and ridicule, Zawech had ceased hoping for some consideration that would help restore his dignity. For most people, he was one huge joke, and nothing else. Even in his death throes, people would laugh at him. Knowing that he would never be taken seriously, he opted to play the fool to make his life bearable.

Zawech rolled his protruding eyes at the people gathered around his table, and waved his crutch to gain their attention.

"Now what?" asked the café owner. "Did the sky fall on your head?"

"I don't know. I was over at El Harrach. All hell has broken loose there. A real *intifada*. Stones were flying in all directions. We were pelting the riot police, and they were chucking them back. I was having the time of my life, throwing stones for all I was worth. I ran through the smoke like a will-o'-the-wisp, hunting for stones to hurl at the pigs. And then I came across two beautiful pebbles, all shining and polished, like offerings, at the corner of the street. You can imagine, I didn't hesitate for a second, I ran over to pick them up. Well, they weren't pebbles. They were a cop's shoes. Suddenly, I get hit over the head. You're probably right, café owner. Perhaps it was the sky falling on my head, because I saw a load of stars dancing round me."

The few laughs that broke out were immediately stifled by a Rasputin character standing in front of the bar.

"This isn't the circus here, Zawech."

"But that's what happened."

"We don't give a damn. We're at war, believe it or not. Keep your silly stories to yourself."

"Yes," added the café owner, wiping the glasses on his filthy apron. "We've got more serious things to talk about. It's not our fault. They've pushed us over the edge. We can't vouch for anything any more."

"In any case, there's no going back now," explained Chaouch, an academic who was considered the local *éminence grise*. "They wanted to dazzle us, and they failed. Their stupid show of strength is the proof that they panicked."

"Absolutely," said Rasputin, "they lost their heads and nobody's going to help them pick themselves up again. Soon we'll be hanging them up in the square until their skin peels away in shreds. Then we'll throw them into the gutter to rid the sewers of rats."

Nafa Walid heard the same old thing day in and day out. Sometimes the arguments caused a crowd to gather in the street and the speakers had to clamber onto the tables to be heard above the din. The Casbah was in a febrile state. The alleyways were filled with ranting and raving, and its spirit was gloomy. The sun no longer ventured to send any light into the city, knowing that nothing would brighten up the future while the Casbah mourned its salvation.

Meanwhile, Nafa mourned his plans. It was his way of being in tune with the grief of his city, of showing solidarity with his people. He stopped looking for Mourad Brik. He no longer hankered to cross the sea. He became resigned. In the mornings, he slept late. After the mosque, he would wander around aimlessly, choose a table at a pavement café and watch the time go by.

Zawech slid his crutch under his arm and dragged his foot exaggeratedly to a table that was empty because of its proximity to the toilet.

"Since we're at war, can I have a free coffee? I've just returned from a pitched battle, I have!"

"No you can't," replied the café owner, firmly.

"I'm a wounded soldier, I'm entitled to be made a fuss of."

"Not here, you're not."

"OK," grumbled Zawech. "No problem. I nearly lost my memory after being bashed on the head, but God doesn't forget." Then, turning to a neighbor, "Have you got a cigarette butt for a hero, my friend?"

"I'm not your friend, loser. I don't find you at all funny."

Omar Ziri appeared on the other side of the street. He

motioned to Nafa to join him. Nafa Walid left some coins on the table and ran to catch up with the "philanthropist" who was disappearing down the street.

Once safe from prying eyes, they stopped under an arcade. Omar Ziri ran his finger under the neck of his shirt and twisted round to ensure that they were truly alone. His exaggerated caution made Nafa feel uncomfortable.

"Are you in trouble?"

"Me? God help me. Whatever makes you think that?" he replied, touchily.

"Nothing. Go on…"

"Imam Younes wants to see you. I'll meet you after night prayer, at my place."

Nafa acquiesced, but not without feeling his heart lurch.

"Can I ask why?"

"Don't you trust me?"

"It's not that. It's just so I can prepare myself."

Omar stared at him for a moment, his eyes unfathomable:

"Nine thirty on the dot, at my place."

"I'll be there."

"I should think so! Right, now wait till I've gone before you go back."

Sitting cross-legged in the middle of an eiderdown, Imam Younes was meditating. He looked grave. He was weighed down with a great sorrow. Behind him, Omar Ziri sat hunched with his eyes downcast, telling his beads. He looked asleep. Only Hassan—the Afghan who has lost an arm in Peshawar learning to make explosive devices—stared at the fifteen or so local layabouts summoned by the imam. Nafa Walid stood in the center of them, observing the Sheikh as he contemplated. Around him, the other faithful waited to learn the purpose of the meeting, their legs crossed and their hands fidgeting nervously on their knees.

Imam Younes finally looked up. His gaze swept over his flock.

In a monotone that betrayed a profound weariness, he recited a verse from the Koran to open the meeting and said:

"How is your father, Ali?"

"He's well, Sheikh."

"I heard he went into hospital this week."

"For dialysis, Sheikh. He can't manage without it."

"That's hard. And what about you, Najib, how is your grand-mother?"

"The same as always, Sheikh. She's hanging on, but without much hope."

"She's a saint. I'm praying for her. And what about you Farouk? I hear that your young wife is ill?"

"Miscarriage, Sheikh. You know how cramped we are at home, with twelve people in a poky little room. I have no work and the old man's paltry pension only makes things worse."

"I know, and I sympathize."

Imam Younes sighed. His expression clouded with suffering and the furrows on his brow deepened. He said:

"We are appealing to you because we know what you have to endure each day. What you do not realize is how lucky you are to be able to return home each evening. You are at the bedside of your sick relatives; you help them in their battle. But there are brothers of ours who, barely a few months ago, comforted us with their presence, and who now spend their nights yearning for their families and worrying about them even in their dreams. Somewhere in the desert, locked up in internment camps, cut off from the world and in the hands of evil torturers, they are mainly wondering whether we have forgotten them. They have left us destitute relatives, distraught wives, and defenseless children. We haven't forgotten them; we don't have the right to forget them.

"As soon as the deportations began, the Front established a support program for these families. An aid fund was set up. Unfortunately, fundraising and the generosity of sympathizers are not enough. There is too much poverty, and galloping inflation does not make our task any easier. So the *Majlis* has instigated new crisis measures. Shops, cafés, workshops and other businesses belonging to deportees will be reopened. We are asking you to run them. We have chosen you, first of all for your integrity, and also because you need to work in order to feed your own families. Brother Omar Ziri will explain what we expect of you, and the percentage that you will earn. I don't need to tell you how much we are counting on your enthusiasm and your loyalty. The families of our absentees are experiencing huge difficulties. Now, as you have seen for yourselves, it is time to do something about it."

Three days later, Omar Ziri invited Nafa to get into a car with him.

"This is your taxi, Nafa. I've just collected it from the mechanic's. It's had a major service and is in perfect condition. Here are the documents. Everything is in order. There isn't a single thing missing. We pay for repairs and petrol. Your salary will come out of the weekly earnings. Statements are made up every Friday at lunchtime. And now, to work. May God bear witness to what we are doing."

Nafa Walid threw himself body and soul into his new job. He was conscious that he was being useful. He was helping provide for families afflicted by the mass deportations, and that was quite something. He was both proud and moved, determined to surpass himself to be equal to the task. He began by strictly organizing his time. He realized how long he had remained idle, when selfless brothers were giving themselves body and soul and he owed it to himself to make up for it. At 5 A.M., he was up, cleaning his taxi. He would polish the bodywork, dust the seats and clean the floor. By 6 A.M., he was at work. At 1 P.M., he took a thirty-minute lunch break. He did not return home until late at night.

On Fridays, at lunchtime, he handed over his earnings to Omar Ziri, who made a note of the takings in a register, signed the receipt and gave him his wages according to the amount earned.

"You're doing well," he congratulated Nafa. "Imam Younes is very pleased with your earnings. If you have any financial problems, don't hesitate to let me know. We have received instructions on that front. We have to protect our employees from temptation."

Nafa did not appreciate that type of allusion. But Omar was known to be tactless. You just had to live with it.

The first months went by without mishap. Nafa was making good money and soon acquired an excellent reputation. Sometimes he found a bonus in his pay packet. Now that he was working to provide a decent living for mutilated families, he didn't see why he couldn't do it for his own. He worked even harder, and felt a surge of pride on noticing that the smells of food wafting from the kitchen were becoming increasingly appetizing.

Meanwhile, his two elder sisters were wed, one to a shopkeeper and the other to a teacher. For the first time, the family was enjoying a sunny period. Things were clearer, and bigger. For the Feast of Ashoura, Nafa gave his parents a wrought-iron bedstead. His father was still annoyed with him, but he did sometimes join his son for dinner. Even though he insisted on staring at his plate, it could be considered an achievement. One evening, encouraged by his mother, Nafa gave his father a kiss on the top of the head. The old man maintained his scowl, but did not push him away. And when the son told him of his plan to send him, with his mother, on a pilgrimage, the old man muttered for a moment and finally acquiesced with his chin, to the family's great relief. Thus Nafa understood that his father had forgiven him, and that he would once more receive his blessing.

Nafa drew up outside Omar Ziri's house and hooted twice to signal his arrival. Omar appeared at the window. He gestured to him to wait.

Zawech was sitting on the pavement, picking his nose and squinting in the sunlight.

"How much is a one-way fare to paradise?"

"A bullet through the head," replied Nafa.

Zawech roared with laughter:

"Trouble is, I can't even afford that."

He stood up and slapped his buttocks, walked up to the car

and rested his elbows on the door. His foul breath hit the driver full in the face.

"Can you spare some money, brother? I've been hungry all day."

Nafa proffered a note.

"You're a decent fellow," Zawech thanked him. "It's no coincidence that God made you so good-looking."

"Be a sport, I'm waiting for someone."

Zawech affectionately stroked the note, and held it up to the sun, then bit it as if it were a gold coin.

"It looks genuine. The other day, someone palmed off a photocopy the color of a ten dinar note onto me. Not only did the café owner beat me up, but he wanted to hand me over to the police too. Now I'm careful."

Omar Ziri cleared his throat as he opened the door. This little cough was to warn anybody hanging around that the women were coming out and they should move out of the way. Zawech pocketed the money and sidled off. Omar's wife—a vaguely human form concealed beneath a *chador*—clambered into the back of the car, holding her little boy. Omar closed the door, cleared his throat again and installed himself in front.

"Drop us at Port Said."

Nafa nodded and set the meter running.

"What are you doing?"

"Can't you see?"

"Are you treating me as a customer?"

"Sorry. This is a taxi, not my own car. I'm trying to provide for the families of the deported..."

"Are you being serious?"

"Of course I am. When I drive my own mother, I put the meter on and I pay for the journey out of my own pocket."

Omar turned crimson. He mopped his face with his *kamis*, his jowls burning. "Humiliated" in front of his wife, he kept the lid on his anger for a moment and then, suddenly, he let out a strange laugh and said, to save face:

"You really are remarkably honest. Of course I'll pay. It was just to test you."

Nafa engaged the gears and drove to Bab El Oued, filled with disgust.

The crowds were milling around the Place des Trois Horloges. It was 4 P.M. The poor part of town was suffocating under a torrid heat. Nafa drove carefully because of the pedestrians spilling onto the road. Suddenly, a gunshot rang out, followed by two more, which echoed through the narrow streets. At the first shot, the crowd froze, puzzled, the hustle and bustle ceasing at once. With the ensuing gunfire, the square was plunged into indescribable chaos. In less than a minute, there wasn't a soul left in the Place des Trois Horloges.

"Don't stop," ordered Omar, "keep going."

Nafa drove to the end of the street. A man lay on his stomach on the pavement, between two parked cars, his head blown open.

"Don't look," cried Omar's wife to her child.

"Let him see," said the father. "He's got to learn how things work around here. You see, Moussa? That's what happens to God's enemies."

The child stared at the body on the ground.

"The man's bleeding, daddy…"

"Even grown-ups hurt themselves when they fall over," ventured the mother, desperately. "When I tell you to be careful when you run in the street, it's to…"

"What nonsense are you telling him, wife? That bastard didn't fall over. Look carefully, son. He's been shot. He's an infidel, a turncoat, and the *Mujahideen* have punished him. They killed him, do you understand? Executed him…"

Nafa accelerated to spare the boy, and to get away from Omar's excited exclamations. He was jubilant, bouncing up and down in his seat for the entire journey.

The slain man was a plain-clothes gendarme, a local boy. The news of the attack spread to the surrounding slums. The people didn't know how to take it. They filled the cafés and discussed the event off and on all day.

The elderly were anxious. The specter of the war of '54 was back to mar their twilight years. They had dreamed of ending their days safe in their own beds, surrounded by their family, amid peace and calm. And now violence had caught their world unawares. Gunfire in the street, in broad daylight for all to see? Was this a return to the days of the OAS? The terrors of the past came rushing back, instilling a profound dread that weighed leaden on people's hearts. The young were heedless. They had not known the Revolution. They demanded their share in the horror.

That same night, another burst of gunfire rang out in a cul-de-sac. In the morning, a terrified group of schoolchildren came across the dismembered body of a soldier. When the ambulance arrived, later that morning, the police escort was caught in cross shooting. Immobilized on the spot, the vehicle caught fire. The smell of burning flesh hung over the impasse for a long time. The sinister abbreviation MIA—*Mouvement Islamique Armé*—armed Islamic movement—stared out from the headlines. Immediately, threatening letters threw entire families into a panic. The elderly put away their stools, gave up *djemaa*—gathering on café terraces to drink tea—and the joys of idleness. Conversations, previously devoted to singers of the past, turned, without warning, into funeral orations.

After the threatening letters, the telephone became a weapon of intimidation; it was an excellent means of announcing reprisals. It rang at all hours. The voice at the other end sent a chill through the listener: "You're going to die, traitor."

These were not empty words.

Each morning, hooded men emerged from their hiding places and shot their targets point blank. Sometimes, a butcher's knife finished off the wounded, slitting their throats. At the mosque, this gesture was explained: a ritual through which death became an oblation, and murder an allegiance.

Soon, the nights were filled with clattering, running footsteps, and hallucinations. The death squads invaded the villages, started fires, burned factories and state institutions, destroyed bridges and taboos, and defined "no man's land" and "liberated zones". Sermons rang out across the mountains, echoing in the villages. Leaflets fluttered on the winds of *jihad*. Spectacular attacks vied with each other to make the headlines. The streets of Algiers, Blida, Boufarik, Chlef, Laghouat, Sidi bel Abbes and Jijel retreated as the march of the Afghans advanced.

Bab El Oued raised its drawbridge. Its undesirable children packed their bags, some didn't even dare come back to fetch them. Their own neighbors spied on them, their fingers on the trigger, flick-knives at the ready. Police, military, journalists and intellectuals dropped like flies, one after another, at dawn, cut down on their doorsteps.

The wailing of mothers mingled with that of the sirens. Burials confirmed the atrocities. Death struck everywhere. Every day. Every night. Relentlessly and without pity. Six police officers were stopped as they turned a corner. Their assailants riddled them with bullets; then, they solemnly pulled them out of the vehicle and decapitated them under the glassy stare of the windows.

Gradually, the Casbah reinforced its defenses. It became a forbidden city. The *Mujahideen* withdrew there after their exploits. This was *their* territory. Distinctive with dark-haloed heads and their pistols protruding from their belts, they strutted about the terraces of the cafés cataloguing their attacks, describing their victims' terror and laughing, pleased with the turn events were taking.

Chapter twelve

One Friday lunchtime, Nafa Walid found Omar Ziri at the back of his restaurant. He wasn't alone. Some men were there and a heated argument was in progress. Everyone stopped talking the minute he drew back the curtain. It was dark inside, despite a window high up on the wall. Nafa recognized Hassan the Afghan, standing slightly apart from the group, stiff in his black burnoose, a scarf wound round his head. He seemed preoccupied. There was also Imam Younes, flanked by Abou Mariem and Ibrahim El Khalil, the two fearsome militiamen from the Kouba mosque. Their nicknames were legendary. They had single-handedly killed three army officers, including a colonel, four policemen, two journalists and a scientist. In the middle of the room, kneeling at a low table, Hamza Youb, the house painter, was pouring tea into glasses arranged in a circle on a tray. His movements were tinged with humility. His eyes remained downcast, as they always did when he was in the presence of an influential member of the movement. Opposite, sitting on cushions, were three men whom Nafa did not know. They stared intently at the taxi driver.

"You didn't tell us you were expecting a visitor, brother Omar," complained one of them, a man in his fifties with a bright, penetrating gaze.

"He's one of us," Omar reassured him.

"I'm sure he is. But the rules are clear."

"I'll leave if you like," volunteered Nafa.

"That isn't necessary," the imam broke in.

The fifty-year-old disagreed, but didn't press the point. He was a broad-chested man, with a protruding forehead and thick eyebrows. His eyes, emphasized with kohl, burned with a fire and an authority that immediately made people feel uncomfortable. One could sense something intractable welling up inside him, like the lava bubbling in the bowels of a volcano.

The other two, half hidden in the darkness, wore thick beards tumbling down onto their *kamis*. Their shaven, oiled heads formed a bumpy, gray shape, as if carved out of a lump of granite, which gave them a taciturn, disagreeable countenance.

"In any case, we have no choice," continued Ibrahim El Khalil, who had been interrupted by Nafa's intrusion. "I agree with Sheikh Nouh."

"We are doing what we can," stammered Omar, sweating profusely. "I assure you we are sparing no effort."

"Emir Jaafar finds it is not enough," said the fifty-year-old. "A handful of volunteers isn't enough to ensure victory."

Omar Ziri rushed over to him with a register.

"You can check: to date, we have one hundred and sixty-three recruits to join the *maquis*."

"A hundred and sixty-three, for a town like Algiers, is a disgrace!" roared the fifty-year-old. "In Boufarik, every night, around twenty new recruits are sent to the training camps."

Then, turning to Imam Younes, he said: "The fact is, Sheikh, that your recruiting agents aren't up to the job, perhaps they're not sufficiently motivated. This is serious. If they're waiting for people to come up to them and present themselves like in an office, they're wrong. You have to go out to people, make them aware, enlighten them, and shake them up. Why not? Many young men are fidgeting with impatience; they want nothing better than to join us. They *want* to do battle. It's just a question of mobilizing them. In Blida, a single street provided more recruits than the whole of Belcourt. Why? Because in Blida, they get straight to the point, they don't beat about the bush. That's why they're successful. They don't just draw up endless inventories and lists and believe their mission is accomplished. Prayer isn't all there is to faith, my brothers. The *kamis* is merely fancy dress if the wearer isn't worthy of it. They pride themselves before you, in their conversion to Islam as if it is a service they have rendered you. Say: *Do not remind me of your subservience to God as a favor on your part. On the contrary, it is God who grants you the honor of helping you find faith if your conversion is sincere.* The Lord Almighty has spoken the truth."

"I think there's been a misunderstanding," ventured Imam Younes in attempt to pacify everyone. "The situation is different in the *maquis* and in the towns. Each sector has its own particularities. I think we are to be congratulated. We have achieved a lot in a year. The towns are not as forthcoming as the villages. Here, it is easier to be discreet, and a good thing too. But that does not mean that what we are doing is insignificant. We are working to protect our networks, our fighters and their families. It's not like in the mountains where there are countless withdrawal zones and the nearby forests. In the city, we have to work in one street and retreat to the next. Besides, we are surrounded by people, and they are not always thrilled to have us so close. Furthermore, we are short of guns. The weapons we gather on our missions are all sent to the mountains. Abou Mariem's group only has one handgun for every three fighters."

"That's not the point," insisted the fifty-year-old. "We have the money to resolve the weapons problem. We have rear-bases in Europe and on our eastern and western frontiers. What worries us today is recruitment. Emir Jaafar is categorical on the matter. We must enroll all the militants of the Front. Without exception. Everybody must take up arms. Anyone who is reluctant must be executed. Quite simply, anyone who refuses to follow us is a traitor. He deserves the same punishment as a *taghut*."

"I absolutely agree with you, Sheikh Nouh," concurred Ibrahim El Khalil emphatically. "Nobody has the right to back down, we have sworn an oath. We will not tolerate any betrayal. We will fight for the FIS and we will die for the FIS. And all our fighters must join the *maquis*. With no exceptions."

"Right," said the fifty-year-old, rising, visibly irritated by Nafa's presence. "We're leaving. Thank you for your hospitality, Sheikh Younes. We've got a long way to go and very little time ahead of us. I hope to see you again soon. As for your request, I will pass it on to the Emir as soon as possible."

The two other men gathered up the folds of their *gandouras* and also rose. The younger man surreptitiously slid a sawn-off shotgun under his belt, took his leave of the imam and went out first to check that the coast was clear.

Omar Ziri closed the door behind his guests and returned to the back room flapping his hand at the level of his chin.

"A tough nut, that Sheikh Nouh. For a simple courtesy call, that was worse than a trial."

"We deserve to be shot," declared Ibrahim El Khalil.

"Speak for yourself. We haven't sinned, or cheated."

"I think we've betrayed our pledge. Because of our laxness."

Omar Ziri ignored him and began tidying a cupboard. He put the registers away in a drawer, piled up some books to conceal them and padlocked the cupboard. Ibrahim El Khalil watched him, fighting the urge to attack him.

"That's enough," said Abou Mariem, "let's all calm down."

"I am calm," said Omar, purposely trying to annoy the young militiaman.

Ibrahim rolled his jaws. His nostrils quivered and he shouted:

"I was in the *maquis*. I saw how things are run there. With a rod of iron! For a cigarette, they'll burn your brains. Result: they're on their toes. Before the summer, the countryside will be completely liberated. Because there, nobody waits for instructions. The emirs take the initiative. And that's what's lacking here, initiative. Recruitment's a priority. It's an absolute imperative. What are they up to, all those layabouts moldering in the shade all day long? We need them to infiltrate the districts, rebuild our broken groups, set up new cells, and blow up this rotten society."

He swiftly eyed Nafa up and down:

"And what do you have to say about all this?"

"I bring in my weekly earnings."

"I'm not talking about that. I'm asking you what you think about..."

"I'm not a layabout," cut in Nafa, refusing to be intimidated.

"Meaning?"

"It's perfectly clear."

The two men tried to out-stare each other, standing so close that their breath mingled. Nafa's face was relaxed. That of the young militiaman quivered with rage.

"Ibrahim," pleaded Abou Mariem, "drop it. You're overworked at the moment. You should take care of yourself."

"I didn't understand his insinuations, and I'm not letting him go until he gives me an explanation."

In Kouba, Ibrahim El Khalil was already feared for his violent temper. He had been sent to reform school several times. Uneducated and unemployed, he had quickly allowed himself to be adopted by the Muslim brothers and had been one of the first volunteers, alongside Abou Mariem, to enroll in the *Dawaa* contingent leaving for Afghanistan. On his return, he had wanted to offer the fundamentalist movement the benefit of his war experience. But neither his feats nor his enthusiasm were enough to elevate him to the rank of emir. His ambition was to command a group and scour the mountains, and here he was confined to the auxiliary post of recruiter, like a common injured fighter. His violent mood swings were beginning to annoy people.

"Do you think your earnings are enough?" he yelled. "Why

don't you join the *maquis*? You're young, available, well built. What are you afraid of? Have you lost your faith?"

"Violence isn't the answer to everything."

"Well, well. A conscientious objector. And yet, not so long ago, you said that you were prepared to die for the cause."

"To die, yes, but not to kill."

"What? Would you say that again, I didn't quite hear you! Where are you from? To die, but not to kill. What the hell is that supposed to mean? So you'd throw yourself off a cliff or under the wheels of a lorry crying: 'Long live the FIS!' and think you were sacrificing yourself for the movement. We don't need your corpse, Nafa Walid, we need you to fight for us. To be ready to die, in the language of *Jihad*, means to go to your limits, to fight to the last bullet, for as long as possible, so as to inflict the maximum damage on the enemy. It is only in this manner that we are entitled to die. Violence is obligatory. You won't defeat the *taghut* with hot air. Let me remind you that we are losing brothers every day: as I speak to you now, some are screaming under torture, while others are dying in internment camps, and still more demand only a penknife to go and cross swords with the traitors."

"That's enough," said Imam Younes, calmly. "Nafa is right: violence isn't the only thing. Just as we need the *Mujahideen*, we also need auxiliaries. War requires us to have at least ten people to support every fighter."

Without taking his eyes off Nafa, Ibrahim El Khalil took a step back, breathing noisily. His face was a grayish hue and there was thick saliva frothing at the corners of his mouth. He spun round and headed furiously for the door. He drew back the curtain then and turned back to the taxi driver:

"One day, I had a toothache. I can't think of anything worse than a toothache. There I was, writhing in pain, about to throw myself out of the window, when I suddenly thought: 'Why does God inflict such terrible suffering on us for a miserable tooth? What kind of sign was it, what prophecy? Something as simple as a bad tooth, and man, that wonderful, almost perfect creation, is reduced to a primitive state with no more dignity than an animal. Isn't that odd? So why, Nafa Walid? If you can answer that, I will gladly renounce violence."

He let the curtain fall behind him.

An awkward silence followed. Omar Ziri was absorbed in contemplating his stomach. Disconcerted, Abou Mariem nodded his head. Imam Younes picked up his beads and retreated to a corner of the room, concealed beneath a heavy veil of shadow.

Hassan the Afghan, who had not said a word throughout, and who was not in the habit of speaking, turned his impenetrable gaze to Nafa. Remaining stubbornly in the background, never taking part in discussions, his face waxen, like a death mask, he never revealed his thoughts. When divisions arose and discussions became heated, he was content to listen to everyone else, as though the question did not concern him. His rigid demeanor and his silence added a disconcerting note to his infirmity, which made his presence as awkward as that of an intruder. So Nafa was completely at a loss when he asked him, in a sepulchral tone:

"Can we count on you, other than for bringing in money?"

And Nafa replied without hesitation:

"Of course."

It was not long before Nafa was called upon.

At first, he was entrusted with "insignificant" missions. He drove fighters on the move from one district to another, picked up "guests" at the station or the airport, occasionally delivered various documents: communiqués urging the young to refuse to do their military service, or shopkeepers not to pay their taxes; leaflets forbidding heretical practises; bulletins detailing the *Mujahideen's* military operations etc. During these trips, he was accompanied by Zawech, whose clumsiness and comic speech distracted the officers at road checkpoints. Gradually, thanks to the hilarious company of his "skipper," Nafa overcame his uneasiness at the sight of roadblocks. He learned to keep his cool and to memorize the locations of the checkpoints on the city's main arterial roads in order to avoid them.

Then, between driving two "agents on the move", he was sent

to pick up the funds that had been raised. He often had to drive to remote villages, during curfew. A fundamentalist panel beater fitted a hatch in the boot of his taxi, under which he hid packages, briefcases, boxes, heavily bound canvas bags containing metal objects—probably dismantled weapons. He did not object, as he was flattered to enjoy such a high degree of trust and respect. On the other hand, he was beginning to enjoy the exquisite thrill of working underground, the risks, the fear that kept him on tenterhooks even while he courted danger, and the almost ecstatic relief that filled him when each mission was accomplished—like a whiff of opium.

For the first time in his life, he was discovering himself, becoming aware of his status, his importance, his usefulness as a person, as a *being*.

At last he was alive.

He mattered.

He was proud, convinced that he was taking part in a grandiose, just and vital scheme. This feeling became a certainty on the day when, returning from the airport where he had dropped some ordinary passengers, he was beaten up by the police. His body and his pride battered, he seriously considered requesting a gun. On second thoughts, he decided it would be wiser not to set out on impulse on a path of no return. Not that it repelled him, but he didn't feel ready yet.

The stiffness of a corpse affected him less than before. He had seen a number of bodies on the road, some mutilated, others—those of the *Mujahideen*—riddled with bullets and exposed to the gaze of passers-by. However he continued to fear the consequences of an action which he was not particularly committed to, but which he would not discount in the event of force majeure.

The terror of the past, born in the forest of Bainem on a night of storms and madness, no longer haunted him. He had attended two summary executions, in the middle of the street, without being seized by panic. The Casbah regularly woke up wallowing in the blood of a traitor. Sometimes a row of human heads sat impaled on a line of railings, or in a square, and the children, shocked at first, began to go up to them to get a closer look, their curiosity gradually getting the better of their dread.

Nafa was not a child.

He was a *moussebel*—liaison officer—an active member of the war effort. True, he was in the wings, and yes, it was still a non-speaking part, but nevertheless he felt determined to give of his best to save the country from the dictatorship of one faction and the greed of another, so that nobody would be abused by over-zealous police, and so that human dignity could be restored once and for all.

One day, Abou Mariem told him about a "sensitive" project. His group was planning to raid a state-owned factory in a suburb that was neglected by the security forces.

"The workers wages will be delivered on Wednesday," explained Abou Mariem. The paymaster is one of our men. He has given us all the necessary information, and we have drawn up a detailed plan. *Not a single shot will be fired.* We just need a first-class driver. You're an ace at the wheel, besides, you know all the shortcuts."

Nafa agreed on condition he did not have to carry a gun. The hold-up went according to plan. Without a hitch. The money slung into the boot of a stolen vehicle, Nafa was clear of the suburb before the alarm could be raised. It was a big day for him, so exciting that he himself volunteered to take part in two similar raids before being chased by a patrol car that happened to be in the area.

"Head for the waste ground," ordered Abou Mariem removing his hood. We've got to shake him off before reinforcements arrive."

Nafa shot through the district, took a stony track through the orchards and arrived at a municipal garbage dump.

"Park there, stop, stop!"

Nafa obeyed with such adroitness that the police car nearly drove into him. The driver just managed to swerve. Abou Mariem was already out of the car. His machine gun sprayed the patrol at point blank range. The three police officers jiggled under the impact, like puppets. Their blood mingled with the broken glass. The vehicle careered on, the siren wailing, and plunged into the ditch. Abou Mariem and Hamza Youb, the house painter, hastily finished off the wounded officers, relieved them of their guns and radios, and ran back to the car.

"Move it! Go!!"

Nafa reversed, drove back through the orchard, turned up an avenue lined with olive trees and drove at top speed onto the bypass, melting into the traffic.

That night, lying on his bed, he was afraid that a nightmare might betray him. Yet he fell asleep like a carpenter after a hard day's work. The sleep of the just.

Omar Ziri checked his watch. He consulted it every ten minutes. Ill at ease in his velvet coat, he continually looked from left to right. The orchard was deserted, meagerly lit by a thin crescent moon. A trail of clouds faded among the stars. It was after 9 P.M. and he was beginning to freeze. In the distance, on the road, car headlights left a phosphorescent trail on the black screen of night. The countryside was slowly dissolving into the shadows, which the barking of dogs infiltrated like spirits.

In the car concealed under an orange tree, Nafa Walid was drumming on the steering wheel. Next to him, Zawech stared at the dark shape of a farmhouse at the end of the avenue. Not a light in the windows. The silence throbbed with the chirring of insects, heightening their agitation. On the back seat, Omar Ziri sat sweating. He was not used to coming out of his lair, preferring to entrust to others the missions assigned to him. But this time, Emir Jaafar had been categorical. There was a very large sum of money involved, and there was no question of just anybody being sent to collect it.

A van emerged across the fields, bumping over the ruts, its lights off. It climbed a hill and onto the track leading to the farm. Nafa switched the interior light on and off twice. In the back, Omar heaved himself, about to extract a gun jammed under his belt.

Thanks to the two signals, the van found its way and approached slowly. A man alighted with a big bag under his arm, and got in next to Omar.

"Burst tire," he said in apology for the delay.

He undid the bag and took out a voluminous bundle.

"Here's the two hundred million, my modest contribution. It is an honor for me to serve the Cause."

The man, a prosperous local industrialist, was admired for his generosity and for his unconditional support of the armed Islamic movement. Nafa had already met him while collecting funds, but this was the first time he had heard mention of such a fabulous sum. He stared at him in the rear-view mirror, but saw only a furrowed face with an impassive gaze.

Omar weighed the bundle in his hand before placing it on the floor.

"I counted it," the industrialist reassured him.

"The emir told me that you've been having a problem with your competitors. He instructed me to resolve it."

"That's true," enthused the industrialist, taking a second bundle out of his bag. "There's another two hundred million in here. To rid me of a rival. Not only is he damaging me commercially, but he's also an enemy of our cause."

"Do you want us to execute him?"

"Not particularly. What I really want is for his factories to be burned down. That way I can double my production and guarantee substantial support for the *Jihad*. Here's a map of the two sites, with their addresses. Security is negligible, and the nearest military camp is miles away. I suggest you burn both of them down the same night. The sooner the better."

"For two hundred million, I'd blow up the whole of Algiers," cried Zawech.

"Shut up," shouted Omar.

Zawech thumped the dashboard violently and hunched his shoulders in a sulk. His reaction annoyed the industrialist. He scrutinized them one by one, asked for permission to leave and returned to his van.

"Why on earth did you bang the car like that?" screeched Omar.

Zawech swung round, his eyes bulging and his nostrils flared.

"Yes, I banged the car. So what?"

"I forbid you to talk to me like that."

"I should care."

Omar could not believe his ears. To be scoffed at by a simpleton, he who inspired both fear and respect among the toughest delinquents of the Casbah! He lunged at the seat in front of him, grabbed Zawech by the collar of his jacket and shook him. Zawech pushed him away firmly, determinedly.

"Don't touch me."

"Is this a joke?"

"Do I sound as though I'm joking?"

Nafa refrained from getting involved. Omar had bullied others so much, it was a joy to see him getting his come-uppance from the lowest of the low.

"Stop clowning around, Zawech," threatened Omar.

"I'll stop when you learn to call me by my proper name. I've spent my life putting up with your stupidity. And for once when I raise my voice, you get angry. Sacrilege. A bird speaking. Well, I'm no feathered creature."

"I don't believe it, I must be dreaming…"

"Well I'm not. I say 'enough!' That's enough! The show's over."

Zawech's face twitched alarmingly. He tore at the seat covers, banged and thumped, giving vent to his fury. His chest heaved, as did his whole being. His fetid breath filled the interior. It was as though he had been waiting forever to spew out the thousands of grievances that had blighted his life.

He got out of the car and slammed the door, walked a few paces and returned, pointing an accusing finger at Omar Ziri, who was literally struck dumb:

"The people, too, have had it up to here. Since '62 they've been taken for a ride. And now they're saying: 'That's enough!' Like me. They've sworn to take their revenge, blow for blow. Like me. I take as many risks as you do, ha! Just you remember that. I'm not some cat that gets run over by a car. And I only have one life. Do I make myself clear, Omar Ziri? I'm a funny guy, not a nutcase. I can see what's happening around me. Spiteful remarks hurt me, even when I pretend to ignore them. The best jokes are short ones. After a while, it becomes a pain. From now on, no more laughing. I've hung up my clown's nose, taken down the big top. I want to forget my nickname and I demand a *nom de guerre.*"

He moved off in the direction of the farm, retraced his steps once again and yelled in Omar's face: "I'll soon show you what I'm capable of, *brother* Ziri."

And he vanished among the trees.

"Well!" gulped Omar, mopping his face on his forearm.

Zawech was killed on the eve of a national holiday as he was trying to break into a military camp on his own initiative. In the Casbah, indignation gave way to consternation.

"He couldn't hurt a fly," said Imam Younes, with a tremor in his voice. "A poor, simple-minded fellow, an innocent soul struck down for no reason by a stupid, thoughtless, fanatical *taghut.*" And Zawech who, when alive, had been emblematic of human decline, was on his death elevated to the rank of martyr and given a splendid funeral. Hundreds of people turned out to accompany him to his final resting place, the notables of Bab El Oued and the Casbah leading the procession, their heads bowed to conceal a rebel tear. For days, all the talk was of this "gratuitous, cowardly, unspeakable murder" that brought shame to a nation for whom the simple-minded were closer to the Lord than the bravest of mortals.

That day, Ibrahim El Khalil found himself flanked by no less than thirty new recruits, when he had merely been hoping for ten in order to reinstate himself in his superiors' good books.

Meanwhile, Abou Mariem made the most of the general mood of affliction to finish off Sid Ali, the poet whom the imams had constantly demonized and whose head the emir himself demanded. He was murdered at his home, very early in the morning. The poet was waiting for his killers. Warned of their plans, he had refused to run away. He had just sent his companion away so as to meet his destiny alone.

Before dying, Sid Ali had asked to be immolated by fire.

"Why?" asked Abou Mariem.

"To bring a little light into your dark night."

Chapter thirteen

The old man lay groaning in the living room. Neither the doctor's frequent visits nor the drugs seemed able to relieve his suffering. Sickness took hold of him, inexorably, gnawed away at him fiber after fiber, surreptitious and methodical, as if seeking to carry him off bit by bit. He did not struggle. Eroded, quavering, he only gathered his remaining strength to beg God to bring his suffering to a quick end. Wrapped in a terry towel, his head shrank like an overripe quince. Between groans, his eyes, sticky from a discharge, rolled upwards, while his flaccid, rancid smelling body lay limp under the covers.

His wife sat at his bedside, collapsing with exhaustion, repeatedly dipping a cloth into a saucepan of cold water and mopping his face.

Nafa could not bear to stand by witnessing their misery any longer. Even if he shut himself in his room, the noise from the living room disturbed his sleep every night.

Putting on a brave face, he sat among his sisters at a low table, brushed aside the few slices of buttered bread that constituted breakfast and asked Amira to pour him a cup of coffee. Then, to cheer everyone up, he surreptitiously poked little Nora who was licking the edge of her bowl of milk.

"You're tickling me."

"Me?"

"Yes, you. I saw you slip your hand behind my back."

"It must have been a spirit-rapper."

Nora shrugged and went back to licking her bowl, watching her brother out of the corner of her eye.

Nafa was concerned about Amira. It wasn't fair, he thought. Despite her great beauty and integrity, she couldn't find a taker. And yet, in her high-school days, when she appeared, all the local youths went into a swoon, entranced by her huge eyes with flashes of jade. Her classmates were envious of her slenderness and grace, and took care not to be seen in her company. Amira was like a *houri* with her dimpled cheeks and long hair that cascaded down her back. Nafa felt sad for her. It was his fault that she had no suitors. He had sent them all away. He had promised her to Dahmane. But Dahmane had forgotten his pledge once he was at the institute of hotel management in Tizi Ouzou. There, the girls were emancipated. Dahmane had always dreamed of marrying a woman from high society, who knew how to entertain and "go out" and talk to the upper classes.

Now Amira was getting on for twenty-four summers, and no swallow seemed to have noticed.

Nora put down her bowl and ran into her room to fetch her satchel.

"Walk her to school, Souad," said their mother. "Tell the teacher I can't see her today either."

Souad nodded. She, too, left the table and took down her *hijab* from its hook in the hall.

Souad was seventeen. Unlike her sisters, nature had not been kind to her. Stocky and chubby, half her face was taken up by a flaccid nose. She was finding it more and more difficult to cope with her unfortunate appearance. It was probably to forget it that she had withdrawn into an embittered, austere and obtuse piety. Nafa could not recall seeing her laugh heartily for a decade.

After the departure of his two sisters, Nafa called his mother to ask whether there were any messages for him. She grimaced, and did not have anything in particular to say to him. She was worried about the old man, but knew there was nothing her son could do.

"I've asked your aunt to come and give me a hand. The lack of sleep is wearing me out. Neither I nor your sisters can cope. We need someone to take turns at sitting with him."

Nafa thought that was a good idea.

Before taking his leave, he observed Amira and wondered whether it wasn't time to find her a husband. He had heard that Imam Younes was planning to take a wife and that he held the Walid family in the greatest esteem.

"It would be a pleasure," he heard himself whisper as he reached the door.

Hamza Youb was waiting for him at the foot of the stairs. He wore a grubby hat pulled down over his ears, paint-stained overalls and tattered espadrilles. Nafa concluded that he was not there for a "mission", but was intrigued by his presence.

"No need to panic," the house painter at once reassured him.

He walked with him to the car park where Nafa kept his taxi, without saying a word. Nafa checked the oil, the water in the radiator, kicked the tires and started up the engine.

"What's up?"

"I'll tell you."

"I haven't worked for two days," Nafa informed him.

Hamza stood aside to allow the car through, and then clambered in beside him. He flipped open the tin of chewing tobacco and helped himself to a pinch, which he placed under his lip, then he wiped his fingers on his knee.

"Now I'll tell you. Yesterday Rachid Abbas was arrested in a café during a routine identity check. As I said, there's no panic. Abbas has never taken part in any operations. He's Imam Younes's right-hand man, and that exempts him from quite a lot of tasks. Only with fellows like that, you never know. Abbas isn't cool-headed. He might panic. The Imam has decided to take the necessary precautions: we must make ourselves scarce for a couple of days, until we know what's going on."

"My father's ill."

"You're not a doctor. Besides, we're not allowed to expose ourselves to unnecessary danger. It could have consequences for the whole group."

"Abbas doesn't know much about me."

"Maybe, but he might rat on someone who's better informed than he is. So, clear off. For a few days. It's not asking the impossible."

Hamza spoke softly, in a monotone, while gazing at the peeling façades of the apartment blocks. Nafa did not trust his calm air. His passenger's words were clear. They had the precision of an order.

"I don't know where to go."

"Nafa, my brother, when will you get it into your head once and for all that we are not alone, that we have a well-oiled organization that looks after every one of us and our families? After you've dropped me off, go back to the Casbah and leave your taxi with Daoud, the mechanic. It would arouse suspicion if you left it in the car park. Tell your family that your car's broken down and that you've got to go to Sétif to buy some parts."

"I told you, my father's very ill."

"He'll be taken care of. Abou Mariem will meet you at Omar's at II P.M., to drive you to a safe place."

After a long silence, he settled comfortably into his seat and slapped Nafa's thigh:

"Relax, *kho*. There's no need to panic, I assure you."

Nafa waited at Omar's until I P.M. There was no sign of Abou Mariem. Late that afternoon a phone call informed them that the scare was over; Abbas Rachid had been released. Relieved, Nafa returned to the mechanic's to pick up his taxi.

For a month, he was left in peace. He wasn't asked to pick up any "special passengers" or collect funds. He went back to work as usual, driving around the city, noticing as he did so the increased police presence around the hot spots, the forces regrouping according to where the threat was strongest, equipping road blocks with barriers and armored vehicles. Although they did not yet dare venture into the Casbah or Bab El Oued, they were gradually taking over the residential districts and the main thoroughfares. Rumor had it that the ranks of the fundamentalists had been infiltrated by police officers. Suspicion turned into spy mania. Informers picked up on the slightest misdemeanor. Kids were recruited to look out both for *taghut* and militant Islamists. In response to the government curfew, the emir decreed another. Bloody purges were instigated in fundamentalist circles, in particular among the support networks. Some of the dismembered bodies found on waste ground by the rescue operators belonged to FIS sympathizers executed by their own side.

Meanwhile, in systematic retaliation for the attacks, the police raids became bolder. The elite police force, the *Ninja-DZ*, operating methodically and efficiently, gradually occupied the ground. They would appear in the night, cordoning off the suspect building, carry off their quarry and disappear at lightning speed. Pitched battles broke out here and there. During the skirmish, obscene insults and taunts could be heard over the gunfire. The first serious losses soon weakened the armed groups from the city center. One night, a surprise attack was carried out on nine fundamentalists in a squalid apartment. At dawn, their unrecognizable corpses were thrown onto a lorry and paraded through the streets. The police fired into the air in triumph. Onlookers watched them make an exhibition of themselves, their expressions filled with hatred. The emirs' revenge was not long in coming. A *Ninja-DZ* patrol was wiped out, in a few minutes, in the middle of a Souk. Once again, horrified passers-by witnessed the slaughter.

Nafa was not worried. At any point. Sometimes he would be stopped during a roadside identity check. His passengers would be ordered out of the car and their luggage gone over with a toothcomb. Sometimes, a policeman would become officious. Nafa did not take the bait. He would wait patiently and bottle up his hatred without a word. They made him wait by the roadside, then let him go.

At home, the old man was slowly, and almost miraculously on the mend. He couldn't stand yet, but with characteristic mood swings, he found he was able to yell at his family again, and it was wonderful.

Nafa was seriously considering marrying off Amira. Imam Younes could not keep his intentions secret. He only spoke through an intermediary, to his close circle. But the whole Casbah knew that he had his eye on the Walids' daughter. In some places, people rose to their feet when Nafa walked past. They went out of their way to cross the street to shake his hand, openly idolized him, and café owners refused adamantly to let him pay. Even Omar Ziri shut up when he was around.

Then, one evening, the police cars in front of his apartment building sent a chill through him. Crowds thronged the street. Whole families were on the balconies, jostling to see.

"They've come to get you," a boy warned him.

Nafa retraced his steps. As he distanced himself, the walls of his childhood swam around him, dissolving like a mirage. His head throbbed, his ears buzzed, his chest caught fire like a bundle of hay. He could hear only his wild breathing, the pounding at his temples, could see only the narrow streets giving him up, isolating him, exposing him. Fear churned his stomach. He suddenly became aware of his vulnerability. Then, half dazed, totally distraught, he began to run, and run and run.

"You'll be able to sleep safely here."

Nafa was shocked. He had never dreamed such squalor could exist. The world Abou Mariem was taking him through was unimaginable. Hundreds of sordid shacks crammed together on the waste land: collapsed roofs, makeshift fences of corrugated iron and bits of cars, windows cut out of packing cases, covered with dusty Perspex and moldering cardboard, puddles of waste water swarming with insects, stripped vans lying across "patios", and mounds of household garbage. In the middle of this Dantean hell, wandered wraiths that virtually fed off the rubbish, their eyes gazing inwards, their faces tense as cramp. They were in the shantytown of El Harrach, on the outskirts of Algiers. Never had Nafa Walid suspected the existence of such human misery at the gates of El Bahja, he who had been born and bred in the insalubrious ruins of the Casbah.

"You thought you'd reached rock bottom, in Souk El Jemaa," said Abou Mariem. "Well, you haven't seen anything yet."

Nafa wondered how human beings were able to *live* amid such ugliness, crammed haphazardly among this hideous scrap metal and the stench, how the kids managed not to poke their eyes out in the alleys littered with iron bars, broken wire netting and barbed wire. What mausoleum had these people desecrated, what curse had they unleashed to merit serving out their sentence in such a filthy cesspool?

"This is why we are fighting, brother Nafa."

"Yes," he sighed.

"You have nothing to fear, here. Our hosts would put up the Devil if he promised to rid them of the bastards who took away *absolutely everything* they possessed."

Before entering a hovel, Nafa considered turning around and fleeing anywhere, far, far away from this chamber of horrors. He was convinced that he would not be able to spend a single night there. He was overwhelmed by a feeling of despair. Suddenly, images began to chase each other around inside his head, and he started to hate all of them, the good and the bad, to hate his family and friends, past and present, to hate his hands, his feet, his eyes, to hate the whole world. How had he reached this point? What was he doing on this forgotten island of humanity, abandoned by angels and demons alike, what had he come to seek here?

He hesitated for a long time before stepping inside the shack.

Like that night in the forest of Bainem, a treacherous force pushed him towards his fate with the placidity of the hangman nudging his victim towards the scaffolding.

He was aware that he did not try to resist, that he had neither the will nor felt the need.

An emaciated old man was crouching in a corner stirring a cauldron with a ladle. His tattered trousers revealed part of his buttocks and his jersey rode high up his back, exposing his deathly pale, naked body. On hearing the sound of footsteps, he glanced at a fragment of mirror on the wall without troubling to turn around.

"That smells good," said Abou Mariem.

The old man sniffed the steam from the pot, replaced the battered lid and rose. With the tip of his worn out slipper he kicked aside a pallet to clear a path, stepped over a low table and greeted the two visitors. He embraced Abou Mariem effusively, greeted Nafa and stood back to stare at him.

"Does your friend like lentils?"

"He'd rather have a good straw mattress to lay his head on."

"Ah, he's passing through."

"He's got the police on his heels."

The old man glanced over Nafa's shoulder.

"I can't see any cops outside. I'd have enjoyed giving them a roasting. Make a change from lentils."

Abou Mariem silently laughed.

He said to Nafa:

"You must have heard of Salah of Indochina?"

"No."

"Well, here he is. He fought in Indochina, in the revolution of '54 and the frontier war against the Moroccans in '63. He's tireless. He still climbs mountains faster than a jackal. He's our guide. He knows the *maquis* like the inside of his pockets."

"Of course," said the old man turning out his pockets, "there's nothing in them."

Nafa felt his stomach contract.

"Is he going to take me to the *maquis?*"

"Not right away."

The old man bade his guests make themselves at home and went out into the courtyard. Nafa didn't have the energy to sit down. He looked about him like an animal caught in a trap. He gulped several times before he could speak.

"I'm not ready for the *maquis*," he stammered.

"Hold your horses. You're going to hide here for a while."

"For how long?"

"That depends on Sheikh Younes."

The old man returned with a plate laden with hard-boiled eggs, olives, round flat bread and cartons of orange juice, placed everything on the low table and sat cross-legged on the floor, waiting for the young men to do likewise.

Abou Mariem helped himself first.

Nafa refused to eat. His face was the picture of despair.

"Something wrong with your friend here?"

"Of course. It's his first time."

The old man swallowed an egg, whole, washed it down with two sips of juice and smacked his lips.

"Hey kid," he said. "It'll all be fine. At first, you feel a bit lost. That's only natural. In a while, you'll feel at home."

Nafa nodded, not convinced.

"Do you believe in fate, kid?"

"My name is Nafa."

"Very well, Nafa, do you believe in fate?"

"I don't know."

"If you start out with the belief that nothing can happen to you unless it is God's will, you're saved. That's fate. The important thing is not to waver in your belief. Isn't that so, Abou Mariem?"

"It is."

"In Indochina, I wasn't twenty years old. I remember, we'd barely set foot in the place and a lorry was blown up by a mine. We didn't have time to scrape up the remains of our mates from the ground before a shell exploded in the middle of the convoy. I didn't know what had hit me, you know. I howled like a kid lost in the jungle. The nights were aflame with flares and explosions. It was hell, lad. I thought I'd go crazy. The mud, the monsoon, the booby-traps in the thickets, but we advanced. Our machetes were blunted by the vegetation. The other side of a tree, the scout got hit by a burst of gunfire in his face. Emerging from a paddy field, the whole section was ambushed. The stretcher-bearers didn't know whether they were coming or going. Some went berserk and hurled themselves at the enemy's machine guns to put an end to it all. Then, one fine day, I said to myself: 'Salah, you've been in this shit-hole for months, and you haven't got a scratch. Can you explain that? I'll explain it, I will. Things will only happen to you if God wants them to. That's the truth. As for the rest, you don't give a damn.' I slogged it out for two years there. It wasn't a country, it was one great, mass grave. We spent more time burying our dead than hitting back at the slant-eyes. I can still hear the chorus of the artillery and the hum of the bombers. When I was demobbed, I said: thank goodness, the storm's over. I can throw my helmet away and wear a turban again. The minute I docked back home, the Revolution was waiting to greet me. Not even time to give my mother a hello kiss. Revolution isn't pretty either. You wouldn't believe it. No less than twenty-eight ambushes. And neither napalm bombs nor the non-stop round-ups got me. Because it wasn't God's will."

"How come with all those wars you weren't wounded?" teased Abou Mariem.

The old man drew himself up. With a theatrical gesture, he pulled up his jersey to reveal his navel.

"What about this then? A bullet went in here and came out there," he added, prodding his backside. "It was probably an unusual missile, because still today, my asshole hasn't closed up."

Abou Mariem rolled onto his elbow laughing loudly.

Nafa did not even smile.

Late that night, Hamza Youb arrived. He found them eating. He sat on a crate looking grim, and let them finish their dinner. Nafa could not stand his implacable gaze. He broke off eating and went to join him.

"Well?"

Hamza stared at Abou Mariem, who got the message. With a nod, he gave him permission to leave. Slowly, Hamza placed his hands on the taxi-driver's shoulders, sensed his quaking, cleared his throat and said:

"I have some very bad news for you, Nafa, my brother. About your father…"

"You're not going to tell me they dared arrest him. He's an old man, he's dying…"

"No, it's worse, Nafa, my brother."

"No, no, I don't believe it…"

"The *taghut* killed him in his home, in front of his family. I am truly sorry."

"No, not my father. He hadn't done anything. It's madness…"

Nafa took his head in his hands and gently slid away to some far-off place.

Part three:
The Abyss

Si tu veux t'acheminer
Vers la paix définitive
Souris au destin qui te frappe
Et ne frappe personne

If you want to achieve
everlasting peace,
smile when fate deals you a blow
and never strike anyone.

Omar Khayyam

I killed my first man on Wednesday 12 January 1994 at 7.35 A.M. He was a magistrate. He had come out of his house and was walking towards his car. His six-year-old daughter was ahead of him, her braids tied with blue ribbons, her satchel on her back. She passed me without seeing me. The magistrate was smiling, but there was something tragic in his eyes. He looked like a hunted animal. He started when he discovered me lurking in the doorway. I don't know why he continued on his way as though nothing were amiss. Perhaps he thought that in shrugging off the danger, he might allay it. I took out my revolver and ran after him. He stopped and turned to face me. In a fraction of a second, the blood had drained from his face and his features were blotted out. For a moment, I was afraid I had got the wrong person. "Khodja?" I asked him.

"Yes," he answered flatly. His naiveté—or assurance—unnerved me. I had the greatest difficulty raising my arm. My finger froze on the trigger. "What are you waiting for?" yelled Sofiane, "shoot the bastard." The little girl did not seem to realize what was going on. Or refused to admit it. "I don't believe it," fumed Sofiane. "You're not going to bottle out now. He's nothing but a swine." The ground threatened to give way under me. I was overcome with nausea, my guts were in a knot, I was

paralyzed. Sensing my indecision, the magistrate thought he had a chance to get away. If he had kept still, I don't think I would have had the courage to go through with it. With each shot, I trembled from head to foot. I couldn't stop firing. I was oblivious both to the detonations and to the little girl's screams. I crashed through the sound barrier like a meteorite, beyond the point of no return: I had just stepped, body and soul, into a parallel world from which I would never come back.

Sofiane held out a glass of water: "How do you feel?"
    I felt nothing.
    I wanted nothing: I did not want to drink, eat, or speak.
    Slumped in an armchair, I stared at the window and took deep draughts of the cool winter air. Outside, a gentle drizzle drenched the garden. A tree, stirred by the wind, was playing hide-and-seek. In the distance, you could hear the whoosh of cars on the wet road.
    I was having difficulty comprehending what had happened. I had the vague sense that I had just crossed a threshold, that nothing would ever be the same again.
    Intermittent flashes lit up the darkness inside my head. For a split second, I could make out a face, a lip, blue-ribboned braids, the pistol shuddering in my hand, the sky and the earth spinning around me as if I were caught up in a frenzied windmill. Then everything went black, was silent, and faded. All that was left was myself, face to face with my conscience. I gripped the arms of the chair to suppress any reaction. No reaction. I felt nothing. My hands were not even trembling.
    I saw myself at the scene of the murder. On tiptoe. In fits and starts. Saw the body crumple under my bullets, get up, crumple, get up and crumple as if the film were out of control. I was oblivious both to the gunfire and to the little girl's screams. I think I became temporarily deaf when I was shooting. Sofiane had put his arms around me and dragged me back to the car. Had it not been for him, I would have just stood there like a scarecrow, gazing at my victim. I had not said a single word since our getaway. I was consumed with an unquenchable rage. I was angry with the revolver that had refused to stop shooting, with my

hand that had not resisted. Above all I was angry with the magistrate who had accepted his fate, just like that, simply because a stranger had decided to kill him in the street like an animal. I was angry with him for having dragged me down with him, implicated me in the tragedy. I was also angry with all men for being nothing but deceptive appearances, common mosquitoes, statues with feet of clay that a bullet a quarter of the size of a dice could annihilate in a second.

I was furious at the disconcerting ease with which man took his final bow, left the world through the back door, he who is made in the image of almighty God.

I had just discovered, in the most brutal way, that there was nothing more formidable, more wretched, less solid than a man.

It was terrifying. Unbearable. Repugnant.

"After the third, it will all seem perfectly natural," predicted Sofiane.

Chapter fourteen

Nafa Walid was advised not to attend his father's funeral, and not to visit his family. They were looking for him in the Casbah and in Bab El Oued, where things were getting complicated with massive police arrests.

After spending forty-eight hours at the home of Salah of Indochina, Nafa felt he would go mad. He blamed himself for the tragic killing of his elderly father. Hunched in a corner, he banged his head, silently ruminating his grief and his hatred, entreating his friends to leave him alone. He refused to eat or listen to reason, and reacted aggressively to their expressions of sympathy. At the end of his tether, he asked to join the *Maquis*. He had only one thing in mind: revenge.

"Don't be blinded by vindictiveness," instructed Abou Mariem, "or you will fail in your struggle. If you seek only vengeance, you risk isolating yourself. We must stay together. Fighting for the same ideal: the Islamic revolution. Your father is dead, murdered by cowards. He is neither the first nor the last. You must get a grip on yourself. We have to remain clear-headed. Hatred is an ugly partner. We must be

wary of it. On the contrary, our war is holy. It is not a personal matter, brother Nafa. We have to be determined but just. Enlightened.
The future of the nation depends on it. We will find your father's
murderers. Inevitably. Sooner or later, we'll flush them out and punish them. In the meantime, join the ranks. We have had to deal with
quite a few similar misconceptions. Okkacha, the hairdresser, lost
his son during a round-up. Without consulting anyone, he armed
himself with a razor and slit the throat of the first cop he met. It was
a stupid and unfortunate thing to do. The policeman was one of us.
He was the one who used to inform us about the raids his colleagues
were planning. So..."

Nafa insisted on joining the *maquis*. At first Sheikh Younes
opposed the idea but then he sent Nafa to join Sofiane's group.

Sofiane was a handsome twenty three-year old, tall and athletic.
His long, tow-colored hair gave him an equine look. With his boyish
features and disarming smile, he charmed both his companions and
his victims. He was in charge of a group of eight handpicked youths
all under the age of twenty-two, sons of dignitaries and industrialists. Their headquarters were at the University where they fine-tuned
their stratagems with surgical precision. With their specialization in
tracking down officials from the legal establishment, Communists
and businessmen, the team was very tight knit, discreet and thorough,
leaving nothing to chance. They were smartly dressed, clean-shaven,
fun-loving students. Some drew their hair back, others sported a
golden earring. At the faculty, they were taken for sons of the bourgeoisie, and were above suspicion. A *fatwa* permitted them to frequent
the cabarets and wealthy circles where they gathered information on
potential targets. Thanks to their casual look, they were able to stroll
up and down the main thoroughfares unimpeded, carrying a briefcase
with a revolver hidden inside a magazine.

From the start, Nafa enjoyed being with them. It reminded him
a little of the luxurious atmosphere of the Rajas', the dazzling lights
of the drawing rooms and the smell of money which, compared to
the shack of Salah of Indochina, was distinctly less oppressive.

For the first few weeks, he stayed with Farouk, the group's

mainstay on campus. Forced to keep a low profile, Nafa devoted himself to his ideological education. He read many religious works, prayed a great deal and never tired of listening to the sermons of the Egyptian, Sudanese and oriental sheikhs from Farouk's extensive collection of cassettes, while the latter wrote manifestos and recruited followers among the students.

Then Sofiane invited him to come and live with him, in a magnificent villa overlooking an orchard, on the Benaknoune heights, which he shared with Hind, his wife. Four years his senior, a frosty, sour *theopath* with a complexion the color of marble, Hind was as averse to jewelry as she was to familiarity. She wielded an extraordinary influence over the group. Nobody dared look her in the eyes. She put everyone in their place, at once, without any qualms, as Nafa found out to his cost at their very first meeting, when he held out his hand to her at the door. Appalled by this "heretical" gesture, she advised him to go back to Koranic school. Thinking she was joking, Nafa smiled; his smile soon faded when he caught a glint in his hostess's eyes that sent a chill down his spine.

It was she who drove the car when they went out on a mission. On those days, she dressed Western-style, wore make-up, and let her long black hair fall over her shoulders. She negotiated the police roadblocks better than an ambulance. Back home, she rushed to remove her make up and change out of her suit as if it were the shirt of Nessus. She would then immerse herself immediately in religious writings.

Nafa had met fanatics, but their extremism was nothing compared to Hind's.

Nafa's accommodation was on the ground floor. His hosts had given him a room with a giant television, bookshelves and a generous wardrobe.

"Make yourself at home," said Sofiane.

"I am overwhelmed."

"One more thing: I'd like you to grow a ponytail. You're a good-looking fellow, may as well make the most of it. With us, the basic rule is simple: combine the useful with the pleasant, in other words take pride in your appearance, strike home and vanish into thin air as if nothing has happened."

The next day, in the basement of the villa, he was initiated into firearms training.

One evening, as a mist was engulfing the town, Farouk turned up. He pinned on the wall photos of a man aged about 40, a lawyer who had upset the armed movement by inadequately defending brothers who had been arbitrarily arrested by the police. Farouk gave a full profile of the magistrate: his habits, the circles he moved in, his movements. Nafa listened attentively, far from imagining that this was to be his first target. His heart came to a standstill when Sofiane promised him that the operation would be a piece of cake and that he would be at his side in the event of any unforeseen complications.

After killing the magistrate, it was not long before Nafa intercepted a judge leaving a village hall at one A.M., in the morning. A doddery character, with a game leg, who was cursing because he couldn't open his car door. Once again, Nafa's hand shook as he placed the revolver against the nape of the astonished old man's neck. The judge did not seem to have grasped that he had the barrel of a gun pushing into his cervical vertebra. When the shot rang out, his dentures leapt out of his mouth, bounced on the hood of the car and smashed onto the tarmac.

To round off Nafa's first month in the group with a flourish, Sofiane made an exception to the rules and offered him, on a plate, a policeman who was so fat that Nafa had to empty his magazine to finish him off. Sofiane had been right: after the "third", it seemed quite natural. Nafa no longer had doubts or pangs of conscience, and started to watch his next victims with the tireless patience that comes with resignation.

"What pleasant surprise have you got for us?" asked Sofiane, who was standing in the hall, his knuckles on his hips.

Farouk wiped his espadrilles on the doormat. He flamboyantly tossed his American baseball cap onto a chest of drawers and brandished his briefcase:

"A hell hound."

Behind him, 'the Mullet' shivered in his flimsy waterproof jacket. He winked at Nafa ensconced in an armchair, briefly greeted him and shook the commander's hand as he waddled in: "It's raining buckets out there."

"Yes, what filthy weather."

"I saw some cops sniffing around."

"So let them, if they've got nothing better to do."

'The Mullet' rubbed his hands together and blew on them. His gaunt face was covered with freckles. The son of a former minister from the sole political party, he had lived in a dream world, spending his holidays in far-flung corners of the earth. At seventeen, he had owned a convertible, which he used to drive to school. In those days, he loved girls, dancing, and giving presents. At university, his teachers and fellow students predicted that he would have an outstanding career. He was gifted, a real genius. He was way ahead of all his contemporaries, but never appeared to be over-stretching himself. He excelled both in the sciences and in general culture, commanding the admiration of the university authorities. And yet, 'the Mullet' was not bigheaded. He pursued his studies with characteristic insouciance. And nobody could have guessed that he would turn into a ruthless killer. His life changed on the day when, at university, Farouk had invited him to second him on the Committee. The latter was brilliant too, from a rich and respectable family. He spoke French, but thought FIS. 'The Mullet' was spellbound by his roommate's rhetoric, his clear vision and his handsome, delicate features. He was soon won over, accompanying Farouk to meetings and sermons, to the mosque and specialist bookshops. 'The Mullet' became aware of the futility of ostentation, the shamefulness of dissipation and the pointlessness of an ephemeral world where showy facades were a poor disguise for internal corruption. So he renounced the superficial to devote himself to the essential. Determined to dedicate his genius to the service of the noble cause, he came down from his cloud and sported a bushy auburn beard which he willingly sacrificed when Farouk explained to him the revolutionary necessity to work in absolute secrecy, to change nothing of their student habits or their friends. 'The Mullet' received the message loud and clear. He continued to flaunt his bourgeois jet-set affectations to mask the ardent neophyte underneath, one of heaven's genuine chosen, for whom a tailor-made mission waited like a Visitation.

His first victim was his own professor, a doctor in mathematics, a childless widower who lived alone in a small old house in east Algiers. The professor had been proud to take his pupil under his wing. He often invited him to his house to share his frugal dinner. They would spend entire evenings proclaiming the merits of such-and-such a scientist, the talent of the Russian writers, and the glory of Marxism. 'The Mullet' lamented the breakdown of the Soviet empire and voiced his anxiety as to the future of the Algerian Communists, which he hoped to revive. Delighted, the widower congratulated him on his sentiments, assured him that Communism in Algeria could look forward to a healthy future, and promised to open wide the doors of his Party to him. That was how 'the Mullet' was able to draw up a list of "atheist" faculty staff headed by the name of his sponsor, underlined in red. He executed the professor on the night of his fiftieth birthday, giving him two large-bore bullets by way of a birthday present.

Nafa had worked with him twice. 'The Mullet' had the discipline and efficiency of a professional killer. He struck fast and accurately using a pistol fitted with a silencer. Once the victim was dead, he would mechanically roll down his sleeves, put his gun back in his briefcase and calmly walk away, like a young man out for a spot of window shopping downtown. Never did his victim's entreaties cause his hand to tremble; never did his ghost catch up with him; but hardly had he breathed his last, when 'the Mullet' was already thinking about his next quarry.

Farouk emptied out his briefcase onto the table in the living room, and picked out some photos, which he arranged side by side.

"A Communist bastard," he declared.

Nafa frowned as he recognized the filmmaker Rachid Derrag.

"Are you sure he's a Communist?"

"Unless you can prove the contrary," sneered 'the Mullet'. "Do you know him?"

Nafa realized his gaffe, and tried to cover up. He picked up a photograph, pretended to examine it and 'changed his mind.'

"It's incredible how closely he resembles a postman I used to know."

"This fellow isn't a postman. He makes subversive films and gets stoned out of his mind every Thursday, at the Lebanon."

Farouk slammed a box file down on the table: "I've got a complete dossier on him: Rachid Derrag, forty-seven years old, married, four kids, resides at Cité Amrane, Block C, apartment 1. Studied film in Moscow. Well-known alcoholic..."

"A filthy infidel," added 'the Mullet'. "Apparently, he's making a documentary on fundamentalism to show at a European Festival."

"I hate artists. Especially those perverse enough to be Communists."

Nafa grimaced to show that he had been mistaken. As he looked up, he met Hind's penetrating gaze.

"How long have you been with us now?" she asked him.

"About ten weeks, why?"

"Have you lacked for anything?"

"No."

"Have you had the impression that we were hiding anything from you?"

"Not really."

Hind banged her fist on the briefcase and screeched:

"So why don't you trust us?"

Nafa recoiled: "Of course I trust you."

Hind's lips curled in an animal snarl. Her eyes creased as she focused the full power of her gaze on the disconcerted Nafa.

"Really? You trust us. That's why you're pretending not to recognize the bastard in the photos."

"I got him mixed up with..."

"Don't lie!"

Her finger jabbed menacingly.

Farouk and 'the Mullet' looked away, mortified.

Sofiane took his hands out of his pockets and tried to step in. Hind told him to stay where he was, and leaned towards Nafa as if she were trying to dissolve him in her shadow. Breathing heavily, her face contorted, she brought her lips close to the ear of the former taxi driver and murmured, in a voice that was inaudible at first, and then became increasingly aggressive:

"We took you on board to please your Sheikh Younes. We're not particular about details, you know. We examined your file and we took you on in the light of the information we found. We know where you come from, how far you're capable of going, who you've worked for and to what extent you can be useful... we know that you've screwed up more or less everywhere, particularly in the cinema, and we know you played a part in an abysmal movie made by that depraved piece of scum in the photo."

"It doesn't matter, Hind," said Sofiane awkwardly. "Nafa is only on his fifth assassination."

"Sixth!"

"Sixth, tenth, what I mean it is, he hasn't found his own level yet. We're fighters, not killing machines. *God only asks of his subjects what they are capable of undertaking.* If Nafa feels that he's not ready to tackle an old friend, he is not letting us down, nor is it a betrayal."

"Yes, it is," she cried straightening up. "There are no double standards in the *Jihad*. Any person condemned by the Movement must be executed. No argument. Parent, relative or friend—it makes no difference. Keeping to this absolute principle is the only way we'll get rid of all the corrupt bastards in power."

She turned back to Nafa and resumed her attack: "And do you recognize the scum in the photo now?"

Nafa ran his hands through his hair and stared at his shoes, His Adam's apple refused to budge.

"Do you recognize him?"

"Yes!"

"Do you have enough faith to kill him?"

."That's enough!" yelled Sofiane. "You don't have the right to treat one of my men like this! I strictly forbid it. I give the orders here. I'm the boss."

Hind glared back at her husband for a few moments before turning her gaze to Nafa's bowed head. Farouk and 'the Mullet' appeared to be absorbed in the photos. She clenched her fists and went back up to her room.

Rachid Derrag was to have his throat slit. In front of his children.

Nafa was to be there.

No matter how tight he shut his eyes so as not to witness the slaughter, it could not prevent the film-maker's horrified screams haunting him during his days and nights: "I don't believe it, not you, Nafa. You don't belong beside *them*. No. You're an artist, for God's sake, an artist..."

Chapter fifteen

Standing at the window, Nafa watched the fog engulf the town like a horde of ghosts coming in from the sea. Thousands of shrouds laden with salt spray unfurled over the buildings, swaddling the districts of the city and rising inevitably towards the shanty town on the hillside. Algiers sat huddled, listening as horror gnawed at her guts and misery gripped her spirit. The shadows hugging the walls revived her insomnia. The city's agony was played out against the lapping waters in the port. Imprisoned in her grief, expecting nothing of men, and nothing from her allies, she had ceased to believe in the open sea and the heavens.

Nafa tried to recall the days when people used to enjoy hanging around the streets, the hubbub of the cheap eating houses, the strains of *haouzi* music, the swarms of kids playing in the squares; he tried to recapture those carefree, spontaneous times, the ribald evenings around a cup of coffee, the wisecracks that sparked like fairground rockets. How far off they seemed, those familiar scenes of long ago. Dead and buried!

"Can I clear away?" asked Hind.

"Of course," replied Sofiane, from the depths of an armchair. "Bring us some tea, please."

Nafa could see Hind's reflection in the window as she collected the plates from the table. From her forbidding look, he knew that she had not forgiven him for lying, even though he had tried to redeem himself by participating in two other spectacular assassinations after that of Rachid Derrag. But that was not enough to put him back into her good books. She was still angry with him, giving him nothing but that cold, disdainful look reserved for people who have proved to be hopeless disappointments.

Nafa turned back to gazing into the night. A police car drove down the street, its revolving red light casting a blood-colored glare onto the walls.

The telephone rang.

Sofiane rose to answer it.

"Is your TV on?" gasped a voice at the other end.

"Yes."

"What are you watching?"

"A French channel."

"Switch over to ENTV... and stay on the line."

Sofiane went back to his chair, picked up the remote control, then returned to the phone. The green-tinged image on the screen faded, and another appeared, ominous. Amid piles of rubble stood a smoldering house. Police stood guarding the scene. The camera slid inside the besieged building, swept across a hall scattered with debris, charred walls riddled with bullets and overturned furniture, then turned to a courtyard where seven bodies lay beside war weapons, home-made grenades, wads of banknotes and fluttering documents.

"Hello, are you there?"

"Yes," replied Sofiane. "I don't understand."

"The national command was double-crossed. There must be moles in high places. It was a top-secret meeting of the utmost importance. Even I didn't know about it."

"I counted seven bodies."

"They were eight. We must watch out. The one who escaped may be in the hands of the *taghut*."

"I didn't recognize anyone," said Sofiane, irritably.

"The entire senior command, I tell you. It's a terrible blow. There will be serious repercussions throughout the Movement."

"Is Emir Jaafer among the martyrs?"

"Yes, and Sheikh Nouh, the national coordinator, the West and North regional coordinators, the emir from zone one, a representative of the organization in Europe, and… is Hind beside you?"

"She's doing the washing up."

"Find a way of telling her."

Sofiane's heart missed a beat.

He gulped and asked:

"Abou Lhoul?"

Silence at the other end, then:

"Yes, he was killed too."

Hind stood framed in the doorway as if alerted by a sixth sense, her arms folded over her chest. She stared at her husband who hurriedly turned away, dripping with perspiration.

"Hello," resumed the voice on the other end.

"I'm still here."

"Tell her how deeply sorry I am."

"I'll tell her."

"Watch out, brothers. It's a terrible blow, but we'll get over it."

"I don't doubt it for a moment. I'll call you back. We'll speak soon."

Sofiane replaced the receiver and wiped his sticky lips with the back of his hand. Nafa, who had seen the images on television, guessed that disaster had just struck the Movement full on. He had not recognized anyone on the screen, except perhaps the corpse in the middle who reminded him of someone he had met briefly one afternoon at Omar Ziri's.

He watched the emir's lips with bated breath.

Sofiane looked up at his wife. He did not know how to tell her the news.

He ventured:

"Something terrible has happened, Hind."

Nafa felt in the way. He coughed into his hand and made to leave.

"Stay," said Hind.

She leant against the doorpost, stared at the ceiling light and turned to follow her husband's gaze.

"Who was on the phone?"

"Ishaq."

"Oh."

"They've just shown what happened on TV. The entire high command has been wiped out. There was Jaafer, Sheikh Nouh, Abou Horeira, Abou Abderrahmane, Zakaria, Slimane Abou Daoud, a brother from Europe..."

"And Abou Lhoul," she added in a calm voice.

Sofiane frowned.

"How do you know?"

"My brother never left Jaafer's side for a moment. If he's dead, my brother must be too."

"I'm so sorry."

Hind straightened up, slowly, with a supple movement of her hips, and rubbed her arm without taking her eyes off her husband. Not a muscle moved in her face. She looked impassive, almost serene.

She nodded and said:

"I'll go and get you some tea."

For weeks, there was an air of expectancy. The country observed a truce. No more murders, no news from the *maquis*. The blow to the Movement was exceptionally harsh. As time went by, the full gravity of the situation sank in. Sofiane ordered his men to suspend operations and go back to the university to wait for new directives. With Jaafer eliminated, there would be a bitter power struggle. Each emir who was killed dragged the microcosm that gravitated around him down too. His entourage and bodyguard were automatically dispersed, his close collaborators relegated and others replaced until things were back on track, vanishing into the night without trace.

Sofiane was worried. His brother-in-law, Abou Lhoul, was no longer there to guarantee his group the relative autonomy they had previously enjoyed, and he feared that some crazy emir might destabilize the network he had spent years putting in place. He was also afraid of being relieved of his functions and transferred to an area where he did not want to be.

Differences—even dissidence—were corroding the Movement's bases. After the MIA, other armed factions gained ground as they became increasingly expansionist. The Islamic Salvation Army was rivaled by the armed Islamic groups springing up all over the place, fearsome and destructive, better equipped, better organized, zealous and terrifying. In record time, they had taken over the *maquis* in the center, west and southeast of the country, had made a display of large-scale ambushes and daredevil attacks on military camps. They were like a frontier army that had lain in wait for a long time, attacking an injured village to finish it off. The founder members of the FIS found themselves a laughing stock. They had lost their authority. As each attack propelled glorious newcomers to the fore, their leadership fell into disarray. It was no longer the moment for rhetoric. Knives spoke louder than words. The sheikhs were silenced by the emirs, the politicians by the warriors. Some imams surrendered, giving in to the authorities. They had no qualms about making a spectacle of themselves on television, demythologizing the *Majlis*, stirring up ill feeling. The exiled leaders contradicted each other, mutually relieving each other of their authority. Demands were met with indignation. In the interior, it was worse. Conflicts broke out all over the place, cracking the framework of the *Jihad*, with new currents emerging in their bloody aftermath. The clans were on the lookout for the slightest opportunity to revive the leadership race: Iranians, Afghans, the *Hijra wa Takfir* sect, Salafists, Jaz'ara, the companions of Said Mekhloufi, disciples of Chebouti, the self-proclaimed general, and other occult, underground and Machiavellian influences stirred up the troubled waters to add to the discord and confusion.

Sofiane was utterly at a loss. He kept close to the phone, his hands clasped behind his back and his head bowed. Every name put forward, every potential candidate for the emirate plunged him into a sort of hysteria, sometimes enthusiastic, sometimes despondent. He in turn put forward names, opposed others, and threatened to set up a breakaway group. His contact, Ishaq, advised him to maintain his composure and assured him of his unconditional support.

In witnessing these highly intense telephone conversations, Nafa shared his emir's mood swings. He sank into despair when he heard him complain, and felt a glimmer of hope when Sofiane relaxed.

Meanwhile, Hind shut herself up in her room. Since her brother's death, she had taken refuge in reading theological works and in prayer, appearing only to cook the meals that she barely touched.

And then, one evening, at eight P.M., the phone rang.

Strangely, Sofiane and Nafa, who were watching the news on television, both felt unusually alarmed.

"Yes?" said the emir, his heart pounding.

He listened, listened, nodded and hung up.

He returned to his place with a despondent step, and slumped down in his chair, sick with exasperation.

"There are so many *éminences grises* in the Movement, yet it's a stupid peasant, an illiterate idiot who's been appointed leader... Odd, truly odd..."

Nafa Walid sat dozing under a pear tree, a book lying face down on his knees. It had rained the day before, and the orchard steamed in the sunlight, lulled by the twittering of the birds. A cloudless sky stretched its blue canvas over the city. Spring strutted its finery, superb in a sultan's tunic, a flower in its buttonhole, a swallow on its turban. Nafa abandoned himself to the delicious caress of the warmth, a blissful smile on his *Jihad*-scarred face, recalling the landscapes that used to delight him in the days when he was a driver for the National Tourist Office.

A shadow blocked out the sun. He waited for it to move. It

stayed put. Then he opened his eyes and saw Sofiane standing before him, his hands in his pockets, his brow furrowed.

"I'm going to miss you, my friend," he announced, teasing a blade of grass with the toe of his shoe.

"Are you leaving?"

"You're the one who's leaving, Nafa. I've received orders to send you to serve under a certain Salah of Indochina. I tried to negotiate to keep you in my team, but they wouldn't have it."

Nafa leaped out of his wicker chair. His book fell to the ground; he didn't notice.

"Under Salah of Indochina?"

"That's what I've been told. You must know him?"

"He's just a support member."

"Maybe you've been designated to an auxiliary service."

"Do you think I wasn't up to the job under you?"

"You were terrific. I assure you, this is nothing to do with me."

Nafa glanced up to the first floor window.

Sofiane stopped him at once.

"Hind doesn't know you're leaving yet. She's hard, but dirty tricks are not her style."

Nafa clenched his jaw and tried to think, to explain the misunderstanding. He wasn't able to concentrate.

He shook his head, wearily.

"When do I leave?"

"Today."

"Well…"

Sofiane grasped his shoulder sympathetically:

"I've greatly appreciated your decency, brother Nafa. You've been brave, friendly and discreet. I am fond of you. I'm really going to miss you. I would have liked to keep you, only with all this turmoil, nobody can guarantee their own future any more."

"I understand…"

"If you need me, you know where to find me."

Nafa thanked him.

He forced a smile to show that he'd manage, and made his way unsteadily towards the villa.

Nafa waited till nightfall to join Salah of Indochina. Sofiane dropped him just outside El Harrach and wished him good luck.

"You'll always be welcome, Nafa."

"Yes…"

"Take care."

"I'll try."

The car reversed, turned around, hit a dustbin and accelerated. Nafa stood in the middle of the deserted street and watched it disappear. Other than one shop that was still open, there wasn't a living soul to be seen. A full moon hung in the sky. The exhalations of the wadi filled the air, indicating the proximity of the social outcasts' colony.

Nafa kept close to a hedge and climbed a steep path up to the group of huts. Dogs were barking their heads off; some would loom out of the darkness, frothing at the mouth, and then slink off, their tails between their legs, pursued by a hail of stones.

In the newfound silence, babies could be heard howling inside the shelters built of scrap.

"I was beginning to wonder whether you'd been put inside," yelped Salah of Indochina greeting him at the entrance to his shack.

Five young men were moping inside. They did not seem thrilled to be there. Nafa recognized Abou Tourab, Abou Mariem's lieutenant. He sat in a corner, hugging his knees, in a foul temper. Next to him, Amar the second-hand dealer was absently fiddling with his *tarboosh.* The three others, squeezed onto a jumbled pile of dirty washing, were talking in low voices.

Salah proceeded with the introductions: "This is Nafa, a brother from the Casbah."

They rose to greet him.

"Right, you know Abou Tourab and Amar. This is Abdoul Bacir, the son of the Imam of Kouba. A brilliant explosives engineer. He was behind last month's bomb. And that's Mouqatel from Belcourt, and over there is Souheil, a deserter. He was involved in the Admiralty attack."

Nafa sat down facing Abou Tourab.

"Coffee?" offered his host.

"No thanks, I can't sleep at night as it is."

Salah crouched down and slapped his knee.

"You do look miserable. What's the matter?"

"You tell me. I was fine where I was serving. Why have they put me under you? Have you been demoted too?"

"Haven't you heard?" asked Abou Tourab in amazement.

"Heard what?"

"About the reshuffle. Sheikh Younes was relieved of his duties and sent to the *maquis*. Ibrahim El Khalil is now head of the West Algiers groups. He appointed Abou Mariem as his deputy and has enlisted all his peons from Kouba. He's seized the stronghold that we built with our own hands."

"Watch your language," warned Salah.

"But it's true."

"All the same, you're speaking ill of an emir."

"What's all this about?" cried Nafa, outraged. "Where are all the others?"

"Booted out," groaned Abou Tourab. "For the moment, Ibrahim has kept on the people who suit him, and got rid of the 'recalcitrant' elements. You should have seen how contemptuously he booted out Sheikh Younes. Outrageous. Then he went for the support network. He executed the main leaders. For the most trivial reasons."

"Not trivial," protested Salah. "They were all unscrupulous bastards."

"What do you know?"

"I know that an emir is always right. That's the rule. Ammi Bachi was a bastard. He abused the wives of our martyrs. In front of the whole of Bab El Oued. The other one, the hunchback, he was a devious character. He was often seen in places he had no right to be. As for Omar Ziri, he dipped into the war chest to build his villa, in Cheraga."

Nafa gave a start: "Omar Ziri's dead?"

"And how!" crowed Salah of Indochina, jubilant. "I was there, and a pretty sight it was too. We went to pick him up from the back of his shop. He was spread over a table gorging himself like a pig. A royal banquet just for him: a huge roast turkey stuffed with mushrooms, baskets of expensive fruit, bananas from Columbia, apples from France, everything imported. In short, he was having a ball. He sat there stuffing himself, sighing with contentment. He was so busy sucking his fingers and licking his chops that he didn't hear us come in. Suddenly, he became aware of our presence, and froze. As he looked up, he nearly choked. Ibrahim said to him: 'Carry on stuffing yourself, you pig. And make sure you chew everything well. I don't want any bones stuck in your throat. I'd hate to ruin my knife.' Well, you can imagine what happened next. A balloon deflated. Omar Ziri, the glutton—the crook of crooks—shat himself. I swear it's true. The place stank of his shit. At first he tried to deny the offences he was accused of. As nobody was moved, he went down on his knees and begged the emir to spare him. It was an amazing sight. As if a barrel full of fresh blood had burst. I tell you, I almost wanted to lap it up. I was jubilant. He'd been acting as if he were God for such a long time."

The five men stared at the old man in horror and indignation.

Nafa mopped himself with a handkerchief.

He stammered, his throat dry: "Can someone tell me what the hell I'm doing here?"

"Tell him," muttered Abou Tourab to Salah.

"Why me? Did you leave your tongue on those boots you were licking?"

Abou Tourab suppressed his anger. He explained:

"Ibrahim is getting rid of Sheikh Younes' cronies, especially the ones he can't stand."

Nafa recalled the run-in he'd had with Ibrahim El Khalil, one Friday, in Omar Ziri's establishment, and felt a tremendous weariness.

"He bears grudges," said Amar. "There's no-one like him. We had a row, years ago, in Peshawar. Over a stupid sheet. Ibrahim needed it for something or other. I told him to use his own. He insulted me. I insulted him back. He left, and he's never forgiven me."

"And as for me," Abou Tourab chimed in, "he's angry at me for having shot the poet Sid Ali. Even though it was Abou Mariem who gave the order."

"Stop there!" interrupted Salah. "The emir insisted the bastard should have his throat slit. And you defied him, you tried to be clever."

"For heaven's sake, he was the bard of the Casbah. The people took it badly enough when they heard their idol had been shot. Slitting his throat would have been…"

"Nonsense! He was nothing but a charmer of idiots. He lulled people to sleep in their shit. The Emir demanded his head. It should have been handed to him, and that's that."

"OK, OK," yelled Nafa, throwing up his arms. "I just want to know why I've been sent to you."

"I'm a guide."

"So?"

"Tonight I'm going to take you into the *maquis*."

Nafa noticed that the others were staring at him. He guessed that they could sense his panic. He clenched his jaws and tried to regain his composure.

"That's just too bad!" he sighed, stoically. "When do we leave?"

"An hour before curfew."

"I must visit the old lady. I haven't seen her since my father's death."

"That's up to you. At 10 P.M. sharp, we're off. I won't wait for anyone who's not here."

Nafa glanced at his watch and rose: "I'll be back in an hour."

"I'll come with you," said Abou Tourab.

Nafa's mother had aged a great deal. A few months had been sufficient to achieve what all those long years of ups and downs and domestic chores had not succeeded in eroding. There remained nothing of her former face, which had always been radiant despite the disappointments. The maternal face, once so comforting, was nothing now but a cracked mask, somber and sad, with two lusterless eyes like candles burning in the gloom of a death chamber.

Nafa was stricken. The elderly woman could barely stand. She gripped the door handle betraying her giddiness.

Clearly, Omar Ziri had forgotten to add her to the list of needy families.

Nora, in the hall, stood stock-still. She wasn't thrilled to see her brother. She stared at the floor, fiddling with her braids. Souad and Amira hid behind a curtain in the kitchen, unaware that their shadows gave them away.

"What do you want?" asked their mother.

"Won't you let me in?"

"You shouldn't have left us."

"I was avenging my father."

"He didn't ask you to."

"He didn't have to. The *taghut* killed him. The rest is my business."

"It's you who killed him. The police were here looking for you. They came to search the place. Your father objected. They showed him what you kept hidden behind your wardrobe. He clutched at his chest and dropped dead. His heart gave out. He couldn't bear that his child, his only son, in whom he placed all his hope, had turned into a terrorist."

Nafa bowed his head.

At the foot of the stairs, Abou Tourab watched the street. In the dark, something was decomposing.

"I've come to tell you that I'm joining the *maquis*."

"You didn't need to trouble yourself."

"I wanted to say goodbye."

"You have."

Nafa bit his lip.

His grief pressed down on the back of his head.

"I assume I don't have your blessing."

"The blessing of your sheikhs should be enough."

He nodded, turned on his heels, and paused on the top step.

Without turning round, after a contemplative silence, he said: "I am not a terrorist."

He heard the door close and set off down the stairs. Like a damned soul descending into hell.

Chapter sixteen

A sympathizer drove them out of the city, aboard a rattling van, before handing them over to another driver, who was waiting for them at a remote farmhouse. After a halt and a cup of coffee, they clambered onto a tractor and made their way through orchards until they reached the bottom of a wooded hill. The remainder of the journey would be on foot. Scrambling up hill and down dale, they arrived at a shimmering plain lit up by the moon as if it were broad daylight.

"From now on, you can sing at the tops of your voices," said Salah of Indochina. "Here, the night belongs to us. No *taghut*—no rebel scum—would dare venture out around here."

Of the seven men, only Salah was armed. He carried an old sawn-off shotgun. They walked some more, and some more, passing through silent villages plunged in a sepulchral darkness, the windows blacked out and the doors barricaded. They imagined the inhabitants clutching their covers, sleeping with one eye open, their hearts in their mouths. The slightest creak, the most innocent squeal made their hearts thump as if they'd been given a drop of nitroglycerine.

Salah knew it.

And that was why, bitten by who knows what morbid bug, he fired into the air as they left one village.

"That'll scare the women," he joked, despite the group's disapproval. It was comforting to remind the ordinary people that big daddy was looking after them.

At the first light of dawn, they stopped in a forest, by a stream. Salah asked them to wait there, and returned after around twenty minutes, with a bag filled with provisions.

"We're going to stuff ourselves until we puke," he promised.

On a rock, he spread out cans of food, bottles of mineral water and biscuits.

"Don't stare at me like that. I'm a magician. I can pull women out of my hat, if you want."

Becoming serious again, he explained that the place was a transit center. The brothers stored food there for itinerant armed groups.

They ate and slept in the copse.

In the afternoon, Salah led them through an interminable maze of undergrowth. The terrain was rugged and hostile. The men were exhausted, their feet burning and their calves numb. The old man refused to let them rest. He seemed to take a malicious pleasure in choosing the most difficult paths out of sheer spite.

"This makes a change from your cushy hideouts, doesn't it?" he chortled.

Nightfall found them struggling along at the bottom of a ravine, tripping over protruding roots. At the top of the slope stood a decrepit cabin, guarded by a tall eucalyptus.

Salah loaded his gun.

"There's a light. I'm going to see what's going on. If you hear shots, beat it."

It was obvious that he was exaggerating, but his companions were too tired to say anything. Salah closed his eyes, invoked the name of the Lord and prayed. He was a good actor. In other circumstances, he would have made a good comic, but there was something heretical about him. Aware of his "impunity", he gave free rein to his talents, knowing full well that he annoyed people. Perhaps that was what he was trying to do: make himself repulsive.

He crawled through the thicket and around a fence to approach the cabin from the rear. A dog barked, then…

After around ten minutes, Nafa grew impatient:

"What the hell's he up to?"

"I hope he gets himself killed," groaned Abou Tourab. "I'm sick of his little ways."

An old woman appeared on a mound and signaled to them to join her.

"It's a trap," said Abdoul Bacir anxiously.

"It's that asshole playing games again."

And it was true: Salah of Indochina lay sprawled on a mattress, his jacket hanging from a nail and his shoes on the window ledge. He had washed his face and was sipping a glass of tea with an affected air and an ironic grin.

"Very funny," grunted Abou Tourab.

An old man was sitting cross-legged in the center of the room. His egg-shaped head gleamed in the glow of an oil lamp. He had a gaunt face and big, bony hands, and looked at least eighty. His clothes were in tatters and he smelled of damp straw.

"I wish I could offer you a lamb," he said in a quavering voice. "But all I have is a little couscous and a few slices of dried meat. My wife and I are poor. Our children have gone to the city to earn their living, and my crops haven't seen any rain."

"Don't worry, *Hadj*," Salah consoled him haughtily. "There's nothing more nourishing than a good Bedouin couscous. Tell me, where are the *taghut*?"

"Who?"

"The soldiers and the police."

The old man smiled. His toothless mouth split his face like a grisly wound.

"I haven't seen a single one since Independence. Even in De Gaulle's day, I didn't see many. This place is the back of beyond.

Nobody comes here or ever returns. My wife and I have no neighbors. We live more or less for ourselves."

The old woman brought in a huge dish brimming over with steaming couscous."

They ate, they drank, and they rested.

"Right," said Salah, "it's time to get out of here."

He asked his host to show them the path to the shrine of Sid El Bachir. In single file, they climbed up a goat track. Suddenly, Salah struck his forehead.

"I left my bag at the hut."

He ordered the old man to take the group to the shrine and ran back to the shack.

The shrine of Sid El Bachir was nothing but a heap of ruins, destroyed by a homemade bomb. The saint's grave had been gutted and burned. On the catafalque, red lettering proclaimed that the GIA had been there.

The old man raised a stone to his lips, kissed it religiously and placed it on a tuft of grass.

Salah of Indochina arrived breathless. He asked his companions to continue straight ahead, without him, on the pretext he had some important information to give to their host. When Nafa and the others had vanished into the woods, Salah turned to the octogenarian and said:

"Thank you for the couscous, *Hadj*."

"Bah, it's a duty."

Salah grabbed his knife and plunged it into the small of the old man's back, then again into his stomach. He fell to his knees, wide-eyed in bewilderment.

"Why, my son?"

"Hey, that's how it is, *Hadj*, the Lord operates in mysterious ways."

Matching his words with action, he grabbed him by the skin of his pate, thrust his head back and slit his throat so profoundly that the blade broke one of the cervical vertebrae. Blood spurted in Salah's face. He relished it fully, as if in the throes of orgasm.

In the morning, Abou Tourab noticed the congealed blood on the guide's collar and chest.

"Did you kill him?"

Salah opened his arms:

"Our orders are strict: don't leave any traces."

"So why did you spare the old woman?"

Salah rolled his malicious eyes:

"But I haven't got a bag."

And he burst out laughing.

Nafa had the feeling that Salah of Indochina was taking them round in circles. They had been fighting their way through the dense forest for hours, through immense trees and tangled undergrowth. Daylight could not penetrate the foliage, which restricted visibility. It was a wild region. No sign of walkers or hunters. Nothing but trunks besieged by wild sprawling grasses, thorny tangles suspended in the void, drooping shrubs masking the horizon. Salah of Indochina plunged into the vegetation, as nimble as a weasel, his gun at the ready. He continued to exaggerate the dangers, and was at pains to draw a red herring across the trail, to disorient his companions who puffed and panted, stumbling along behind him, their bodies covered in scratches.

The next day, they arrived at a fundamentalist camp set up in the folds of a valley. It was a medical post built of pillboxes and camouflaged under thick branches. The master of the house was a gangling doctor who was bald and myopic, assisted by four nurses in fatigues. Some twenty warriors in Afghan dress guarded the place.

The arrival of Salah of Indochina stirred the place out of its lethargy. Jibes flew, there was much embracing, hugging and hearty claps on the back. Salah knew everyone, including the girls, who were visibly pleased to see him.

Nafa saw the injured lying on camp beds inside the bunkers. Others were convalescing, hobbling about on rudimentary crutches or sitting dreaming at the foot of a tree. A robust fellow with both legs amputated was reading the Koran at the entrance to a shelter. Nafa greeted him. The maimed man did not reply. He merely raised his book higher to conceal his face. Nafa looked to see if there was anyone he knew among the men gathered in the heart of the forest, but in vain. He was offered some rice, and then they ignored him. Nafa ate in silence, then went off on his own to a clearing and took off his shoes to let his feet breathe. His socks were soaked in blood. He rolled up his trousers above his knees, exposing his legs to the sun and dropped off to sleep.

When Nafa awoke, he found a man sitting beside him nursing a rifle between his thighs. He was wearing a parachutist's jacket and faded canvas trousers.

His bushy beard mingled with his long white hair, which cascaded down his back.

"I never thought I'd bump into you here," he said.

Nafa raised himself onto his elbows and stared at the man:

"Do I know you?"

"You really have got a head like a sieve."

Nafa cast his mind back in vain. The man's eyes were familiar, their expression belying his smile, but it was impossible to place him.

"War changes a man, doesn't it?"

That voice rang a bell, but Nafa was still mystified.

The man fished a bullet out of his cartridge pouch, weighed it, closed his fist around it, breathed into it and opened his hand again. The bullet had disappeared.

"Yahia, the Bensoltane's chauffeur!" he exclaimed, relieved to meet up with an old friend at last. "The musician who could conjure *houris* out of his mandolin."

"In the flesh."

They embraced, laughing.

"So, Nafa the actor, you finally made your choice?"

"So did you, it appears. Are you based here?"

"I'm just passing through. I've brought back a wounded man. What about you?"

"I don't know. I was operating in the center of Algiers. The new emir decided to dispense with my services. What's it like here?"

Yahia pulled a face:

"I miss my mandolin."

"How long have you been in the GIA?"

"About two years. I worked in Sidi Moussa. My group was busted. I retreated to Chréa."

He scraped a hole in the ground with the butt of his gun:

"It was ugly, very ugly."

"It's what you wanted.

"You think you want something at first. But actually, you take what comes and learn to live with it."

Yahia suddenly turned bitter. To calm himself down, he raised his hand to Nafa's neck, produced the bullet and rolled it sadly around in his palm.

"It's slower with a bullet. When it comes to conjuring tricks, nothing beats a good silver coin. Besides, the problem with a gun is that it's hard to play a good tune. I'd give my right arm to get my mandolin back. It's true that I used to be angry. My frustration affected my judgment. If I had known that things would go this far, I'd rather have remained a loser..."

He fell silent for a moment, gazing at his bullet, then he went on:

"I didn't join the *maquis* out of conviction. When they began to shoot people who had nothing to do with the system, I tried to keep out of it. That wasn't what I was hoping for from the Islamic Revolution. But I wasn't given any choice. My eldest son was an FIS activist. He was deported to Reggane. I said it was bound to happen and I resigned myself. Except that the gendarmes wouldn't leave me alone. Every week, they'd turn up at my place, make a bloody mess, cart off one or two boys and beat them up. I went to see their officer. He called me a filthy fundamentalist and threw me in solitary. I was tortured. When they let me go, I didn't even have the time to dress my wounds before the cops moved in. My wife became diabetic. It was hell. After a few months of persecution, I couldn't take it any more. So I took my two boys and I yelled: 'Death to the bastards!' There are limits, *kho*. I'd rather die than put up with some things.

The youngest was killed at Sidi Moussa. He died in my arms. You haven't got kids, have you?"

"No."

"You can't imagine what it's like. If an angel had come to comfort me, I'd have made mincemeat of him. I went crazy with grief. The sight of a uniform would send me into a fury. I wiped out at least a dozen of them, in Sidi Moussa. The more throats I slit, the more I wanted. I was insatiable, but it did not diminish my suffering. I didn't even wait till it was dark to act. I attacked in broad daylight, in the middle of the street, in full view of everyone, *kho*. I wanted everything to be clear. It was them or me. My other son was wounded. I left for the *maquis*. I was put in charge of a *saria* of around fifteen seasoned fighters. I burned down schools and farms, blew up bridges and factories, set up false road blocks and forced whole villages to flee… Then, I don't know why, a woman fighter accused my son of sexual harassment. She was lying, of course. My son was deeply religious. He didn't even touch the women they brought back from the raids. He was a believer. He fought out of conviction. The emir didn't want to know. My boy was executed the same morning that his eldest son joined us after being released from an internment camp. There are coincidences of such cruel irony that I shall never understand their purpose. I went berserk. As a precaution, they disarmed me. If it hadn't been for my eldest son, who knew an influential member of the Council, they'd have done me in too. Nowadays, I deal with transporting the wounded. That's my story."

Nafa was silent.

He did not know what to say.

Yahia began playing with the bullet again.

"It's funny. That's the first time I've told anybody about all that. Here, you confide in someone and they'll stab you in the back."

Nafa realized that the Bensoltane's former driver was suddenly wary of him. He slapped him on the thigh:

"You have nothing to fear from me."

"I'm sorry."

"You don't need to apologize either."

Yahia relaxed.

"I can't help it. I had to pour my heart out…"

"Go on my friend. I'm a bottomless well."

A multicolored bird landed in front of them, and hopped around in the grass. Yahia watched it, pensively. Unable to stop himself, he let out a sigh and said:

"Once, Sid Ali the poet caught a praying mantis in a field. It was a beautiful spring day. There were flowers everywhere. Sid Ali showed me the insect and asked me if I knew that originally, the mantis had been a leaf. I said I didn't. Then Sid Ali told me the story of a rebellious, arrogant leaf who couldn't stomach the idea of being dropped from the branch simply because it was fall. She considered herself too important to molder among the dead leaves, humiliated and blown into the mud by the wind. She decided to go it alone and swore she would only rely on herself, like a big girl. She wanted to survive the winter. And Nature, impressed with her grit and determination, turned her into an insect to see how she would fare. That was how the Praying Mantis was born, fierce and taciturn, more ambitious than ever. The miracle went to her head. She began to scoff at her branch, to trample on it. She became a cruel, haughty predator, and her impunity soon blinded her to the point where, to prove something or other, she began to devour everything in her path, including those who love her."

The bird flew off.

"A nice story," said Nafa.

"Yes… We should have listened to the poet."

"Hey, handsome!" yelled Salah of Indochina from the top of a rock. "Come on, we're leaving."

Nafa pulled on his socks and shoes, rolled down his trouser legs and stood up.

"I have to go, Yahia. I'm glad I met you."

"See you soon, Nafa the actor. If you come back this way, ask for Issam Abou Chahid. That's my *nom de guerre*. I'm in *Katiba El Forkhane*. I'll be delighted to see you."

"I can't give you my address. I don't know where I'm going."

"It's no problem, I'll find out."

They shook hands, avoiding each other's eyes, both overcome with emotion, and then they embraced in silence for a moment.

"Look after yourself, Nafa."

"Goodbye."

Nafa stepped over a bush and hurried to join his group. Turning around on top of the rock, he saw Yahia standing in the clearing, waving.

They were never to see each other again. Yahia was killed at the close of summer. Irritated by his magic tricks, his emir had him executed for sorcery.

Chapter seventeen

The mountain hamlet of Sidi Ayach was not able to withstand the fundamentalist demands for long. Its proximity to heaven did not mean that its prayers were heard. It tolerated racketeering, harassment and abuse, allowing itself to be depleted in order to feed its persecutors, but the day after the massacre of a rural policeman's family and that of a retired soldier, the villagers piled children and belongings onto makeshift carts and fled. The *katiba* took over their shacks, set up their headquarters and requisitioned the abandoned homes.

Surrounded by forests and ravines, the hamlet was perched at the top of a sheer peak that dominated the area and controlled the only road that encircled the mountain. The risks of a military operation were minimal. Any distant hostile movement, no matter how slight, could be detected; a single bomb under a bridge would put a stop to it.

The *katiba* comprised around a hundred men under the command of Emir Chourahbil, whose native village was a few hundred meters below. He was a huge fellow with flowing locks, endowed with Herculean strength—he could knock out a donkey with his fist. A veteran of Afghanistan, his troop was made up mainly of relatives and neighbors, and he ruled unchallenged over his constituency, combining the offices of mayor, judge, notary and imam. The population worshipped him. Thanks to him, they had enough to eat. When Chourahbil looted the state supply center, he distributed three-quarters of the plunder among the poor and to his relatives. In winter, when he hijacked entire truckloads of gas canisters, he kept a few for his own personal use or for making bombs, and gave the rest to his tribal allies. He was a "lord" in the feudal sense. He looked after the elderly and the children, never burned down a school without opening a Koran school at the same time, rid the villages of corrupt officials and mesmerized the young with his gripping sermons. People brought their disputes, their worries and their quarrels to him, and he took them all very seriously. His decisions were final. He blessed marriages and circumcisions, handed down divorce judgments, and settled old differences in accordance with the *Shariah*, thus familiarizing his subjects with the administrative procedures of the imminent Islamic state.

Chourahbil was just. His charisma was equaled only by his ruthlessness. He instilled terror into his enemies and his men alike. He had appointed his brother deputy, a cousin as executive officer, a brother-in-law as secretary to the unit and a nephew as paymaster. His bodyguard was made up of relatives and local men. They enjoyed boundless privileges. They were entitled to marry and live with their families in the hamlet. They occupied the best houses, were free to come and go as they pleased, and to help themselves at leisure. The rest of the *katiba* was a ragbag of deserters, escaped convicts, thugs, teachers and engineers hounded out of the cities, and young peasant farmers kidnapped during expeditions and recruited by force. These fighters were subject to draconian rules, treated with suspicion, and they paid with their lives for the slightest misdemeanor. They had to find their own food.

Nafa and his companions were not greeted by the emir, who hated city-dwellers and considered their transfer to his command as a disciplinary measure. He sent Amar and Mouqatel to another *katiba*, kept Abdoul Bacir whose bomb-making skills Salah had vaunted, and handed Abou Tourab, Souheil and Nafa Walid over to a caustic, punctilious corporal who refused to give them weapons and assigned them various chores. He declared that they were not allowed to join the bodyguard, or to mix with the fighters, that their tasks were to keep the unit supplied with drinking water which they had to fetch from a spring several kilometers below, to build secondary bunkers for use in the event of withdrawal, take care of the *katiba's* mules and old nags, and, if need be, bury the dead. At the same time, they were to train in close combat like new recruits and follow indoctrination classes morning and evening taught by a *mufti*.

Souheil had not been expecting such a welcome. He had been an NCO in the navy and enjoyed a certain esteem in the Admiralty. Having betrayed his unit, killed a barrack-room mate and two soldiers in passing, and then packed his bags and left, he was convinced that he would immediately be made an emir. Had he not, in his possession, three machine guns, two handguns, a crate of grenades and the complete list of officers? Hadn't the brothers promised to send him to the rear base in Europe as soon as possible, and that in the meantime he would only act in urban areas? His naval training had not prepared him for the rigors of bivouacking or in harsh mountain conditions. He had been a radio operator, nice and comfortable in his cabin, the collar of his tunic neat and his hands as delicate as those of a pianist. His arrival in Sid Ayach still rankled. He felt he had been taken for a ride. In addition to the sense of total disorientation, he was increasingly afraid of the men of the *katiba*. They were filthy, repulsive, shifty and had an evil look. They ate like animals, slept like animals, never laughed, prayed all the time without performing their ablutions or removing their shoes, and talked about nothing but their sharp knives.

Souheil informed Nafa of his intention to return to Algiers. Nafa advised him to calm down and make the best of things. Souheil waited a week. One morning, he was reported missing. There was a general scramble. Celebration. Tracking the quarry.

The next day, when people rose for dawn prayer, they found

Souheil hanging from a pole by his feet, in the village square, stark naked, his body flayed and his throat slit from ear to ear.

Nafa swore he would not end up like that.

"It's as clear as daylight, as easy as falling off a log," the *katiba mufti* informed the new recruits gathered around him in a clearing. "There are only two ways, not twenty: the way of the Lord, and the way of the Devil. And they are diametrically opposed. You start out from a given point. The more you advance, the closer you get to one extremity and the further from the other. You can't have one foot in the east, and one in the west. It isn't possible. When you have chosen your destination, you go towards it. There are paths like that, so straight that you have just enough room to put one foot in front of the other. You can't go round in circles without disturbing the order of things, without knocking over a signpost and straying as a result."

The new recruits nodded in silent agreement. The *mufti* smoothed his henna-red beard with a translucent hand, tapped a hefty volume of *hadiths* and added, in his deep, singsong voice: "Do not think that we are privileged. God enlightens all beings, every single one. There are men who recognize His benevolence, and others who refuse it, choosing instead the shadows of blindness. We are fortunate to be among the former. We have renounced all that is sham and illusory and chosen the path of nakedness, where all is visible, without pretension or camouflage. On the Last Day, the illusory will remove its mask, the ostentatious will be exposed: the only thing that will be revealed to the gaze of the All Powerful will be the bare truth of our deeds. That day, we will not have to blush at our nakedness. Today, it is the proof of our sincerity; it confirms we have nothing to hide. Here, we are the soldiers of God. Those who have refused to join us fester in the shadow of demons. These people should no longer matter to us. They must be weeded out. Our path will be all the easier for it, and no malicious roots will trip us up. The GIA is our only family. The emir is father to all of us, our guide and our soul. He carries within him the prophecy. Follow him with your eyes shut. He will lead us to the Gardens of the Just, and the splendors of Eternity will

208

be ours… If your natural father is not on your side, he ceases to be your father forthwith. If your mother is not on your side, she is no longer your mother. If your brothers and sisters, your cousins and your uncles are not on your side, then you are no longer one of them. Forget them, cast them out, they are nothing but diseased branches that you must prune to preserve your genealogical tree. If it comes to choosing between God and your relatives, there is no option. You do not compare heaven with an air bubble. You don't choose between the universe and a mere speck of dust."

A youth raised his hand, breaking the spell of the moment. His neighbors nudged him, urging him to lower it. He refused to give in and waggled his hand until the *mufti* took notice of him.

"Yes, son?"

The boy became confused.

"Did you want to ask a question, son?"

"Yes, Sheikh," stuttered the disciple. "What should my attitude be towards relatives who fight for the Islamic Salvation Army?"

A shocked muttering broke out among the assembled men. They were soon silenced by the *mufti*'s august hand.

"The Islamic Salvation Army is a vipers' nest, my boy. They are *bughat*—rebels. They are in league with all sorts of people and would flirt with Satan if he were prepared to let them touch a corner of his throne. Those people are slippery, manipulative and calculating. They are opportunists pretending to be good Samaritans, wolves in sheep's clothing, fortune-tellers who convince the poor to accept their wretched lot in the belief that miracles happen in dreams. They are worse than the *taghut*, their allies. They use the Faith for financial gain, bartering their share of the cake with the official swindlers. They don't give a damn about anybody or anything.

"The GIA does not bargain. It will never sit down at a table with the enemies of the Word. It will not be tempted by any concession, any gain, any privilege. We are unable to be diplomatic when God is offended. We will fight whole nations, if need be, for Him. And this corrupt country of ours, which is being paralyzed by drought because of our sins, this country is suffering and begs us to deliver it from the grip of the traitors and the claws of the vultures. That is the oath of the GIA: war, nothing but war, until the total extermination of the *taghut*, the *bughat*, the infidels, the freemasons and the lackeys—especially the lackeys, for there is only one way of putting the world to rights: and that is to get rid of all those who kow-tow."

"So we should consider relatives who fight for the Islamic Salvation Army as our enemy," inferred the youth, glowing with satisfaction.

"Absolutely."

"You see," he said to a neighbor, who immediately hung his head. "What did I tell you?" Then, turning to the *mufti*: "Can we try and persuade them to follow us?"

"They're not worth the trouble. How many of them are there in the Islamic Salvation Army? A few hundred gangsters, a few handfuls of ogres, just about able to scare kids at night? We have no use for them. For us, they are the dead that the gravediggers are loath to bury. The fate of the nation is in our hands, it is up to us. There are thousands of us in the *maquis*, millions in the cities; we are already the nation of tomorrow. The proof is all around you: these mountains where not a *taghut* dares venture, these crowds who tremble at our footstep, these roads that shudder at the explosion of our bombs, these cemeteries that take in, every day, the decaying carcasses of the corrupt officials who are becoming a dying breed. Is there any doubt in your mind?"

"No, Sheikh."

"I didn't hear you."

"*No!* Sheikh!"

"Anyone who doubts our word doubts the word of our Lord. They will witness the burning lava of hell turn his cries into eternal flames. Beware of the Devil, my brothers. He is watching for the slightest chink in your resolve to enter your spirit. A *mujahid* must remain vigilant. Never, never, never doubt your emir. It is God who speaks through his mouth. Do not think, do not question your deeds and actions, banish all thoughts from your minds, all hesitation from your hearts, and be content to be the arms that deliver the blows, that carry the green standard and the torch. And remember this, remember it day and night: if something shocks you while you are spreading death and destruction, say to yourselves that it is the Devil who, aware of your imminent victory, is trying to tempt you away."

The *mufti* snapped shut his book. The lesson was over. The military instructor, who had been sitting open-mouthed in the shade of a bush, stood up and clapped his hands. The new recruits rose, formed a square, and fists on their chests and knees to their chins, they dived into the woods yelling like commandos. The instructor, a former parachutist corporal, swung his bludgeon and barked at the stragglers, demanding they close ranks. The ground trembled as his cubs marched to the beat of rousing songs.

Abou Tourab went over to the *mufti* who was sitting on a carpet, busy gazing at his expressions in a fragment of mirror.

"You are the most brilliant orator I have ever heard, Master."

The *mufti* winked, as cunning as a djinn: "It's because you never bothered to unblock your ears before."

"Truly, master," insisted Abou Tourab, sanctimoniously, "your words are like a magic potion. They are balm to the soul."

"Alas! They don't stop yours from sounding false, brother Tourab."

"I mean it."

The *mufti* stowed his fragment of mirror in a secret pocket in his *kamis*, and rose. He was two heads taller than Abou Tourab and Nafa, which made him all the more imposing.

"My dear brother, if I allowed myself to listen to the song of the sirens, I would have run aground on a reef by now. Thank God my hearing is acute and infallible. It always warns me in time. If fate had made me king, with ears like mine, my palace would be a charnel house. My courtiers would be hanged by their tongues and the conspirators eliminated faster than they could think. Do you know why?"

"No, master."

"Because I never hear a word without dissecting the thought behind it. Sycophancy bounces off me like hail off a suit of armor. So stop beating about the bush and get straight to the point."

"Very well, master. Earlier on, you said a *mujahid* must never doubt his emir."

"I did."

"Should one doubt a *mujahid*?"

The *mufti* flicked a length of his turban over his shoulder and climbed a steep path.

"What are you driving at, brother Abou Tourab?"

"Brother Nafa and I arrived in the *katiba* in spring. Now summer's drawing to a close, and we still haven't been given a gun. New recruits have been trained and given a baptism of fire, while Nafa and I are still looking after the mules and twiddling our thumbs, even though we proved ourselves in Algiers and killed lots of infidels."

"And why do you think your former emirs didn't keep you?"

"Our duty is not to ask questions. We must have unwittingly let them down in some way. If that is the case, we would like to redeem ourselves. I was Abou Mariem's lieutenant. I must have disappointed him, unbeknown to me, but I have never betrayed. We would like to be put to the test. If we fail again, then leave us behind for good. It is humiliating doing chores, master. War is raging, and we want to be part of it. We took up arms to win or die."

"Then speak to the emir."

"You would plead our cause better than we could ourselves. Your ear is so acute, I'm sure you can hear my sincerity."

The *mufti* cleared his throat and gazed at the two men. He took out some amber beads from somewhere about his person and fingered them while he considered.

"Well, I'll see what I can do. In the meantime, go back to the mules. Sometimes their company is more instructive than that of horses."

"So you want us to believe that you're not shirkers?"

Abou Tourab and Nafa Walid were in their shack, making lunch, when Abdel Jalil's powerful voice boomed out behind them. They froze in mid air, and straightened up, surprised to receive a visit from the *katiba*'s most intrepid warrior.

Abdel Jalil was a real colossus, so huge that he couldn't find shoes his size. Tall and broad, his chest crossed with cartridge belts and a machete in his belt, he could have killed his victims just by narrowing his eyes at them. He was straight out of a nightmare, with his plaited hair making him look like Medusa and a voice that carried further than a musket shot. When he inspected his men, his animal air made them tremble from head to foot.

Abdel Jalil was not only flesh and blood; he was death on legs. A cousin of Chourahbil, he was in command of the unit's itinerant section, the one that appeared anywhere, any time, as destructive as an epidemic, as devastating as lightening.

"The emir has instructed me to see what I can get out of thugs like you."

"It would be an honor to serve under you," cried Abou Tourab.

"I'm not deaf."

He had to bend double to enter the shack.

He inspected the nooks and crannies, turned over a mattress with his toe, crouched in front of the cooking pot and lifted the lid:

"What are you cooking up?"

"A stew."

"I don't mean this shit, but what's in your scheming minds?"

He stood up, unsheathed his machete, and rapped it against his palm.

Nafa stiffened.

Abou Tourab struggled not to be intimidated. It was clear that their fate depended on the next few moments. Concentrating hard, he took a deep breath and replied in a clear, strong voice:

"We only have one mind, and it is that of the emir."

Abdel Jalil brandished his blade so that it caught the light filtering in through a hole in the wall. He waved it adroitly in front of Abou Tourab before sliding it under Nafa's chin.

"Cheats don't survive long in my outfit. You can't imagine what I do to them."

"They deserve no less," approved Abou Tourab, his heart thumping.

Abdel Jalil stretched his lips. His manic eyes pried, watching for a suspicious shudder, or a flicker of hesitation. Satisfied, he cleared his throat and walked past the two men standing to attention like two kamikazes posing for posterity.

He replaced the machete in its sheath and left without another word.

Abou Tourab let out a sigh which bent him in two.

Nafa took longer to realize it was finished.

A few days later, they were given shotguns, cartridges and bulletproof vests improvised from old inner tubes filled with sand, and they joined Abdel Jalil's section.

The first expedition took them some fifty kilometers away to a valley where the army had just set up a camp. Chourahbil was keen to give the *taghut* a warm welcome to *his* district. Two home-made bombs concealed in the middle of the track, around thirty warriors hidden in the thicket, and in less than ten minutes, the ambush destroyed a truck and a jeep, wiped out seventeen soldiers and yielded a dozen machine guns, as many conventional bullet-proof vests, crates of munitions and a radio.

On their return to Sidi Ayach, the heroes were given a memorable party. The success of the operation even delighted the regional emir—the commander of all the *katibas* in the area—who turned up, at the head of his escort, to congratulate Abdel Jalil in person.

"The country is ours," he solemnly declared.

He was right. The country was in the hands of the armed fundamentalists. The *katiba* could go wherever it pleased, without fear. The fighters requisitioned hauliers' trucks intercepted at fake roadblocks, stole them from municipal car parks, flouted the police, and paraded through the villages in broad daylight, their heads held high. The people gave them a heroes' welcome, acclaiming them with great ovations. As soon as they appeared on the horizon, children came running to meet them, the farmers abandoned their fields to come and greet them, while the women's ululations rang out across the countryside. The village notables laid on lavish feasts in the square, with a dozen spit-roast lambs and dishes of couscous, honey and green tea. Religious songs filled the air and the ordinary people, trembling with emotion, shed tears of joy at the approach of the saviors. Sometimes, Chourahbil rode a white mare. On those occasions, with his dazzling white turban, silk burnoose and gold-embroidered oriental slippers, he embodied some messianic imam whose figure aroused the crowds to mass hysteria. After the festivities, to which everyone was invited, the population gathered around the mosque, and the *mufti* expounded his theories. He spoke of a fabulous country, of dazzling lights, where men would be free and equal, where happiness would be within everyone's grasp… a country where, at night, people would hear the rustle of the Lord's gardens just as they heard, each morning, the muezzin's call to prayer.

Autumn shrank in the face of the *katiba's* advance. Chourahbil carved out a legend for himself. He had a wife in every village, and a war chest in each *maquis*. They collected funds by the sackful, and they racketeered in the villages that were reluctant to pay. Sometimes, to subdue the allies further and bring the rebels to heel, they would massacre a family here, burn a few farms there, as the fancy took them. When a village was beyond reproach, they inevitably found an undesirable notable or a reprehensible element to punish. Television sets and radios were banned, and their owners whipped. They tracked down conspirators, unruly imams, emblematic figures of the past, brazen women and the families of the *taghut*. These people had their throats slit, were decapitated, burned alive or quartered, and their bodies exhibited in the village square.

At the same time, they rooted out Islamic Salvation Army factions to drive them far from the towns and the sensitive spots, cutting them off from their logistics bases so as to starve them and force them to come begging to the GIA. A few skirmishes broke out in places, but these were negligible. Under-equipped and less motivated, the *bughat* soon fled, leaving behind their hideouts and their documents. Sometimes a cornered group would hand over their weapons. They would be reduced to downright slavery before ending up in the ditch.

What was more, army raids, still somewhat haphazard, invariably proved fruitless. Too cumbersome, the military betrayed their presence from the outset, and always arrived too late. Chourahbil simply had to step aside to allow the storm to pass before attacking isolated units on their way back from operations. Thanks to Abdoul Bacir's genius, they mined the tracks and booby-trapped vehicles intentionally left at the scene, inflicting losses on the enemy without having to cross swords.

The population cooperated with the emir. People informed him in good time of the army's movements, their planned itineraries, the composition of the units and their intentions. As soon as a camp was set up somewhere, it was identified and assessed. The military police stations, built in "absolute secrecy," were dynamited the night before they were due to be occupied; sometimes a bomb turned the opening day into a slaughter. The more the *taghut* tried to gain ground, the more the GIA expanded its living space. The rise in the number of attacks, in the heart of the towns and villages, the mass rural exodus that swelled the suburbs, the general sense of panic, kidnappings under the nose of the vigilantes, the blowing up of dams and ambushing of patrols, explosive devices planted in military complexes and barracks—this huge avalanche of strikes and harassment destabilized the "authorities" and placed the rest of the country, the countryside and the road networks in the hands of the *katibas*. Then came the division of the enemy whose influence was shrinking away, and the increasing greed of the emirs who, intoxicated by their impunity, began to harbor excessive ambitions and dream of fabulous empires.

The demons of discord awakened.

Greed knew no bounds.

The throne became shaky in the turmoil of changing alliances and internal struggles.

One morning, Sidi Ayach was in an unusual state of feverishness. The men went about their chores, distributing new trainers to the new recruits, dressing everyone in Afghan robes; an eminent commander was honoring the *katiba* with a visit. Chourahbil donned his ceremonial costume, the one he wore when he toured the elated villages. Twenty or so sheep were slain. For the first time, the bodyguard mingled with the ordinary fighters to conceal their scarlet faces and embarrassing paunches. At midday, the vanguard arrived, inspected the camp, and positioned sentries everywhere. Late that evening, the stony-faced Emir Zitouni marched in with his awe-inspiring troops. He refused to partake of the banquet but locked himself away inside Chourahbil's house for hours with the main *katiba* leaders. When the meeting ended, he left the village in the dead of night.

Abdel Jalil explained to his men that a dissident group comprising four hundred traitors was threatening the unity of the GIA.

"Salafists," he railed, making a vomiting motion, "little shits who don't even wipe their asses. Well, we'll just see whether they've got the balls to put their words into action."

He was referring to the troops of Kada Benchiha, a barber from Sidi Bel Abbes, a club-footed megalomaniac, who had been leader of the western *katiba*, before being relieved of his command and sentenced to death by the National Council. A legendary figure, he had made a name for himself by carrying out the most murderous attacks on major garrisons in the Oran area. His men were highly dangerous Afghans. They had state-of-the-art weaponry and were the only ones who had artillery and bazookas. The emir had demanded part of their arsenal to give to the Algiers troops. Not only had Kada Benchiha refused, but he had also demanded to be appointed leader of the GIA, which was why he was marching on the national headquarters in order to take it by force.

Chourahbil assembled his units and headed immediately west. On the way, they were joined by other *katibas*. Hundreds of men, some on mules, others aboard stolen or borrowed trucks, converged from all over the *maquis* towards the Ouarsenis massif where the Salafists were resolutely waiting for them.

The battles were titanic. Dozens of dead. A windfall for the army, which took advantage of the appreciable presence of the fighting factions to decimate them at the scene of the conflict.

The withdrawal was utterly chaotic. Helicopters pursued the fundamentalist mob, the artillery caused havoc and the parachutists trapped them mercilessly. Abou Tourab was shot in the back. If it weren't for Nafa, he would have died. Abdel Jalil loaded his dead onto trailers and his wounded onto mules and miraculously carved himself out a path through the confusion of gunfire. It took him several days to reach the *katiba,* which had been severely crippled and was fleeing south.

The losses were soon forgotten. The battle of the Ouarsenis was considered a victory. The Salafists had been defeated, and that was what mattered. Emir Zitouni made no secret of his relief, but felt that the atmosphere was still poisoned. He launched a vast purge. The regional emir was court-marshaled and sentenced to death for having secret dealings with the Salafists, and for abuse of office and heresy. His head was suspended from a lamp-post in his native village. Other leaders met the same fate. Units were disbanded or transferred amid bloodshed. The reorganization brought everything back into line.

Chourahbil became the regional emir. To celebrate his promotion, he returned to his family village and married a cousin. Once the marriage was consummated, he ordered two elderly men to go and find the soldiers and tell them that the emir was dying and that eight "terrorists" were waiting in the village to bury him. It was a juicy bait. A military convoy soon turned up. As it rounded a bend overlooking a precipice, it entered the trap. The first and last trucks were blown up. Caught in a stranglehold, the rest of the company was decimated by the hail of gunfire. Thirty soldiers were killed. The wounded were piled onto a vehicle, doused with petrol and burned alive. Their screams rang out across the mountains like a chorus of the damned. Neither the icy winds nor the heavy winter snowfalls could cool them down.

"Come in," roared Abdel Jalil, motioning Nafa to sit on a sheepskin on the floor.

Nafa obeyed. He sat cross-legged on the rug, and folded his hands between his thighs.

The room was poorly lit. A steaming earthenware pot filled the air with the smell of food. There was no furniture, other than a tiny coffee table in the center of the room. On the bare walls hung a few war trophies: two crossed sabers, a dented soldier's helmet, and a *sahd*—a home-made bazooka taken from an Islamic Salvation Army unit, ineffective and ludicrous.

Draped in a regal burnoose, Abdel Jalil sat imposingly on an upholstered dais, dangling a set of beads from his finger. Appointed chief of the *katiba*, he no longer needed to burden himself with cartridges and a machete. His word was law, his wrath punishment, and in the halo that surrounded him believers could doubtless discern the surreptitious beating of an angel's wing.

"How is your friend?"

"He'll pull through, Emir."

Abdel Jalil's beard nodded. A fluttering standard was that blessed beard.

After a moment's reflection, he declared:

"You've convinced me, brother Nafa."

A young fighter brought in a pot of tea, served the emir and then Nafa and tiptoed out.

"Relax and drink."

Nafa took a sip which scalded the roof of his mouth, then another and a third, until his throat was on fire. He did not even realize that there was no sugar in the tea.

"I've been watching you since you came to us. I watched you at Ouarsenis and during the retreat. You were courageous. And you do not seem to harbor any personal ambitions. In short, you are selfless. Unassuming and efficient. The sort of man I'd like to have working for me."

"I am very…"

"Don't say anything," cut in Abdel Jalil, rising.

He paced the room, his hands behind his back.

"However, you do have one fault."

Nafa put down his glass, suddenly on the defensive.

Abdel Jalil planted himself before him.

"A chink in your armor, brother Nafa... an unfortunate crack: your eyes. You are too quick to cast them down."

Ashamed, Nafa bowed his head.

"You see? You're always staring at your feet, and that is not good. You can't see where you're going. Hold your head up, brother Nafa. Someone with your courage should hold his head high, very high... do you know why I summoned you?"

"No, Emir."

"To put blocks under your chin to keep your head up."

"That won't be necessary, Emir."

"Well stand tall, because from now on, you will be in command of the mobile *saria*."

"Me?"

"Do you see anyone else in the room? They're a hard-boiled lot; it's a tough unit. They need to be ruled with a firm hand, I warn you. There are bound to be some who are envious of your appointment. There are fighters who are more qualified than you and more senior, and who are desperate to be in command. Their problem is that I hate those who are in too much of a hurry. They will trample on their neighbor's body to achieve their ambitions. And I won't have that. Have I made myself clear?"

"Yes, Emir."

"Good. Now stand up."

Nafa rose to his feet.

Abdel Jalil placed his hands on his shoulders, crushing him with his weight. It was a sign of great respect.

"Congratulations, *emir* Nafa. May God guide your steps and your hand. Now, you are a leader. You will enjoy all the privileges that are your due and you will fulfill your responsibilities alone. Your orders will be carried out to the letter. You will not accept the slightest hesitation or misplaced remark. Your men will be the fingers on your hand, and nothing more. Do you understand?"

"Yes, Emir."

"I am relying on you to get it into the head of your subordinates. I demand a fierce, authoritative command, and that you keep your head high and your eyes wide open."

"Very good, Emir."

"Crush the envious. In the event of force majeure, you are entitled to eliminate one of two of them to set an example."

"I hope I shan't have to do that."

"But *they* won't hesitate."

Nafa nodded.

Abdel Jalil turned his back to him.

The interview was over.

It was not necessary to be heavy handed. Abdel Jalil's visit to the *saria* had made an impression on the men. Nafa had no trouble in taking charge. Apart from Khebbab—a former aviation captain who had become a bomb maker—the others kept a low profile. The section was a mere shadow of its former self. The rout at Ouarsenis had brought the fighters down to earth with a bump. With ten dead and eight wounded, they dared not make a fuss.

The harshness of the winter restricted the number of missions, both in distance and in time. Nafa began his rule with a few modest forays, here and there, a few symbolic fake roadblocks, and returned to Sidi Ayach to enjoy a hero's rest.

His position as emir exempted him from a certain number of mundane preoccupations. He no longer had to worry about board and lodging. An obsequious servant ran around after him, ready to fulfill his wishes with the alacrity of a genie.

He lived in comfortable accommodation. A fire burned day and night in his hearth. In the morning, as well as a gargantuan breakfast, he found hot water to wash in.

He was an emir.

He discovered the giddiness that comes with power and esteem. There was nothing more wonderful, he felt. Like God's chosen, strolling through Paradise, he merely needed to snap his fingers for his slightest wish to be granted. Often, he did not even need to go to the trouble. His men thought for him. They all strove to earn his approval, to please him.

Nafa was amazed at the simplicity of things and of people. His transition from fighter to emir was remarkably easy.

It was magic.

The thawing of the snows began in the warbling forests. The thundering cascades drowned the silence in crystalline symphonies. The orchards emerged from their snowy mantle. The earth became verdant again under warm skies. When Nafa looked out over *his* territory, it was his corner of Paradise that opened its arms to him. He loved standing on top of a rock and spending hours listening to his flapping robes applauding him in the breeze. Standing high above the mountains and men, he merely had to raise his arms to take wing.

Chapter eighteen

A whistle rent the air, followed by an explosion.

A few hundred meters from the village, a cloud of dust rose up in the middle of the forest. Nafa Walid leaped out of his sleeping bag and rushed outside. A group of fighters stood paralyzed in the alleyway staring in the direction of the explosion.

"What is it?"

"It must be one of Khebbab's apprentices, Emir."

Nafa frowned. He returned to his room to fetch some binoculars and scanned the countryside. Nothing suspicious as far as he could see. It was daybreak, and the sky was just beginning to grow light. The empty, winding road that curled around the base of the mountain glistened with dew. In the distance, the lights of the villages faded in the dawn.

"Go and see what's happening."

Abdel Jalil and his wife came and stood outside their house too. The emir made a motion with his hand to inquire what was going on. Nafa yelled that he had sent his men to find out.

"It's probably a bomb gone wrong."

Abdel Jalil nodded. As he turned to go back inside, he heard a chorus of whistles cross the sky, like the rending of a curtain being torn. Immediately, explosions ripped through the village's outlying houses. Stones and roofing sheets were sent flying in a tornado of dust and flames.

"It's artillery fire," yelled Abdel Jalil. "Everybody to the woods for shelter."

A second salvo rained down on the square, killing several beasts of burden. Houses that had been hit collapsed, blocking the alleys with rubble. Screams, women's shrieks, then chaos. The fighters rushed out of the houses, leaped out of windows and bolted in all directions, their wives close behind. A third salvo shattered the peak, destroying in its wake a paddock and a hangar. The wounded screamed under the debris, others dragged themselves along clutching the walls. The village suffocated under a dense brown pall, while a fire broke out in the woods and began to spread through the forest.

At the foot of the mountain, the leading trucks of an endless military convoy invaded the road.

Abdel Jalil ordered Khebbab to take his team of bomb makers and to blow up the bridge. The former captain loaded the homemade bombs onto mules and raced into the thickets.

In the burning village, the shells fell relentlessly on the stragglers, who kept going round in circles, disoriented by the explosions.

Suddenly, shots rang out below, followed by heavy blasts.

Nafa called Khebbab on the radio: "Now what's going on?"

"No way can we get near the bridge," replied the captain. "The place is crawling with paras."

"Are you serious?"

"I tell you, the bridge is surrounded by paras. What shall I do?"

"Mine the tracks."

"I'm right up against them."

"Place your bombs on the access routes. That's an order."

A swarm of helicopters appeared over the mountain.

"Shit!" cried Abdel Jalil. "We weren't expecting this."

The *katiba* retreated into the woods, abandoning the dead and the wounded where they lay. Helicopters flew low over the village. Their rockets whined through the air before gutting a block of little houses. They returned to bomb the outskirts of the village, landing under cover of the pall of smoke over the mountain. Teams of parachutists poured out and ran to position themselves on the high ground before regrouping to move in to the attack.

Rooted to the ground, the *katiba* lay low in their hiding places, unable to retaliate or to maneuver without laying themselves open to attack from the air. Down by the bridge, the volleys of firing died down. Khebbab informed the emir that he had run out of ammunition and that he was going to pull back. Down below, the military convoy advanced relentlessly.

"We are going to retreat immediately," decided Abdel Jalil, "otherwise we'll be done for."

A group stayed put to block the paras and attempt some diversionary skirmishes. The rest of the *katiba* headed into the forest to escape the helicopters. Around midday, they reached an opaque crater, about ten kilometers down below. The cover party signaled that the helicopters were bringing in reinforcements, and that the convoy was setting its troops down on the northern flank of the mountain ready to comb the area. From his observation post on top of a rock, Nafa saw more convoys arriving from east and west to take the mountain in a pincer movement.

"We need a miracle," he groaned.

Within a few hours, the military vice tightened. Hundreds of soldiers were swarming through the woods, dynamiting arms caches, burning the provisions they found and occupying the water supply points. The *katiba* tried to break through the enemy lines. The men were driven back. They tried again a bit further on and met the same resistance. By nightfall the losses amounted to twenty-five dead and as many wounded. Impossible to go on. Abdel Jalil ordered his platoon to pull back and withdraw to the crater. The *katiba* managed to inch their way among the valleys, arriving at an overgrown riverbed. They concealed the wounded and the women in caves and went back up in a bid to provoke the enemy to distract them and draw them away from the crater. The clashes were even fiercer than before. Slowly, the line of operations shifted, to the warriors' great relief. The *taghut* advanced on several fronts, cutting off suspect areas, inundating them with mortar fire before going over them with a toothcomb. They could be heard over the radio reporting on the results of their attacks and the number of fundamentalist dead they had come across. Thanks to this leaked information, the *katiba* found it had considerable breathing space.

"We must hold out until nightfall, whatever the cost," explained Abdel Jalil. "Then we'll move up to the enemy lines to find a breach."

"How?" asked Nafa gloomily.

"Very simple. We advance, we shoot; if there's a riposte, we retreat and do the same again a bit further on until we meet no resistance, a sign that the coast is clear."

The emir's strategy paid off. Before daybreak, the *katiba* located an opening and headed into it at once. The men ran into a wooded valley and hid until the army had finished combing the place, which took five days. They held out against hunger and thirst. Unable to move under the sky throbbing with helicopters, they sat at the foot of the trees and stayed still, sustaining themselves on edible plants and wild fruits. When the army raised the siege, Abdel Jalil realized that he could no longer return to Sidi Ayach. The army had installed two detachments of commandos there, and set up roadblocks everywhere.

Nafa was sent back to the crater to fetch the women and the wounded, a third of whom had died for lack of treatment and food. Then began a life of wandering and misery. There were ambushes everywhere. Patrols criss-crossed the hills. From time to time, helicopters flew over the forests, flattening suspect areas and withdrawing after dropping baskets of leaflets calling on the fundamentalists to lay down their weapons and surrender. The sky would be full of sheets of paper fluttering like thousands of giant butterflies that settled over the clearings. But woe to anyone who dared pick up a leaflet. Thirsty, exhausted, hounded on all sides, going without food for days and days, the *katiba* asked for permission to return to the regional HQ. Chourahbil categorically refused. He ordered Abdel Jalil not to let the mountain fall into the hands of the *taghut*, and to somehow keep in touch with the allied tribes whom the rebel villages massacred at the first opportunity.

Abdel Jalil chose an abandoned Islamic Salvation Army camp halfway between Sidi Ayach and Chourahbil's native village. The place was built around two streams, it was wooded and on a hill, but it was not big enough to accommodate everybody. They built more bunkers and planted explosive devices all around to fend off a potential attack, as the surrounding villages were hostile to the GIA and had been won over to the cause of the *bughat*. The *katiba* was going through an infernal phase. Living conditions were horrendous. They had left everything behind in Sidi Ayach: bedding, clothing, cooking utensils, medicines and food, and had to start from scratch with only what they had to hand. No more living in luxury, in proper houses with a fire burning in the hearth and food stocks. Open to the elements, uncomfortable and gloomy, the bunkers and caves of the new camp filled them with weariness and bitter despair. Sleeping in them at night made their blood run cold. They would huddle in a corner, on the freezing ground, without blankets, their hands between their thighs and their knees drawn up to their chins. By morning, their limbs were numb with cold, and even the toughest cried out in pain. Confronted with the low morale of his men, Abdel Jalil decided to take things firmly in hand. It was risky appealing to neighboring villages for help. One indiscretion and the police would show up. Diminished and left to its own devices, the *katiba* would not survive a second attack. Nafa and his *saria* were forced to operate miles away so as not to betray the unit's so-called living quarters. At the head of his trustiest henchmen, he roamed the hills and woods for days and nights on end, hijacking a truck on a lonely road, stealing livestock from remote sheepfolds and stripping itinerant vendors of their wares, taking care to cover their tracks as they returned to camp. He also attacked a center for the disabled and a mosque, to requisition supplies, religious books and rugs.

Meanwhile, things had become considerably more complicated. Military harassment was being stepped up, and the armed groups were retreating further and further, allowing the *taghut* to gain ground. Barracks were springing up even in the forests, and others in the villages. At the same time, the population was beginning to switch allegiances. The first patriot groups were beginning to form…

One evening, Nafa Walid was summoned by the emir of the *katiba*. Inside the cave lined with stolen wall hangings, Abdel Jalil had a sinister expression. Next to him sat Zoubeida, his wife, a woman of iron, wearing a tightly belted, multicolored outfit, espadrilles on her feet and a pistol in her belt. She was stately and beautiful. Her mesmerizing gaze always disconcerted Nafa, who never dared return it for more than two seconds. Behind her, sitting cross-legged on a mat, was Othmane, a former imam from Blida, who looked worried. Opposite him, standing on his squat legs, a certain Ramoul was anxiously kneading his fingers.

Ramoul was a rich local livestock merchant. His farm was at the edge of the village of Ouled Mokhtar, on the other side of the forest. In his early fifties, he was the picture of health underneath his worn, smelly garb. Visibly ill at ease, his eyes darted around beneath his grimy turban. He shook Nafa's hand, bowing like a servant.

"Do you know each other?" asked the emir?

"We bump into each other from time to time."

"Well, Sy Ramoul has confirmed the rumors that a section of the population is mobilizing against us. What we thought was propaganda orchestrated by the *taghut* turns out to be a fact. And it is spreading. Villages are preparing to welcome military detachments so as to set up their own resistance groups. The villages of Matmar, Chaib and Boujara, and the tribes of Ouled Mokhtar, Riah and Messabih are turning against us. According to Sy Ramoul, applications for guns are being made to the military police every day."

"It's true," said Ramoul, shaking his head.

Abdel Jalil banged on a coffee table to bring him to order. He narrowed his eyes as he went on: "Thank God the rot has not yet affected our area. But there are scattered outbreaks of disease. The

regional emir does not want this sickness to spread in his constituency.
He has ordered shock treatment to get rid of it once and for all."

"It's true," added the incorrigible Ramoul, sniffing a pinch
of snuff. "It mustn't be allowed to spread. I'm a livestock merchant
and I travel a lot. What I've seen is incredible. Do you know that
in Kabylia there are so many militiamen that the population doesn't
need the army? It's true, I assure you. I've seen it with my own eyes.
I was in Dahra too, to sell a hundred or so head, and there again, I
saw, as I'm seeing you now, patriots building roadblocks. I thought
they were our people, and there were gendarmes helping them. It's
true, I swear. If I hadn't seen it with my own eyes, as I'm seeing you
now, I wouldn't have believed it. And near Tiaret, there things are
really serious. The patriots have organized patrols, and even ambushes.
Our groups can't move around the way they did before. Sometimes,
they can't find anything to eat."

Abdel Jalil banged the table.

"If I were you, Sy Ramoul, I'd think carefully before opening
my mouth."

"Why?"

"You're engaging in subversion."

"Me?"

"Shut up!"

Ramoul stepped back a couple of paces at the emir's out-
burst.

"Go and wash your filthy mouth out with soap and water seven
times before coming out with such disgusting nonsense."

The livestock merchant felt his legs go weak. He turned ashen.
His legs buckled and he sat down, trembling, his Adam's apple bob-
bing up and down like a faulty piston.

"Listening to you, anyone would think that the boot was on the
other foot. We are still masters of the situation. All this masquerad-
ing is a futile gesture. There are, of course, a handful of traitors who
allowed themselves to be lured by the *taghut*, but it's not the end of
the world. How many are they in Ouled Mokhtar, in league with
the infidels?"

"Six," stammered Ramoul, taking a crumpled piece of paper out of his pocket.

"And you call that a militia?"

"No, *sidi*. I simply exaggerated to make sure we took the problem seriously."

"It's not your problem."

"Absolutely, *sidi*."

"Were you worried, on your farm?"

"No, *sidi*."

"So, keep it shut."

Pale and perspiring, Ramoul wiped the corners of his mouth with his thumb and tried to make himself inconspicuous.

Abdel Jalil held out the list to Nafa: "Sy Ramoul will show you where these scum live. I want their heads to be displayed at the entrance to the town hall."

Nafa arrested four of the six traitors in their beds at three in the morning. An old man, a former *mujahid,* his son, his nineteen-year-old grandson and a *fellah*. He bound them with wire and dragged them to the village square, where the population had assembled, guarded by around thirty fundamentalists. He announced that anyone who demanded arms to fight against the Islamic revolution and God would receive the same punishment. Imam Othmane recited a *sura* that talked about ways of dealing with infidels, explained to the crowd that they had a duty to be wary of rulers who tried to involve them in devilish tricks, promised them that the day of victory was nigh and withdrew to allow the executioners to decapitate the four traitors.

Far from allowing themselves to be intimidated, the people of Mouled Mokhtar buried their "martyrs" swearing on their graves that no murdering fundamentalist would ever leave their village alive again. While waiting to obtain the guns they had requested from the authorities, they fashioned sabers and slings, made petrol bombs and organized the defense of their integrity. Nafa came back to watch them, certain he could frighten them away merely by crowing. He was hounded out with stones and incendiary devices.

In the following weeks, three detachments of the village guard set up around the camp, forcing the *katiba* to move to another forest, deeper in the interior.

Rumors of an election spread through the *maquis*, sowing doubt and amazement: they were planning to hold presidential elections. The fundamentalist troops were cut off from the rest of the world—the radio and newspapers were banned, only communiqués from the National Council were distributed—and this news was a huge blow to their already dented morale. In places, there were instances of insubordination, which were routinely and bloodily repressed. The blind tyranny of the emirs, who were clearly unsettled by the turn of events, combined with the overwhelming misery of their men, thrown out of their "citadel" and doomed to keep on the move to escape the air raids and police sweeps, aggravated by the noticeable withdrawal of assistance from the allied villages whose support networks were breaking down, plunged the guerilla forces into a profound gloom. The specter of discord and suspicion came back to haunt the fundamentalists and deplete their ranks. Every day, fighters went missing, some executed on simple hearsay, others preferring to give themselves up rather than live with a sword of Damocles hanging over them. Each defection saw the *katiba* on the road again. The "penitents" collaborated with the *taghut*, leading them to the camps and acting as guides for military operations. To contain the surrender, Chourahbil ordered the canceling of leave and deemed any fighter found outside his camp a deserter to be executed on the spot.

"You ought to keep an eye on Omr and Haroun," murmured Abou Tourab in Nafa's ear. "They've been behaving oddly recently. They shut themselves away, and won't leave each other's side."

"So what?"

"They've been like that since the helicopter dropped leaflets on us. In my opinion, for what it's worth, you'd do well to sniff around and see what they're up to."

Nafa didn't need to be told twice. He went and found the two suspects, searched them and found *taghut* leaflets concealed in their bags.

"What's this?"

Without waiting for an explanation, he whipped out his gun and put bullets through their brains, surrounded by the rest of the platoon having their lunch. This warning paid off. Terror quelled any thoughts of defection. The men died on the steep paths, they were blown to bits by the mortars and fighter planes, but at no point did they dream of parting company with the group. To nourish such suicidal thoughts took at least two, to egg each other on and devise an escape plan. But the individual fighter had never been so abandoned. The slightest look, the slightest gesture, might bring down the wrath of his superiors on him; he walled himself up in silence and said nothing. Docility became his only means of survival. He must not appear over-enthusiastic or too distracted. Simply obedient. Like a robot. Come when called. Speak when spoken to.

During a meeting at the regional HQ, Chourahbil tried to be optimistic. He promised that the presidential elections would be a fiasco, that the population would boycott the polls, for, according to the experts at the National Council, the people demanded an end to the thug system running the country. Nevertheless, the instructions did not exclude applying dissuasive measures, for whatever purpose they might serve. But Chourahbil was wrong. Khebbab's bomb, planted at a polling station, killed ten and injured sixty, but the voting went ahead. Worse, the population was massively behind the *taghut*'s charade. It was the most disastrous day since the Redemption. Punitive expeditions against the villagers, massacres on the roads, bomb blasts in the souks—all the rivers of blood and tears did not quench Chourahbil's thirst for vengeance.

Chapter nineteen

I can't wait any longer," said Abdel Jalil. "I'm going to have to go and have it out with Chourahbil. The replenishment he promised me is taking forever to get here. It's impossible to work in these conditions. It's not long till Ramadan, and I'll need more than fifty fighters if I'm to stop those traitor bastards fasting in peace."

He adjusted his Afghan tunic, took down his machine gun and placed his predatory talons on Nafa's shoulder.

"I'm leaving you in charge of the *katiba*. Don't try anything in my absence. Our men are exhausted. I'll be back within a week."

"Do you need an escort?"

"No point. I'll take Handala and Doujana with me. They're worth a whole *saria*. My wife will come with me too."

"May God protect you."

Abdel Jalil automatically checked the magazines of his gun and walked out of the bunker. Handala and Doujana were waiting on the path, with a mule laden with gifts for Chourahbil. Zoubeida was in fatigues, radiant as an Amazon queen. Her gaze sought out Nafa's but she was unable to catch his eye.

"Goodbye, then," said Abdel Jalil. "No point in tiring the men. No excesses before my return. I hope to come back with reinforcements. Otherwise, I don't see how we'll be able to honor our commitments during holy month."

"Very good, Emir."

"One other thing: try to keep your eyes and ears open. Desertion happens fast."

"It won't happen."

Abdel Jalil joined his wife and invited his two companions to precede them.

The sun was setting; the tentacular shadows of the trees were preparing to greet the night. In the woods, a cuckoo mocked a blackbird. Nafa watched his leader disappear. Zoubeida turned around. Her bewitching eyes said farewell. He smiled. It was the first time he had smiled at the wife of an emir and wondered whether that boded ill.

Two days later, the radio operator informed him that Abdel Jalil was wounded. Nafa took an escort, a medic, and went to assist his superior. He found him lying on a blanket inside an abandoned shack, with an ugly wound in his stomach.

"We saw an isolated house and decided to spend the night there," explained Zoubeida. "Just as we pushed open the door, a woman shot at us. The buckshot hit Abdel Jalil point blank."

The medic examined the injured man pessimistically. He cleaned the wound, dressed it and advised Nafa to get the emir back to camp immediately. Abdel Jalil was battling against death with the energy of despair. Lying across the mule, he shivered with fever and was delirious. He was bleeding to death.

He was carried into his bunker and placed in the care of a medic.

The radio operator informed Nafa that Chourahbil had been surrounded and wasn't able to dispatch a doctor.

"It doesn't matter," said Abdel Jalil.

Just before breathing his last, he added: "Shit! Abdel Jalil killed by a woman. I'll never get over it, not even in Paradise."

He was buried at the foot of a solitary olive tree, on top of a hillock. Imam Othmane wept his heart out and vowed to erect, on the site where the martyr lay, a monument where schoolchildren of the future Islamic state would come to reflect.

Chourahbil mourned the loss of his cousin and exhorted the squadron, the *katiba,* to live up to his sacrifice. He asked Nafa to take over in the interim, until a new emir was appointed.

"Why the interim?" protested Zoubeida. "The *katiba* is yours by right."

The radio operator who had just delivered the regional instructions stared at his feet.

Zoubeida asked him to go, and to leave her alone with Nafa.

"Do you want someone else to come and usurp your position and perhaps relegate you to the role of a simple *mouquatel?*"

"What can I do? It's Chourahbil's decision."

"Let's call him back and tell him there's no need to look for a chief because there's one here."

"He'd accuse us of mutiny."

"Don't let them walk all over you. They'll end up flattening you."

"Don't go on about it. I don't want to be in their sights."

Zoubeida moved towards him, more arousing than ever. She placed her hand on his shoulder, slid her fingers one after the other towards his neck and caressed his beard.

Nafa looked away.

"Don't hide your blue eyes from me," she murmured. "You're depriving me of the color of the sky that I most love."

"Please," stammered Nafa. "Abdel Jalil has only been dead a week."

"The dead have no sense of time."

Nafa felt a stirring in his belly. Something vacillated inside him. For a second, he wanted to grab the widow's hand on his beard, and press it to his lips. Then he regained his self-control.

Nafa lay on his pallet staring at the dim glow from the oil lamp. He could not forget the burns Zoubeida's fingers had left on his neck.

No matter how conscientiously the *sabaya* massaged his legs, it was the widow's hand that obsessed him. His flesh trembled, and the ardent stirring in his belly a few hours earlier turned into fire. In the hope of quenching it, he turned his attention to the *sabaya*, a teenage girl kidnapped during a punitive expedition and whom he had deflowered himself. She was beautiful, with firm breasts, full hips and, even though he possessed her every night, neither she nor the other *sabaya* had aroused in him a desire as pressing as that caused by those inquisitive fingers on his shoulder, neck and beard. He had always been fascinated by Zoubeida. He had dreamed of her since he had first set eyes on her, one morning, at Sidi Ayach.

The curtain of the bunker opened, and, as if by magic, she entered. Nafa sat up with such alacrity that he hit his head on a joist.

Zoubeida looked the *sabaya* up and down. Her hands on her hips, she sent her away. The girl waited for her master to dismiss her.

"Go," he said.

She rose and went outside.

Zoubeida folded her arms on her chest. Her huge, overpowering eyes swept the squalid room, lingered on the oil lamp, then dwelled longingly on the emir.

"You've been watching me for so long in secret, and now that I'm free, you run away from me."

"I'm not running away from you."

"Then recite the *Fatiha*."

"Why?"

"I want to be your lawful wife."

"Don't you think it's a bit soon?"

"We're at war. Nobody knows what tomorrow might bring... Unless you don't want me any more."

"Me?"

"In that case, what are you waiting for? Read the *Fatiha!*" Issuing her challenge, she unfurled her belt with a languid gesture.

Nafa put his hands together, his palms upturned, and recited the *Fatiha*. He was trembling like a child.

Zoubeida shook her long hair that cascaded down her back and began to unclasp her jacket. Nafa's throat was dry at the sight of her magnificent breasts.

"Tell me you like me, *husband*."

"I like you."

"Tell me you want me."

"I want you."

"Put out the lamp."

"I'd rather gaze at you first."

She kneeled down, hitched up his robe, brushed his downy legs with her lips, gradually moving up his powerful, trembling thighs.

"I liked you the day you arrived at Sidi Ayach," she whispered. "I was fascinated by your blue eyes. I only lived to bathe in them one night, with the radiance of your smile for moonlight."

Nafa extinguished the lamp. It was the most exquisite night of his life.

Chapter twenty

I've thought long and hard," Zoubeida told him, pecking his lips. "If there must be an emir for the *katiba*, it will be you. There's no question of saying no. We're going to shut them up. You only have to want to, my love. Do you want to be emir?"

"I do."

"Excellent. All we have to do is pull off something that they won't be able to challenge, or undermine. Something sensational, that will knock them out. Don't interrupt me. If you want to get ahead, listen to me."

"I'm listening."

"They say that Abou Talha* loves huge massacres, that the more victims there are, the happier he is. Well, this will satisfy him. Shhh! I have an idea. I was planning to discuss it with Abdel Jalil. Now I'll put it to you. Do you know the village of Kassem?"

"That's in the hands of the Islamic salvation army?"

"Exactly. They've refused the weapons offered to them by the

---

* see entry on Abou Talha

taghut. They think the *bughat* can protect them. What they don't realize is that we're going to wipe them out in one fell swoop."

"There's a barracks less than fifteen kilometers away."

"The army won't intervene. They know the village is fundamentalist and have kept their distance since the two ambushes. Even with advance warning, they're wary of traps and won't be able to do anything until daylight."

"Go on, this is interesting."

"I have a foolproof plan. We're going to slaughter those scum. And when Abou Talha hears that the village of Kassem has been wiped off the map, he'll want to know who was the genius behind it. And then, my love, I wouldn't be surprised to see you in charge of the entire region."

"Do you really think so?"

"I'm certain of it."

She kissed him tenderly on the mouth.

"I'll make you a *zaim,* a charismatic *jihad* leader. And, on the day of victory, I'll be by your side to conquer other areas. In life, my emir, you have to dare. The world belongs to those who go out and seize it."

Nafa raised himself up on one elbow, cupped his cheek in the hollow of his palm and gazed down at his wife's exquisite face:

"Now tell me about your plan, you brilliant darling. I don't know why, but something tells me we're going to sorely miss the village of Kassem."

After dawn prayer, Nafa ordered Abou Tourab to assemble the men for a mission of the utmost importance.

"How many should we leave behind to guard the camp?"

"None."

"In that case, what do we do with the *sabaya*?"

"Slit their throats."

Kassem should not have set its heart on that barren hill lost in the depths of the forest. Neglected by the gods and man, it was to pay dearly for its asceticism. It was a wretched little village, with tumbledown hovels scattered higgledy-piggledy among the fields, without streets or even a mosque; just a jumble of homes with their backs to each other that were barely more than animal pens. Ragged urchins played in the orchards, despite the rain and squalls. Their shouts mingled with the yapping of the dogs. On the only muddy track that led to the village, a group of men were trying to repair a tractor. Women could be glimpsed bustling around their courtyards, a cloth wound around their heads. Smoke was rising from a few chimneys and the odd window banged, but Nafa saw no reason to abandon his plans.

In the sky swollen with copper-tinged clouds, the evening sun refused to show its face. As if what was about to happen was not its concern. A flash of lightening preceded the roll of thunder. The rain poured down on the village, without alerting it to its fate.

"Don't spare their kids or their animals," cried Zoubeida.

Divided into four groups, the *katiba* surrounded the village. The farmers around the tractor did not have the time to realize what was happening. The first axe blows split their skulls. The children were silent. Suddenly, they understood their misfortune and fled towards the shacks. It had begun. Nothing could stop the wheel of fortune. Like ogres of the night, the predators fell upon their quarry. Sabers struck, axes shattered, knives slashed. The screams of the women and children drowned out the howling of the wind. Tears spurted higher than blood. The flimsy doors of the houses were easily smashed. The killers massacred effortlessly, without mercy. Their swords stopped the children's frantic race in its tracks, tossed up the souls of victims. The corpses soon began to pile up inside the houses, and the puddles of rainwater turned red with blood. And Nafa killed, killed, killed. He could hear only his rage thumping inside his head, could see only the horror of tormented faces. Caught in the whirlwind of cries and fury, he had entirely lost his reason.

When I regained my senses, it was too late. The miracle had not occurred. No archangel stayed my hand, no flash halted me. I was there, suddenly the euphoria had subsided, a blood-soaked baby in my hands. I was drenched in blood up to my eyes. In the midst of this nightmarish shambles with the bodies of children scattered everywhere, the mother was no longer pleading. She held her head in her hands, incredulous, numb with pain and grief.

Outside, everywhere you looked, bodies lay among the carcasses of disemboweled babies. Flames engulfed the houses, lighting up the scene so that we were in full view. The smell of burning bodies lent an apocalyptic note to the whole spectacle. It was Dantean, for certain, but it was ordained.

Sitting on a rock, Imam Othmane wept.

"If nothing is worth consideration in your eyes, it's because you are not worth much," he chanted.

"What are you on about?"

He pointed to the village with a horrified gesture: "Our great feat speaks for itself."

"We are at war."

"We have just lost, emir. A war is lost the minute children are massacred."

"On your feet."

"I can't."

"Stand up. That's an order."

"I can't, I tell you."

I pointed my gun at him and killed him.

We headed into the forests, walked through the night and came to a halt in a riverbed. And there, listening to the trees shudder at the swish of our blades, I wondered what wolves dream of, deep in their lairs, when their tongue quivers in the fresh blood of their prey hanging from their putrid mouths, like the phantom of our victims clinging to us.

The next day, probably appalled at their own savagery, six of my men slipped away.

We never saw our camp again. An AIS squad fell upon us in a clearing. The confrontation lasted for hours. Then we had to beat a retreat. Further on, two helicopters caught up with us on a ridge, and held us there until the arrival of the taghut. I had to sacrifice one platoon to save the rest. When we came within view of our living quarters, we could see thick plumes of smoke rising from the camp where other soldiers had marched in. We fell back on a village to stock up on food and drinking water. Local guards greeted us with absolute fury.

Like hunted jackals, we took to the woods, unable to find a breach through which to escape the enemy's tentacles.

Chourahbil called me on the radio:

"I've been trying to contact you for days. Where are you?"

"I don't know."

"What's this huge military presence in your sector?"

"They're after me."

"What's going on?"

"I attacked the village of Kassem."

"What? So it was you? What on earth got into you? Who gave you the order, you fool? You dared flout my authority. Where do you think you are? I told you to wait for the arrival of the new emir. As a result of your actions, he was killed on the way. What were you trying to prove, you idiot? You were trying to run before you can walk, weren't you?"

"I thought I was seizing an opportunity."

"Idiot. What are your losses?"

"Huge."

"I want figures."

"Twenty-one dead, seven wounded and six missing."

"Oh no, I don't believe it! You can't do this to me! Not to me. Not now. That's a dirty trick. A betrayal. I'll never forgive you. I want to see you at HQ! Now! Now!"

The radio operator turned pale.

He could already see my ghost.

"Don't let yourself be beaten," said Zoubeida, unruffled.

"It's your fault."

"We took an initiative, now let's take responsibility for it. It was a good plan. If it hadn't been for those bughat scum, we would have left the area in time. Besides, we hadn't anticipated the defection of our men. They're the ones who betrayed us. The game isn't lost until it's won."

Her coldness terrified me.

She took me aside and told me:

"Abdel Jalil amassed a fortune when he was leading the mobile saria. I know where he hid it. There's enough money and jewelry to form our own katiba."

"I'll go and see Chourahbil, I'll explain."

"He'll kill you, in any case. Please don't do anything foolish. Abdel Jalil's fortune is immense. We'll have enough to set up two or three sarias."

"Chourahbil will wipe us out. So let's go back to Blida or Algiers. With our money, we'll buy safe houses and send our groups to attack the ministries."

"Listen to me—"

"Be quiet. For the love of God, give me time to think."

I shut myself away in a cave all night.

By morning, my men had vanished. The radio operator had probably informed them of Chourahbil's threats and they had decided to make their way back to the regional HQ without me. Their consciences were clear.

The only ones left were Handala—his brother was asthmatic and he was keen to take him home, Alik and Rafik, cousins who had joined us recently and who were finding it hard to acclimatize, Doujana, leader of the saria whose head was likely to roll alongside mine, and Zoubeida.

"So Abou Tourab, my best friend, has deserted me."

"He hasn't gone," Zoubeida told me. "He's somewhere over there, behind that hillock."

Abou Tourab was leaning against a tree and absently throwing stones into a clump of dwarf grass. His gestures were those of a man who was losing his grip.

I crouched down facing him.

He refused to meet my eye and carried on throwing stones in a different direction.

"I thought you'd left."

"Where would I go?"

"Nothing's lost yet."

"I don't agree."

"We're going back to Algiers. Zoubeida has told me about a hidden treasure trove. As soon as we've got it, we'll go home. We'll buy safe houses and we'll set up our own group."

He looked at me in disdain.

"That's all you can think about: carrying on the fight."

"It's not over."

"It is for me."

"Are you planning to give yourself up?"

"To the taghut, to the bastards who have turned me into a monster? Never. I'll find a way of getting ID and I'll get the hell out of this country. It isn't mine any more."

"You're not serious?"

"I never have been, but this time I am."

"Do you have any idea where you'll go?"

"I'll see. For the time being, I'm not out of the woods yet."

"We're going to carry on the struggle, Abou Tourab. The Islamic state is just around the corner."

"You must be dreaming! Look around you. The temple is destroyed and nobody wants to listen to us. We've gone too far. We have been unjust. Vile monsters let loose, that's what we've become. We are haunted by millions of ghosts, we taint everything we touch. We are no longer worth anything. Nobody wants us. Even in hell, the damned and the demons will protest and ask God to transfer us to another hell, far from theirs."

"Don't blaspheme."

"It's incredible how you've changed, Nafa. Ambition has blinded you. All that glitters is gold as far as you're concerned. You want to be pampered, worshipped and feared like them."

I straightened up.

"I forbid you to talk to me like that. I ought to decapitate you."

"What's stopping you?"

I regained my composure: "You are the only friend I have left."

"You see, you only think about yourself."

We gathered the few things that the others had left us and walked until we were out of breath. Surrounded, left to our own devices, we were treading on broken glass. We had to leave Chourahbil's territory as quickly as possible. Zoubeida led us, as nimble as an Indian. We rested by day and set off again in the evening, moving in precise stages, giving a wide berth to places likely to conceal an ambush. Sometimes an innocent crackling of a twig would immobilize us for hours on end. We sniffed the air like wild animals on the alert for any suspect scents. After a week of forced marching, dropping with hunger and thirst, we attacked a farm in search of food.

On the evening of the eighth day, Chréa welcomed us with open arms. How thrilled we were to gaze at the lights of Blida, of civilization. At last, we were emerging from the mists of time. The apartment blocks, tiny at the foot of the mountains, seemed to us taller than the Tower of Babel. It was a fairytale vision, so unreal that we felt we could hear the roar of the traffic, despite the distance.

We slept in the open air.

That night, I dreamed of my father.

"Nafa," Abou Tourab was shaking me.

It was daylight. The sky was blue, and the mountain majestic. However, Abou Tourab's face had a look of disgust on it.

"Zoubeida has disappeared."

We hunted for her all morning. At a bend in a river, we came across her discarded bag containing her fatigues and espadrilles.

"She probably had a civilian outfit in there. She changed and ran off," groaned Handala.

"She enticed us with her story of loot to get us to escort her to the outskirts of the city. She's probably miles away by now."

"She can go to hell!" I cried.

But nobody believed me.

It was out of the question to go back to Algiers in the state we were in. The police would identify us without any difficulty. We needed to shave and get rid of our Afghan tunics. We located an isolated house. There was a mirror on a wardrobe. On catching sight of myself, I nearly fled. I was shocked. I was unrecognizable. There was nothing human in my reflection. It was that of a beast straight out of the imaginings of a deranged mind.

We shaved our beards, cut our hair and had a bath in a drinking trough. Our white cheeks stood out in stark contrast to our sunburned faces. Algiers would have to wait. While waiting to look human again, we hastily built fake roadblocks on the secondary roads and stripped travelers of their money, jewelry and clothes. We also stole a mobile phone. During one of these raids, a big car caught our attention. A man had just finished changing a wheel. Just as he removed the jack, he found us surrounding him. Dumbstruck, he put his hands in the air and backed away.

He was a strapping black man, built like a boxer, with a squashed nose and a fighter's forehead.

"Small world," I said.

His eyes widened:

"Nafa?"

"In the flesh, Hamid. What on earth are you doing around here at this hour?"

He asked if he could put his hands down.

I didn't make things any easier for him.

"We're coming back from Mrs. Raja's funeral. The poor woman died yesterday. She wanted to be buried in her native village."

"She was a good woman."

There was a man dozing in the back of the car.

I banged on the window with the butt of my gun to waken him.

"Good old Junior," I sniggered. "Still festering."

"He's taken it very badly," Hamid tried to mollify me.

I opened the door and yanked Junior from his seat. He panicked, flapped his hands and blinked madly, only half awake, and turned pale at the sight of our guns. His breath reeked of alcohol, making me reel.

"Where are we?" he stammered. "What the hell have you got me into, Hamid?"

Then, realizing the seriousness of the situation, he raised his hands.

"Don't kill me, I beg you."

"It's me, Nafa. Don't you remember me?"

His eyebrows almost disappeared. At last he remembered me and didn't know whether to be pleased or afraid.

I didn't make things any easier for him either.

"Are you going to kill us?" asked Hamid.

"Why shouldn't I?"

Junior swayed, clutching the door.

"On your knees," I said. "Now, I'm the boss."

"I beg you, Nafa. We were friends once. Don't you remember the good times we had?"

"When? When that bastard gave me hell, when I was nothing but a doormat for him to wipe his boots on? On your knees."

Junior suddenly straightened up.

"No way."

"Do what he tells you," pleaded Hamid.

"Oh no. A Raja has never bowed down to anyone."

"He doesn't know what he's saying," Hamid implored. "It's grief…"

"On your knees, bastard!"

Junior was adamant: "That's asking too much."

"Don't be an asshole," panicked Hamid.

"I might have had one too many, but I can stand up. In any case, they're going to butcher us. They're just bloodthirsty terrorists.

All they know how to do is kill. If my life ends here, I may as well die on my feet."

I slapped him.

He lost his balance, but didn't fall.

"Sure, you're going to die, Baby Rose. But before you do, I swear you're going to crawl, lick my boots and beg me to finish you off."

"Don't bank on it."

"He doesn't know what he's saying," Hamid sobbed with rage. "He's out of his mind with grief."

"I know what I'm saying, kho. Would you like to live in a place where thugs like this think they're heroes?"

"Shut up!" screamed Hamid.

Junior turned on his bodyguard, blind drunk, gesticulating wildly and his voice thick:

"You're talking to a Raja!" Then, turning back to me, he said: "I never took you for a doormat. You were the driver, I was the boss. That's life. Poverty and wealth are mere facades. Each person carries their misfortune within. Whether he's dressed in silk or dew, it makes no difference. The proof," he added, flinging open his arms. "The poor accuse the rich of being the cause of their suffering. The rich think that the poor have only themselves to blame. It's not true. That's the way of the world and it's nobody's fault. You just have to learn to put up with things. Fate would be a right bitch if she didn't hide her hand. Life wouldn't be worth living if we didn't fight back. You think you know, but you know nothing. In refusing to accept it, you go raving mad."

Abou Tourab unsheathed his knife.

Hamid landed his fist in his face, held him in a lock and, disarming him, held the blade to his throat.

"One move and your friend's had it. Back, back…"

I signaled my men to obey.

"Get in the car and go, Junior!"

"I won't leave you alone with these beasts."

"Get out, dammit. I'll manage."

Junior scrambled into the car and drove off at speed.

Abou Tourab was choking. A thin stream of blood trickled down his neck.

"I told you, Nafa," retorted Hamid. "Junior's my manna from heaven. I won't let anyone touch him. Back."

He looked to the right and to the left.

"When I think you threw your chances out of the window for a stupid junkie."

He dragged Abou Tourab to the edge of a ditch, threw him into it and jumped in after him. We couldn't fire without hitting our companion. Hamid took advantage to run zigzagging into the woods.

Handala telephoned his uncle.

"He's someone who we can absolutely rely on. He lost a son in the maquis. He'll put us up until we can think about the future calmly."

Abou Tourab didn't agree. But he had no alternative suggestion.

At nightfall, Handala's uncle came to pick us up from the roadside in a tarpaulin-covered van. He drove us to an apartment block in the suburbs. The third-floor apartment was tiny.

"I have to drop in and see my old lady," I said.

"Wait a few days," advised Abou Tourab. "We're not home and dry yet."

"I won't be long."

Then, to Handala's uncle:

"Could you drop me off?"

"I'm at your service."

It was Amira who opened the door.

At least, what was left of her. Her vacant eyes barely took me in.

"You've got fatter."

That's all she could say, after more than two years of separation.

She, on the contrary, had become very thin. She returned to the living room. Her hair uncombed. Wan. Lost in her black dress. She was the shadow of a distant sister. She crossed her feet on a burst pouf and took up her knitting. It wasn't like her to turn her back. There was something wrong with Amira, she wasn't herself.

The living room was a mess. Cushions lay scattered on the floor. The upholstered benches were battered. Of the three light bulbs in the ceiling light, only one worked. It was dark in the house.

"Are you alone?"

"I'm alone."

"Where's mother?"

"She isn't here any more."

"When will she be back?"

"She won't be back."

She carried on knitting. Ignoring me.

Then, in a monotone, she told me:

"She went out to buy some sandals for Nora. A bomb went off in the market. All they found of Nora was her headband."

She knitted, knitted.

Putting down her needles, she seemed surprised to find me still there.

"I thought you'd left."

In the van, I realized I hadn't asked after Souad.

"Hey, wake up!"

Rafik pulled me out of bed.

Handala and his younger brother were already up, standing stupefied in the corridor.

It was still dark.

"What's up?"

"Something's happening on the stairs," said Abou Tourab, pulling his pump-action shotgun from his bag.

"Where's your uncle, Handala?"

"I don't know."

251

Alik was listening at the door.

"It sounds as though they're evacuating the building," he whispered.

He tried to look through the keyhole, then through the spyglass. A shot, and his head was blown to bits.

"Oh my God!" swore Doujana. "We've had it."

Glossary

Abou Talha—Nickname of Antar Zouabri, the GIA's national leader, the successor of Jamal Zitouni who was assassinated by his peers. He was behind the large-scale massacres and *fatwas* against the entire Algerian people.

AIS—Armée Islamique du Salut (Islamic Salvation Army)

Al Asr—The late afternoon Prayer, the 3rd compulsory Prayer of the day

burnoose—hooded cloak

Bughat—The infidels

chador—Full-length veil with peepholes for the eyes

Da Mokhkess—A sort of "Big Brother", the origin of all Algeria's troubles

dawaa—contingent

falaqa—Beating on the soles of the feet

Fatiha—Opening *sura* of the Holy Koran, that doubles as the creed of Islam and as a salutation that expresses strong feelings and important happenings in life, such as love, fidelity, births, marriages and burials.

fellah—Peasant

Feast of Ashoura—Commemorates the 7th-century death of the Shiite Imam Hussein.

FIS—Front Islamique du Salut (Islamic Salvation Front), founded in 1989

FLN—Front de Libération Nationale (National Liberation Front), founded in the 1950s, to fight French colonialism

griot—the caste of storyteller's in W. Africa responsible for passing on the tribe's history

gandoura—tunic

Hadith—The body of traditions relating to Muhammad, which now form a supplement to the Koran, called the Sunna.

Hadj, Hadja—A man or woman who has made the pilgrimage to Mecca

Haouzi—Haouzi songs belong to the oral tradition of the Arab Haouz tribe of Marrakech (Rehamnas, Sraghnas and Zemrane). They recount the story of the region and sing of love and nostalgia for the brave old days.

hijab—Veil

Hijra wa Takfir—Sin and Atonement (sect)

houri—one of the beautiful virgins of the Koranic paradise

Jaz'ara—"Algerianists"—a student intellectualist Islamic group

Jihad—Holy war

kamis—Loose shirt

katiba—*Author's note:* "In the underground fundamentalist movement, the death squadrons are made up of irregular numbers. A *katiba* is a batallion, made up of 150 to 200 fighters, but sometimes operates with less than 100. The *katiba* is made up of three or four *saria* (companies), each comprising 25 to 50 fighters, sometimes as few as 15."

kho—Brother

Majlis—Fundamentalists' consultative assembly

maquis—Underground fighters

MIA—Mouvement Islamique Armé (Armed Islamic Movement)

minbar—Pulpit

mouquatel—Fighter, soldier

mufti—Muslim legal expert and adviser on the law of the Koran.

mujahid— (plural: *Mujahideen*) One who takes active part in a Jihad.

OAS—Organisation armée secrète, (the secret army) a militant terrorist organization which carried out a ruthless campaign against the FLN and the French government during the War of Independence.

qacidas—A monometric or isometric poem with a uniform rhyme scheme.

sabaya—Women or girls kidnapped during massacres and false road blocks. Considered as war booty, the fundamentalists treated them as whores. At the first sign of pregnancy, they were routinely decapitated or quartered.

saria—Platoon or company—see note on *Katiba*

Sura—Any of the 114 chapters of the Koran

Shariah—Islamic law

Sidi—term of respect, 'master'

Sy—Polite address for an elderly man

taghut—One who exceeds his legitimate limits. In Koranic terminology it refers to the creature who exceeds the limits of his creatureliness and abrogates to himself godhead and lordship. The ultimate stage is that man not only rebels against God but also imposes his rebellious will on others. All those who reach this stage are *taghut*.

zaim—Leader

zorna—Oboe

Key Dates

1954–1962—Algerian War of Independence

1962—Algeria gains independence from France

1965—Colonel Houari Boumediene grabs power in a coup as a single-party Socialist state is consolidated

1988—Serious demonstrations to protest against commodity shortages and high prices broke out in Algier, Oran, and other cities in October. When the police proved unable to curb the outbreak, troops supported by armored vehicles assumed responsibility for security. Large demonstrations were staged by Islamist groups inspired by the *intifada*, the uprising of Palestinians against Israeli rule on the West Bank of the Jordan River and in the Gaza Strip. It was estimated that more than 500 people were killed after ill-trained soldiers used automatic weapons against the demonstrators. More than 3,500 demonstrators were arrested, but most were released without charge before year's end. Allegations of arbitrary arrest, unfair trials, mistreatment, and torture compounded public anger against the government.

1989—Islamic Salvation Front (FIS) founded

1990—FIS wins 55% in local elections in first free vote

1991—June: FIS calls a general strike. Military declares a state of emergency; November: first armed Islamist attack in Guemmar, in the east; December: FIS comes top, with 47% of vote, in first round of national elections

1992—January–February: Parliament dissolved by decree, state of emergency continued, army grabs control; March: FIS banned

1992—Armed Islamic Groups (GIA) formed

1994—General Liamine Zeroual becomes President

1995—Exclusion zones set up in south to protect Algeria's vast and rich oil and gas fields

1997—Anti-Islamist militias legalised. Non-extreme Islamic political parties allowed to stand at elections. 700 killed in massacres at Bentalha, Sidi Hamed and Beni-Messous

1998—Zeroual stands down, Abdelaziz Bouteflika takes over

2001—80 killed in riots in Kabylia supporting autonomy for Berbers.

About the author

Yasmina Khadra

Y asmina Khadra is the pseudonym of the Algerian author Mohammed Moulessehoul, who was born in 1956. A high-ranking officer in the Algerian army, he went into exile in France in 2000, where he now lives in seclusion. In his several writings on the civil war in Algeria, Khadra exposes the current regime and the fundamentalist opposition as the joint guilty parties in the Algerian tragedy.

Before his admission of identity in 2001, a leading critic in France wrote: "A he or a she? It doesn't matter. What matters is that Yasmina Khadra is today one of Algeria's most important writers."

The fonts used in this book are from the Garamond family

Other works by Yasmina Khadra
also available from *The* Toby Press

Autumn of the Phantoms
Double Blank
In the Name of God
Morituri

The Toby Press publishes fine fiction,
available at bookstores everywhere. For more information,
please contact *The* Toby Press at www.tobypress.com